Scenic Overlo[ok]
Book Prize, s[…]
Long Live the […]

Praise for Scenic Overlook

"In her novel-in-stories *Scenic Overlook*, Anne Ray surveys our cultural topography through the eyes of a young woman who, escaping the realities of grief and family dysfunction, sets out across the country searching to define herself in a landscape of casual ambiguity, populated with drifters and soul-searchers who become the driving force of Ray's perceptive and original voice. An impressive debut."

—Elizabeth Brundage, author of *The Vanishing Point*

"Anne Ray's *Scenic Overlook* is a startlingly good collection. With an expert mix of heartbreak, joy, and humor—and with its gorgeous language and nuanced insights—Ray has created a character and world that readers won't soon forget."

—Thomas Grattan, author of *The Recent East*

"In her gripping debut, *Scenic Outlook*, Anne Ray writes piercingly about grief, work, loneliness, and the relentless past. I love how passionately her heroine Kate tells her stories and I love how she almost always acts in her own worst interests. The huge accomplishment of this marvelous book is to show Kate, despite everything, towards the light."

—Margot Livesey, author of *The Boy in the Field*

"Anne Ray is a true artist of storytelling, and *Scenic Overlook* is a masterpiece of a collection. In this powerful and profound journey through grief and self-discovery, the prose shines like jewels—bright and breathtakingly beautiful, sharp enough to draw blood. Through the lushness of Ray's attention to detail and the depth of her emotional intelligence, the world of her characters is at once strange and exotic and achingly familiar, creating the kind of experience that simultaneously transports the reader into the narrative and reflects back to them their own desires for love, connection, and belonging. It's an exquisite book."

—Aryn Kyle, author of *The God of Animals*

"There is an attention to the in-between spaces in *Scenic Overlook* that left me breathless. A lobby, a casual remark, an errand in a new place, a series of years in a service job, the time after sudden death. Anne Ray has figured out how people behave in these extra-normal spaces. There doesn't seem to be any detail that her prose can't notice and, in noticing, honor. This attention charges every page with something like lightning, electrifying every sacred drive. In searing, deft prose, Anne Ray has mapped American daughterhood. How dearly we need it! *Scenic Overlook* will take its place alongside the keenest observers of the profound mundane. Less a debut and more a vector-shifting arrival."

—Marie-Helene Bertino, author of *Parakeet*

SCENIC OVERLOOK

Anne Ray

ACKNOWLEDGMENTS

Grateful acknowledgement is made to the publications in which the following stories originally appeared: *The Adirondack Review* ("Guidance & Control"), *Sequestrum* ("Scenic Overlook"), *Story* ("Noe Valley"), *CALYX* ("Clinic"), *Cut Bank* ("Novio, Novia), *Gettysburg Review* and *Pushcart Prize Anthology 2018* ("Weekend Trip"), *StoryQuarterly* ("The Pool"), *North American Review* ("Spine"), and *LIT* ("Warning Sign" as "We Were Blamed for their Deaths").

Scenic Overlook © 2023 Anne Ray

Published by Awst Press
P.O. Box 49163
Austin, TX 78765

awst-press.com
awst@awst-press.org

All rights reserved.
For permission requests, please contact the publisher.

Printed in the United States of America
Distributed by Small Press Distribution

ISBN: 978-1-7367659-7-5
Library of Congress Control Number: 2023945434

Cover design by Claire Krüeger using paintings by James Isherwood
Editing by Tatiana Ryckman
Copyediting and typesetting by David McNamara / Publish Publish

CONTENTS

Pavement	1
Guidance & Control	41
Scenic Overlook	73
Noe Valley	103
School for the Deaf	147
Answering Machine	179
Clinic	201
Novio, Novia	215
Weekend Trip	239
The Pool	267
Road's Edge	291
Spine	321
Warning Sign	351

PAVEMENT

Tonight, as I put dishes away, laying one on top of another, a slew of days came back to me from the year I lived at home, the year my father died. I blinked and I was twenty again, and it was March and raining, the dying end of winter, and I was in the kitchen trying to win the nightly argument with Danny, my brother, about which one of us would get to use the car—that white Chevrolet that smacked of police cruiser—while my father's car, forbidden to us, slept in the garage.

Sometimes, as on that night—probably it was a Monday—it was his burden to drive me home from the publishing house where I worked as an unpaid intern, after his day at his tech support job. For this, he hated me. That night this argument began as soon as we got home, to the house wedged in between other houses of the same phylum, a split-level in dark brown planks amid pebbly cul-de-sacs and pine trees that dropped thickets of needles. The house we'd grown up in: Chicken-

and-rice casserole. Our basement, floor covered in beige carpet remnants. Lawns, hidden in dark. Garage door, opening and closing. Worry, a taste like a walnut.

Danny wanted to drive 450 miles to Massachusetts to meet up with college friends at some metal band festival that weekend. "I told you I wanted to use it Friday," I said. I pulled out a chair at the kitchen table and its legs screeched across the floor. "If you're going to leave for five days, let me use it this week."

"All week?" he said. "Fuck no."

He had a curtain of dyed black hair that covered the back of his neck and an already-thinning hairline, even though he was twenty-two. He always wore a rubbed-leather motorcycle jacket that would have been cool if it wasn't eight sizes too big. He had a habit of not taking it off when he was inside. He had an earring and lines of pale brown fuzz crawling up his thin forearms. There were girls, also with dyed black hair, who were really into him.

"I will not be gone for five days," he said. "I have said this before. But I will be gone."

That way he had of eschewing contractions, as though he were a Russian count.

My mother had left a casserole on the stove. She clinked dishes, wearing yellow dish gloves. Danny and I were crowding her, bursting the silence with our momentary commotion. She drank wine the color of ammonia from a glass misty from washing, getting soap from the gloves on the stem.

We were still arguing. Our father had been dead three months and this is what we were doing.

"At least let me use it tonight," I said.

"What for?" he said. "What are you even going to do? You do not have plans."

"How would you know? Mom," I said, and stopped myself. A childish utterance was about to come out of my mouth. He's not letting me use the car. That year we'd gone backward in time in our dealings with each other.

"Hmm?" she said, wiping the countertop. And then, from nowhere, "Did you have a good day, Katie?"

She has been doing this since we were children. We would cry about a dropped ice cream cone and she would say, Where's your bathing suit? Now this habit seemed worse, in the lifeless, bleary place she was since my father had died. When I was a child, her hair was sandy and touched her shoulders. Now it was dyed dark brown, the color of mine, and stiff around her head.

I was about to answer her and say, Yes, it had been a good day: I'd heard a rumor that there'd be a job opening. The same job we were doing, only, paid. Of the interns, it was probably just me and my friend Andrea who had a shot at it. She and I had become fast friends. Maybe she hadn't heard yet. I thought I had a good shot, even though I had left off that I hadn't technically gotten my diploma—my mother had summoned me home for the funeral right before fall semester finals, and I hadn't returned. The publishing house had hired me anyway—

I'd faked it on my résumé. Before I could say anything about this job, Danny sighed the weight of a zeppelin, and acquiesced:

"Fine," he said.

"Are you still going to drive all that way this weekend?" my mother asked him.

"It is not that far."

"You'll drive up on Saturday?"

"I already said, I will leave after work on Friday and drive at night."

My mother peeled the gloves off, dropping them in the sink.

"That's a long way," she said, her mouth a flat squeeze of irritation. "It's not safe to drive after dark."

"I know, Mom," he said, but she was already in the den, on the couch, the TV talking.

I ladled on a spoonful of casserole on a plate, sat on the other end of the couch. After a while my brother joined us. I ate, he ate, and we watched television. My brother put his empty plate on the floor. His legs were stretched out like a plank, his face hidden by the wing of the easy chair, my mother coiled against the arm of the couch. I hadn't told them the day's news about the job. But it didn't seem like the right time. My mother was biting her thumbnail, grinding it slowly.

The carpet turned gray from the light of the TV, which, on occasion, made us laugh.

After a while I got up to go out. "I'm going," I said to the den.

"Okay, sweetheart," my mother said.

"Keys?" I said to Danny.

He fished in his jacket pocket and gave them to me, brushing my palm like bird claws.

Most people my age were in the back of a movie theater, at a house party, at art class, at band practice, taking gravity bong hits. I often went to the library, or, just drove around.

I pulled out onto the highway, a glittering six lanes. A car flicked its lights at me. Cops ahead. My brother'd had a car. He'd bought it himself, a metallic blue hatchback with duct tape on one window. That winter, it wouldn't start. The local garage wanted more to tow it to the repair shop than it was worth. We later watched as some charity came and pulled it away.

Out the windshield: sky behind a tree with no leaves, stars seen through branches like iron rods. I swung around our town's crowded loop, lit by rust-colored streetlight. In the loop's bullseye was a mall, with a dollar store, a food court. On this ring was the regional hospital in which Danny and I had been born, and where my father had spent his end, hooked to machines, seething, his disease thickening his veins, and the community college where I'd taken classes for an interminable semester, until I transferred. If I keep driving, I thought, I will drive past it all. Past the soft-serve yogurt place with the plastic swirl on its roof. Giant Foods, its orange neon G. Strip mall with a pool hall where I'd spent hours in high school. Exit ramp, west: Every time I fought an urge to speed down it, keep driving, end up on a sliver of the moon.

After an hour or so I went home. As the garage door opened, a sound like a drill, the shape of my father's car loomed.

It was a maroon Citroën, somehow both boxy and sleek. My mother drove it when she went out, which was seldom. My father'd always said: Not maroon. Aubergine. Before he got sick, he'd taught at a private boys' school where another teacher drove one. So, my father bought one too. The Citroën was heavy, a little bit fast, a manual transmission. The eggplant paint was coated in a thin layer of dust. I ran my finger over it.

Upstairs, my mother was asleep in her room. Light shone around my brother's door.

When I knocked he looked up, a surprised expression on his face like someone had just walked in that he didn't recognize. He lay on the bed reading one of his mutant comic books. He had my father's same sharp shoulders, only, hunched; he'd never learned to stand up straight. The room smelled of feet and phlegm. It was perennially filthy, today's filth being a half-drunk milkshake on the desk.

"It smells like shit in here," I said.

"I am aware of this," he said. "You are in no way original in your observations."

He was smiling as he spoke. He was good at amusing himself, had an inner life that I envied. I bumped my foot against a floppy paperback in a heap on the floor. It was a study guide. He'd been living at home already when I'd come back, working at Kmart until he'd found this tech support job and discovered he needed expensive classes to get some kind of certification. He was saving up to pay for these, and we were both saving to move out. We were in a little war about who would get there first. He would, I assumed, since I'd lost my paid job. I'd been working part time at my old high school job, at a coffee shop in the nearby shopping center. The kind, sharp Korean man who owned it had given the job back to me. But almost as soon as I started, it went out of business. There'd been paper hearts taped to the door for Valentine's Day. I'd gone into work and he said, We close tomorrow.

Danny stuck out his hand. I threw him the keys.

"Is Mom driving you to the rail station in the morning?" he said. She often said she would give me a ride to the commuter train. But sometimes, she would be in her bathrobe still when I was ready to leave. On those days I'd walk to the station through a field and up a long stretch of road with no shoulder. I nodded, and a palpitation of relief passed over his face.

"Sleep well, fool," he said.

"Stop calling me that," I said, and turned to go.

"Door," he said, and I closed it behind me.

In my room, I opened a window, the knocking blinds cracking the quiet. The small rush of air called up in my mind a hissing sound—the sound of a machine my father had been hooked to as he sat in a chair, near the end. My father had always been building something, always in the backyard hammering, sawing. By then, he had to make do without this, but still, he had sat sanding a thin piece of wood. What it was for I don't know. I rarely knew what he was making until it was a finished work of precision and craft. He'd carry in stacks of wood and hammer more, breaking the quiet of our house, and molding would appear where there hadn't been any. Voilà, he'd say. As he sanded, dust fell on the blanket over his lap, and the sounds of the sandpaper and hiss merged.

I lay down on my unmade bed. I slept fractured that year, waking and getting up and repeating. On my bed with my clothes on. On my bed in pajamas with the light on. Finally, under the blanket, light off.

The next day, my mother—awake, alert—drove me to the train station and I arrived in my business casual clothes at the publishing house, deep in an office park with an address in the ten thousands on a fake road. Our job that day was to mail brochures that were stacked in the mail room adjacent to the warehouse, which was filled to the roof with academic monographs. The interns that day were Andrea and me and Seth, the other intern, who was slouchy, boyish, with a swishy haircut and dimples. Andrea was a sunny person who knew everything about rock music and sometimes wore her hair in pigtails. She had the dark, tiny eyes and fidgety manner of a finch. Our boss was a statuesque woman from Slovenia named Lola. I wanted to ask Andrea if she'd heard the rumor—the paid job—but didn't want to say it in front of Seth. As an intern he was incompetent, bordering on lazy. He never volunteered for any task, which Lola somehow never picked up on. She sometimes offered to teach him things, even things he should have known how to do and that she shouldn't have had to bother with, like how to do a mail merge. He was banking on his various varieties of charm.

Lola came in from her office—which had a sliver of window looking into the hallway—to check on us. Her perfect oval face was marred only by a slight smudgy haze around her teeth, probably from smoking.

Seth sat up. "Slavoj Žižek!" he blurted. "That's the guy I read in college whose name I couldn't remember yesterday."

Lola scoffed, smiling. "Everybody knows him," she said. "Do you even know where Slovenia is?"

He grinned, shrugged, his eyes wide like a pony's, and even I thought he looked adorable.

The minute she left his manner shifted to sullen. We sealed envelopes for a while.

Seth said, "So where'd you go to college?"

He hadn't gotten to this yet in the time-passing chatter we'd exchanged. "Oberlin," Andrea said.

"Where'd you go?" he said to me.

A lumpy crash came from the warehouse—a box falling. One night, at happy hour, I'd told Andrea I'd never gotten my diploma. "Who gives a crap," she'd said. She'd said that if I explained to Lola what happened, she'd understand. I looked at her now, and she peeled off another sticker.

"St. Mary's," I said. He slid brochures across the table to me. His face had become sallower. He thought this place was grim. I thought, he wasn't wrong.

Lola returned, waving a transmittal form. "Anybody want to do this one?" she asked.

"I'll do it," I said, whizzing my stack of brochures to Seth, who, as usual, had not volunteered.

On the way out that evening, Andrea and I stood in the parking lot as we often did before leaving. The sun was sliding down, the sky an iridescent blue. The squeal of rushing traffic from people pulling onto the highway, alone in their cars, droned in the background. The whole world coated in traffic.

"Were we ever that ass-kissy?" she said. "As Seth?"

"He never read Slavoj Žižek," I said. "Hey listen. I heard a rumor."

"You talking about the job? I was about to say the same thing." She'd heard the full story: they were hiring a full-time editorial assistant in the group that did political, religious-y books, this weird hybrid that I found totally unreadable.

"Is that a job that one wants?" I said. "I might make more money working retail."

"That book they did about the Pope," she said, "Terrible."

She wasn't wrong.

"You going to apply?" she said. The secret about my unfinished degree hung between us, but her upturned eyes repeated what she'd said before: who gives a crap.

"Probably," I said. "You should too." She nodded, and said, "Hey, do you want to come to the Drain on Wednesday?"

The Drain. A pocket of resplendent hideousness in Baltimore.

"Hell yes," I said.

Andrea drove me to the train station, and the grimness dissipated in the guitars on her stereo. The train dropped me off, I walked the half hour home in my flats, the cold snaking up my sleeves.

It was 7:49. The white car was gone, Danny was out. I peeked upstairs and saw a seam of light around my mother's closed door. The floorboards creaked, probably her padding around. I ate leftovers standing by the sink, my damp flats on the stained faux terra-cotta tile.

I went down to the basement, a thing I would do around that time. I would wander to a part of the house and try to see it anew. I found some of my old notebooks and brushed through the pages of one, but I didn't want to read it and put it back. I found a book of photography, of Western, empty landscapes, and leafed through page after glossy page.

I opened a photo album, its outside puffy and varnished. Sometimes I'd look for photos of my sister. In them I could see my own thin nose, my clefted chin.

I see now that this business with the car, and that whole spring, really, was because of our sister, our own particular tragedy. The night my sister died, my brother and I had been alone in the house with her. My parents thought that would be fine. For some reason she had gone out, and she hadn't ever returned. She had taken my parents' other car, and had been hit by another driver. She was sixteen, had gotten her license perhaps a week prior. Leaving us alone, that was uncharacteristic of my parents. Probably, Danny and I know so little about what happened to her because my parents had to piece it together themselves. Almost as soon as she was gone, they stopped speaking about her. For months I didn't understand that she was not merely absent but dead. What I know about her was fixed in the mind of an eight-year-old and had faded and yellowed. Her death had slipped into a sort of family lore. It's hard to admit that I've forgotten so much of her, that this is what it felt like. In that rainy March, I remembered less than ever about her.

The photos that contained her were not there. Only hopscotch squares of empty plastic slots. Upstairs, the garage door started to grind; Danny had come home.

I stopped on a photo of my father and removed it. He slouched over a stove, the floor tiled black and white. He smiled back at the camera over his shoulder, wielding a spoon over a sizzling pan. A dog with perky ears looked up at him. His long hair, like David Partridge's, was a wave of pale brown that dusted his eyebrow, the color of my brother's. He wore a loose corduroy jacket. I'd never seen him with anything other than his ink black hair, cut high and tight. Did he dye it, like my brother? When had he ever slouched?

On the back was written in lilting ballpoint pen: Sunday.

When I opened my eyes I heard my mother's slippers dragging ghoulishly down the basement stairs.

"Katie?" she called. Before I answered, she was peering down at me, eyes on the photo.

"Did you have a dog?" I asked, hearing my voice rise cheerfully. "And I found this beautiful book."

She didn't answer, only pulled her robe closer.

"Where was this?" I asked, pointing at the photo.

I figured she would change the subject with one of her non sequiturs, like, to ask me to unload the dishwasher. Her face was a razor-sharp mask.

"Put those away," she said.

The next day, Tuesday, I think, was a borrowed day. A day with no work. With no plan whatsoever. The weather turned foggier, spongier. Grass clippings, flotsam on the curb. I suppose I could have worked more days at the internship. But what was the point? I sat at the computer and sent out résumés, clicking away, my completed degree there in black and white.

A while later my mother and I went to the back of the house, where houses lurked just beyond the line of pine trees and the air-conditioning box loomed in the hedges, a gray square. She and I had been repotting her geraniums, when she felt up to it. The day unfolded well: She had gotten out of bed, she was outside. She had not gotten dressed as if to go to work, even though she had not worked since my father got sick, and climbed back into bed with all her clothes on, which she had, in what I see now were the worst moments, done a few times. The day was good enough that it gave me the nerve to ask.

"Mom," I said. "Did anyone from St. Mary's call?"

"Those bureaucrats? Not that I know of."

She shook dirt from her gloves. The details of re-enrolling overwhelmed me. They'd called to explain but my mother had accidentally erased the message before I'd fully understood all of what I needed to do or even written down a number to call, for which she was immediately apologetic. I'd called various offices a few times and had not gotten anywhere. Maybe I could at least make up some finals and not lose the fall semester. When I thought of asking for help, I could hear my father, saying, You just need to get to work. My mother too did not like the idea of special circumstances. She wouldn't have called if I'd asked her to. She'd never really wanted me to transfer from the community college. I didn't ask more. It was a good day; I didn't want to push it.

In the afternoon, she said she wanted to go out to do an errand, and I said, Great! I was still at the geraniums when I heard her come home.

In the kitchen, she'd unplugged the coffee maker. A new one sat on the counter, a stack of coupons she had been clipping shoved out of the way in a messy pile. She spooned coffee grounds into a filter.

"I got us a new one!" she said, and clapped her hands. She pressed the start button. We watched the machine working away.

"There," my mother said. "So that's all taken care of."

She poured a cup; I watched her take a sip. But then, a little while later, I heard her door close. Her mug was on the counter, cold. My mother was someone who would find a useful thing and do it. Someone who dressed and applied lipstick and a chalky powder that matched her fair skin perfectly. But now it was as though she only had so much she could give to any day, and once that was expended, she collapsed in on herself. She certainly wasn't going to cook. And maybe she wouldn't even eat.

Danny came home. He'd pulled his hair into a stringy ponytail, making him look even balder and thinner. I was clipping the rest of the coupons. Carolina Rice, Hellmann's mayo. He must have seen my look.

"She's in her room?" he said. I nodded. We went upstairs and hovered outside her door.

"Should we knock?" I whispered.

He cracked his reddish, knobby knuckles.

"Nah," he said. "Let's make dinner."

But then we discovered there was no food in the house. So, we had to go back out to Giant Foods.

"I can go," I said. "I can drive."

"I will drive," he said, grasping the keys.

"You're such a tyrant with that thing. Can't I even drive to the store?"

"Possibly," he said. "But not now."

And then, of course, in the Chatham Town Center parking lot, for no reason, he wanted to wait in the car.

Inside, I went to buy some frozen pizzas. We were keeping it simple. It seems now like we should have at least been able to eat actual food, and buy, for instance, a head of lettuce. I rolled up my sleeve to avoid the dreck of condensation on the inside of the case's door. Just then, two people walked down the aisle and I recognized the woman: hair like a triangle, a purse tucked over her arm. I'd gone to high school with her. We were nominally friends. With her was a tall blond man wearing boat shoes. She was the big high school winner. Her name returned to me. Melanie.

"Katie!" she said, spotting me. "Are you home visiting? Weren't you at St. Mary's? It's so great to see you."

"Here I am. So where are you these days?" I asked, trying to dodge the subject of me.

She'd been in Germany studying economics. "I'm going to the Sorbonne in the fall. I'm terrified," she said, her eyes giddy.

"It is going to be very hard," said the blond guy.

"This is Dolf," she said.

"So nice to meet one of Melanie's friends from home," he said.

"We're trying to decide what to make my parents for dinner," Melanie said. "Where are you working?"

When I didn't answer, she changed her question.

"Or will you be back at St. Mary's?"

The list of arrangements unrolled in my mind: The two hours to campus. A form for an extension due to extenuating circumstance, which the message had said was now lost? Maybe? It seemed I needed the form to not lose the tuition. All I wanted was to set off into the desert with a sunset in front of me. I couldn't answer, and I shrugged, and saw myself, shoving a pair of glasses back up my nose, a pair I wasn't even wearing. I smiled at them, smiling at me.

"We'll see!" I said.

We stood between the freezer cases, the piped-in music eating my brain.

"Does this store have a bakery?" Dolf asked Melanie. "Do these markets have bakeries?"

Pointing, I said, "That way." Melanie nodded, as if she hadn't spent her whole life coming to this Giant Foods, which hadn't even had its floors re-linoleumed since elementary school.

We parted with an awkward hug. "See you soon!" she said.

I thought, Not so.

Outside Danny was not where we parked. I waited on the chilly asphalt, and the car rolled up slowly, the way he always drove. I got in and slammed the door. He was drinking from a 7-Eleven cup filled with a slushy green liquid.

"Dude," I said. "What is that? It looks like ectoplasm."

I saw Melanie and the boyfriend exiting, her purse stapled to her forearm. They waved.

"Who were those people?" Danny said.

"Don't worry about it," I said. I shoved the sleeves of my sweatshirt right up to my biceps.

At home, my mother was up, and I was filled with tepid relief. I could see that Danny was relieved, too, even through the hollow face he made as he slurped. I heated the frozen pizzas and we picked at them. Later, I got the book of desert photography from the basement and sat in the den, idly turning the pages.

Danny came in. "It is time for me to get a milkshake and go peruse some records," he said, with a shrug that said, come along if you must.

I ran upstairs to change, threw off the sweatshirt and watched it land on the closet floor, and we took off.

In the night the landscape felt like a destroyed dream. He cruised through the drive-thru: halogen peeking through a cracked acrylic sign, the pictures of food a hot, overcooked fantasy. Beige concrete, shattered curb, the orange neon G. Car lot: windshields brushed in mist. Highway: slash of black-and-white fluorescent deleting the forest. In ten years, every edge of it will be flossed by subdivisions, four-story townhouses with no front door and no yard. But it was 1998 and the stereo pulsed with rage and spite, saying, my whole existence is flawed, and it is this way for all of us in the Tower Records parking lot: Everyone asking, Please let me someday be a person with ideas. The same prayer, the same song. Tower Records: the only store open, like a beacon, with an acre of empty parking lot behind us.

We stayed until closing. As we left, the white lines of the parking spaces looked like graves. He blasted the radio. We got into a disagreement about jam bands.

He turned down the volume. "Was that not Melanie Tucker? At Giant? Her brother was in my year."

"Good to know," I said.

"What is your problem?" he said.

"She was with her European boyfriend," I said. "I was buying a frozen pizza."

His look had a wisp of sympathy in it. I guess this was all I needed to pour my heart out. Not that he cared. Maybe he did. I didn't even want to do all those things, I said, I didn't want to go to school for economics, didn't want a Dutch boyfriend or whatever, and I definitely did not want to make dinner for anyone's parents.

He sighed. A drop of rain hit the windshield.

"What you must learn," he said, "is that there is no point in doing anything. So people like that are just spiders."

I looked at him driving in his grandmotherly way.

"But I just want to go somewhere not here." I heard my voice and I was whining.

"Then, do," he said. "Except going nowhere may be your lot in life."

The metal on the stereo seethed; I wanted to flick Danny's scrawny wrist for saying that. But he was right. At least he earned an actual paycheck.

As a truck roared past us, spitting water, he slowed.

"Do you ever get scared of getting into a car accident?" I said. "Is that why you drive so slow?" I said.

"I do not drive that slow."

"You kinda do."

"If I do, it is because people are idiots, and because the car is a delicate machine."

"This car?" I said. "It handles like you're driving a beach ball."

Danny turned on the windshield wipers and they squealed across the glass.

"You didn't answer my question," I said.

In his pause I could hear the sound of metal breaking against metal.

"Yes, I do at times fear this," he answered.

Rain sped down the windshield, until the wipers wicked it away.

"Did you know that Mom took all the pictures of her out of the photo albums?" I asked.

He twitched his head over at me.

"The pictures of Dad too?"

"Those are still there," I said.

The rain became steadier, and he turned the wipers up. "I am sure she kept them. They must be somewhere."

"Maybe it was all too much," I said. "She doesn't seem good."

"No. She does not."

"Should we do something?" I said. "To help her, like, go back to work or something. Or just, take her out more."

He glared at me. "She is better than she was," he said. "And you know as well as anybody that she would refuse any such efforts."

He was wasn't wrong. I pictured one of us going to sit on her bed and saying, Hey, Mom, patting her hand. It wasn't us. I didn't bother to answer Danny. I knew he was right. I watched a droplet of water skim down the windshield. I couldn't help her, she couldn't help me. I had been sending those résumés, listing my false diploma. I had a vague idea that I'd move out, grab a room with some people, but I couldn't think past that. Danny would move out, if he didn't spend all his money on CDs. Maybe my mother would snap out of it. The prospect of that job at the publishing house washed over me. Despite myself, I felt that I was winning. Whatever race there was for a not-well-paid job, I was in the lead. If I had it, I could've told Melanie I had an actual job. The distant myth of my sister came back to me. She'd had only that one half night of freedom. I wondered what job she would have wanted—probably not this one, or Danny's. The droplets grew, and my thoughts swirled.

"I don't know why," I said. "I'm not scared of getting in a car accident. I'm scared of being here forever and getting sick and dying."

"You could die when Wile E. Coyote chases you off a cliff," Danny answered.

"Every time I have a serious thought you say something like that," I said. "Don't you ever have even one serious thought?"

"All my thoughts are serious," he said. "Listen to this chord."

He stuck a brand-new CD into the stereo.

The next day, I had the car. I had won for the moment and went to the internship. We were compiling a list of names of faculty in anthropology—applied, forensic anthropology—by searching through directories on college websites. All afternoon Seth had been talking in a fake accent, a lisping, twerpy Foghorn Leghorn.

"Hickety boo!" he said.

Andrea laughed, and I heard the production manager sigh from the office nearby, closing her door.

I went to the kitchen for a cup of the terrible free coffee, and overheard Lola and one of the editors talking: The rumor was true. The editorial assistant position was real.

Back in our office I felt like I'd heard some wicked secret. I wanted to tell Andrea, only, not in front of Seth, who was barely working.

"I shay, we've got to proofread theshe catalogsh," he said, Andrea laughing.

Even though I was tired of it, I laughed too, which felt like fresh air. I waited for the right moment to catch Andrea. In the meantime, Seth went back to work at last. Just then Lola came in, tall as a scarecrow.

"Kate, handle this for me?" she said, lilting some paperwork into my hand and flitting off.

It was typewritten corrections from an author who had probably never touched a computer. We were still in that age. I fixed it and sent it back to her.

A little while later, Lola returned, popping her head over the edge of my cube's wall.

"Finished already?" she said. "How fantastic you are!"

The overweening compliment made me blush with happiness as she went back to her office. Andrea and Seth had heard it, no doubt.

"Katie," Seth said, "Here's a professor from St. Mary's. Isn't that where you went?"

"Right," I said.

He kept talking. I heard it was this kind of place, etc., on and on, like a fingernail digging into my palm. Him smiling, so wide and unencumbered. I felt the fresh air evaporate, and heard myself. Mmm. Right. Guess so.

"Geez!" he said. "Whatsa matter?" His expression turned to that of a sad puppy. He rested the knuckle of his index finger on his cheek and twisted it.

I wanted to squirt hot, bad coffee at his adolescent face. I turned to the desk, pushed the escape key. I heard Andrea clicking, she'd turned away too.

"Chill out," Seth said.

"I'm pretty chill," I said. "It's cool."

Uncharacteristically, Seth worked all afternoon. The two of them left before I did; there was no chance to catch Andrea. I drove home, one mile an hour in a terrible backup. Seth had riled me after all. I thought of that message from St. Mary's. As I drove, sun setting over the highway's concrete barriers, it occurred to me that if my father had wanted me to go to class—Learn at least one thing, I heard him say—my mother seemed to object. Maybe she'd even erased the message on purpose, which was a horrible thought. Maybe it was the cost. My father'd had a life insurance policy, which I gathered was why she hadn't gone back to work. But I was the one who'd pay tuition, the one with the huge student loan. I fumed, until I only heard the talking of the news radio, clenching my teeth, seeing Seth's pony-cute face.

When I got home, Andrea called. They were going to the Drain, remember? "Thank god," I said.

My mother had made dinner; the scent of sautéing onion filled me with relief. I went upstairs and changed, checking my outfit: a black vest, my black boot-cut pants, purple shirt with a highish neck with this long extra fabric that I tied in a sort of scarf. Downstairs my mother wanted us to eat at the table together. She took a pile of knives and forks from the cage of the dishrack.

Danny said, "This Friday I will be driving to Massachusetts."

"Let's set the table, shall we?" she said, and stuck a spoon in the casserole, making a noise like a boot sinking in mud. Then she whipped her head around, like someone had rung a bell.

"What? All night? No. Leave Saturday."

"I want to be there for all of Saturday."

"Why do you get the car the whole weekend?" I said. "I'm taking the car on Friday."

Danny said, "You have somewhere to go? You do not. This is because you have no life."

"I'm going out tonight," I said. "And I'm taking the car on Friday. You're being such an asshole."

"Katie, don't call your brother an asshole."

"Can I get the keys?" I said.

Neither of them responded. Danny scraped casserole onto his fork. My mother drank her wine.

"You're not going to drive at night like that," my mother said.

"Statement," Danny said. "I am driving to Massachusetts."

"Why is it about when he's going to drive the car, and not about whether he has to share it?" I said.

"Katie, don't yell at your brother."

"I'm not yelling at him. Keys?"

My mother said. "Katie, please load the dishwasher before you go."

"Can't Danny load the dishwasher?"

For some reason Danny picked that moment to look at me askance. "What are you wearing? Are you in the marching band?"

"Hey, shut it," I said, clenching my fork upright, its end pressing into the table. But it was true. It was all polyester. "You think all I do is nothing, so what do you care? You're such an asshole."

"You have to load the dishwasher because Danny did it yesterday," my mother said.

"We didn't even eat together yesterday," I said.

"Katie, stop being such a child. I will never understand why you act like such a child. I ask you to do one simple thing. How can you talk to your brother like that." She turned to Danny.

"And you," she said, her voice pitching upward. She stared into her napkin, put it against her face and began to cry, speaking to us both. "You make me feel disgraced."

Danny and I sat, a cold harpoon jutting into my chest.

"Mom," I said. I touched her shoulder, her bones like gears. "Mom, I'm sorry."

Danny looked like he'd swallowed something awful, his lips pressed together.

"Mom, it's okay," I said. "See? I'm doing it."

I opened the door to the dishwasher, and it bounced on its hinges.

She rubbed her face, her eyes red-rimmed. The harpoon drove farther into my sternum. She brushed one side of her hair with her fingers, gently, then the other.

"You have to run water over them first," she said, as if teaching me for the first time.

Danny must have seen my face, which must have said: If I spend one more minute here, I'll die. As I loaded the plates, he put the keys on the countertop. The florid hum of the dishwasher began, and then I was swinging the car around the cul-de-sac, past dark houses, to the thumping pavement, and I was gone, gone, gone.

I opened the door to the Drain: dense rock and roll hammering, black walls spattered in chalk and decaying posters. Andrea and some loose crowd of people I barely knew were inside. Red tin ceiling, red glitter vinyl couches, neon juke box. A friend of hers in a black jacket with a wallet on a chain bought drinks because he was twenty-one. He took the crumbled money I gave him and returned with another tumbler. We sat in a booth, smoking.

"Hey, you know this book?" Andrea said, and reached into her bag. It was one our company's titles. Surprisingly, she was carrying it around with her. Something about English labor markets, and it filled her with ideas—it related to punk! she said. I'd forgotten about the job opening since the kitchen. I needed to ask her.

But the thought was lost in the tumble of money we threw on the table, and the conversation changed back to music, and more drinks, and pool, and cigarettes, and soon we were out of range of it. Something under my skin loosened, after those glasses of amber whiskey. That place had a halo of delight that kept people inside till they zombified. There was steam inside me that needed to be blown off. It was too good, it was too fun, and the job seemed to not matter, nothing mattered except the laughter and the juke box blaring, you don't remember, you don't remember. We went to the roof deck, under the moon. We should go to New York, we should start a magazine. Yes, yes, yes! Watching an idea passing through my mind felt like seeing a unicorn.

"What should we do now?" someone said. A holy question.

The night spun out, and we stood on the sidewalk. I felt like the weather was wonderful. Even though it had started to rain an icy rain.

"Everything's turning," I said.

They all looked at me. "Hey there," Andrea said. It was decided that they had to take me home. I sat in front while Andrea drove the white car and the black-jacketed friend drove Andrea's car to my house, dropping me off. For a second, I stood on the dark porch and watched Andrea's car puff away.

Upstairs I went to the bathroom. I threw up, the white basin filled with green-brown swirl. I thought, Try not to wake up Mom.

I went to sleep and already had a hangover, and when I woke, I had a hangover still. It had grown like a horn in the middle of the night. Danny drove me to the office, a pungent taste in my mouth that not even the sour office coffee could cover. When I finally arrived, Andrea grinned. I said, "I'm alive."

"You live it up last night, Kate?" Seth said. "Too many Jell-O shots?"

I didn't answer. I went to the kitchen, and on the company bulletin board, beside a bratty sign about the microwave, was a job posting. The Editorial Assistant.

As I sipped the coffee, I thought of my mother. She'd worked in human resources, and later as a fundraiser for nonprofits. She'd been good at talking to strangers. I had the feeling that the posting was meant for me: paycheck, desk, Lola's easy tasks. But what if I wanted to move to New York? What if I just wanted to go to New York? Or the desert, wind on my face. If I took that job, I wouldn't be able to do any of those things. But I was not doing those things. I was not getting on buses, I was not scheming to leave town. I sighed. It was time to make a decision.

In the narrow hallway, I rounded a corner and almost smashed into Lola and Andrea.

"Oh, hi there!" said Lola. I answered cheerfully. They walked quickly by, Lola's swishing blue jacket brushing me. "Hey," I said to Andrea, but she only gave me a nervous look.

I knew what it was. Lola was telling Andrea about the job. The race I'd imagined was happening.

I returned to my desk and tried to get back to work. Seth teased me about my hangover, and at 12:01, went out to lunch, tossing his shoulder bag on jauntily. I wanted to ask, What is even in there? You're just going to your car. He was gone for ages. Perhaps Lola was on her way to me, for my turn. I waited for her as long as I could, until I was so hungry and queasy that I walked to the deli buried in the next boxy office park over, where I spent some of my saved coffee shop money on an order of fries, and ate, sitting on a hard, plastic bench.

When I returned, through the skinny glass panel of Lola's office, I saw Seth talking, her amused smile as he gesticulated, pen in hand. He was wearing glasses.

Him? I thought. Really? He had never once worn glasses. I was glum, and went back to work on the mailing list. Merge! I said to it. But it spat errors back at me. It was getting late. Seth came back to his desk, removed the glasses. Without Andrea around—she hadn't come back yet—just Seth and me, the air was tense. He slouched in his chair, looked at me for a split second but said nothing.

At four o'clock, still no Lola. Andrea came back at last, carrying the box of brochures we had to mail.

"You done that list yet?" Seth said. He was picking up and putting down an object, something soft and blue. A miniature foam computer.

"You wanna try?" I said, not looking up.

"No thanks," he said, standing and stretching. "Guess these can wait till tomorrow." He stood, stretched, and left.

It was just me and Andrea.

"Want some chips?" She tilted a plastic sack in my direction.

I was glad to see her face. I took a giant handful, so did she, and we scattered crumbs on the keyboard until we fixed the stupid mailing list. Take that! Andrea said, jabbing her finger at the Excel document. For a while we sat sealing brochures with white, round sticky disks while talking about bands. Post-punk versus proto-punk. As we came to the end of a stack, I looked at the clock. It was 5:30. There'd been no Lola.

A hundred things went through my mind. In the grayish industrial carpeting, a paper clip was buried. I shoved it with my shoe. Andrea creased brochures, her cramped face peaceful. I thought of that book shoved in her bag, of her pouring over flap copy, skimming bibliographies.

As I tried to free the paper clip, it came to me that I'd naively thought that it would be me they picked. But I was fraudulent. I should have known: I was wrong for that job, and it was wrong for me. Somehow, even Lola had seen it. Her compliment—in that moment I finally saw it—she felt sorry for me. Was I not even as good as that lazy ass-kisser? I thought of all those résumés I'd sent out and they seemed right then like scraps of paper, thrown out the window of a moving car.

I looked at the clock again, and realized, I didn't need to stay.

"You heading home?" I asked Andrea.

"Not just yet," she said.

"Thanks for the snack," I said. And turned to go.

As I did, Andrea called. "Kate. Did Lola come talk to you?"

The sound in her voice was longing. I shook my head.

"Did you apply for it?" I asked, and she nodded. Her expression turned tense.

"So did Seth," she said. "What if they offer it to him?"

"They can't do that," I said. "They just can't. Jesus Christ, he's so annoying. And he barely works. He left an hour ago, for Christ's sake. I thought you liked him."

"He's not that bad. He's amusing sometimes." And then she smiled, mischief in her face. "Actually, he is pretty bad. He was wearing those damn glasses."

"For sure they were fake," I said, and we both laughed hard, Andrea grabbing that blue squishy computer and saying, Guess we'll just mail these tomorrow.

"Hey listen," she said. "I didn't say anything. About you know, what you told me. But I'm sure if you said something, they'd understand."

"Nah, it's okay," I said, scraping the paper clip in the carpet with my shoe, flipping it like bait, caught on a fishhook. "I don't think I deserve it."

I wanted her to contradict me. But she didn't.

"One day you will," she said.

I felt a tremolo in my lip, but it dissipated, and we were sunny again. I was envious, and happy for her that she wanted something that much. I wanted to want something that much.

Before I left, I went to look for Lola. I had to tell her that she shouldn't hire that twerpy kid, that it was Andrea who deserved it, who was real, and Seth was fake and she shouldn't be fooled, but Lola wasn't there. I asked a man reading a manuscript in the next office if he'd seen her.

"Who?" he said.

I never found Lola. In the end it didn't matter, because they gave it to that idiot. As for Andrea, she was undeterred. She ended up working in foreign rights and moving to London. I still see her from time to time. But I gave up sending résumés for the rest of that year—the giving up being a kind of freedom—and instead, I waitressed. As for Seth, he's probably still an editorial underling.

That night my mother and Danny and I were in the living room, watching television.

"Are you still driving to Massachusetts?" my mother asked.

"Saturday, I suppose," Danny said, and she seemed calmed.

A thicket grew in the air, my brother's hand on the back of his head, scratching, all of us probably thinking of a car, hitting another in the dark. His stiffened arm, a nervous move.

The next day I woke and it was 11. The weather had changed to balmy, heat in the air as though a storm approached. In the upstairs hallway, my mother was painting the molding along the floorboards, and seeing her, my relief was no longer tepid; I could picture her as she'd been, doing project after project, taking phone calls, scribbling in her day planner. She crouched, laying drop cloths. I changed my clothes, and we painted.

"You don't have to help if you don't want to," she said.

"No," I said, "I want to."

"Thank you, Sweetheart," she said. The sound of our brushes overtook the hall.

"Mom," I said. "Am I remembering it right that you and Dad went to Paris? From that photo?"

She didn't answer for a long time.

"No," she said. "He did that on his own."

"When was that?"

"I can't really remember," she said.

Something downstairs made a thump. "What was that?" she said, putting her brush down. I followed, and at the bottom of the stairs, she held the clock from the powder room wall.

"Fell right off the wall!" she said. "Didn't even break! Can you believe that!"

She laughed, and as she did a cold shiver ran up my arms. On her face was an astonished look, an expression I hadn't seen in so long. Maybe I had never seen it.

In the afternoon, she worked in the yard. While she was out, I hung the clock back on the wall. I tapped the nail back into the wall, just an inch or two higher.

I cleaned up the paint, and as I carried it to the garage, I saw my mother in the yard, looking at the horizon, where the clouds were lifting. Another system was moving in. Sometimes it seemed that without my father, there was not the right amount of space for her. Too much, or not enough. But, seeing her, out in the yard, a figure alone, she didn't seem sad. She seemed homesick.

The afternoon had spilled out into evening. Danny would be home soon. My mother took a shower, and I watched the news.

In the kitchen, she said, "I'm going to make chicken stock. It's not going to make itself, is it?" She opened the refrigerator and began piling things on the counter.

"Mom," I said. "Why don't we go out? We could go to Cliff's."

"I don't know," she said, letting the refrigerator door drift closed. "We should be frugal. And I don't think I want to go out. But you can."

"How 'bout a pizza? That's cheap. Bring it home, so no one has to cook."

"Well," she said. "All right."

I phoned Ledo's. "Get a large," my mother said. "So there'll be some for Daniel." After a while I put on a jacket and she gathered her purse. She was going to come too.

Without thinking, I asked: "You want me to drive?"

Then, without a word, as though handing me an egg, she gave me the keys to the maroon Citroën.

It felt smooth under my hands as I drove, and yet, with a growling heat in its engine. I drove gently, like Danny would have. The air was so warm that we had to roll the back windows down. The streets were wet, the air smelled of grass clippings. After a while Danny would come home. Maybe he and I would go somewhere later.

Ledo's was crowded, and she and I waited, the smell of tomato sauce in the air, the hostess neatly stacking menus. My mother touched a small cut on the back of her hand. The noise of the place buzzed. The hostess brought our food, and my mother held it on her lap on the drive home.

"It's making me hungry," she said, and we both laughed.

My mother lowered the sun shade and looked at her teeth in its miniature mirror. I glanced at her, and in the short second that followed, a squirrel darted across the road. I hit the brakes.

"Katie!" she said, grasping the door handle. The heavy car sent us both wagging forward tightly against our seat belts, and she grabbed the pizza box.

But it was already over, the squirrel was gone; we were fine.

A memory caught me. I was small, maybe eight. After my sister died. My father took me somewhere to eat. A fast-food place. My mother wasn't there, neither was Danny. Where had they been? Outside it was raining hard. Inside, the smell of burned oil, the floor greasy. There was a counter where you could load up your burger from a sort of salad bar. My father was impatient. He left the booth and went to that little station, for, I don't know, pickles.

I remember his back, in a faded wooly plaid shirt. He sat down, ate a bite or two.

"This is terrible," he said, as though to himself.

Before he'd said it, I'd liked the way the drops formed on the window. How it blurred the outside world. Waiting in line was fun, how my father leaned down and said, What do you want?, handed me a stack of napkins, and said, Hold these. Just us, just me and him. But as he spoke, I saw where I was. In a fast-food place with scum on the floor, rain pouring down on a broken parking lot.

In the car, my mother said, "Didn't you see that?" a tone in her voice like she thought I was blind.

"I saw," I said.

At home, the stuff for the chicken stock she'd wanted to make was sprawled on the counter. Neither of us had noticed. I put it all away. We ate in front of the television. Neatly, off china plates, the way my mother liked to eat takeout. When the program ended, she loaded the dishwasher, returned to the couch.

"Where's Danny?" she said. "It's getting late."

It dawned on us both at the same time.

"Do you think he already left for Massachusetts?" I said.

"He said he was leaving tomorrow," she said.

She went to the phone. "Maybe he's working," she said. "I'm calling his desk."

It rang for a long time, her face clamped in worry.

"No answer," she said.

We sat, an antsy feeling around me. He had taken the car. I went to the phone, looked out the window. I dialed Andrea's number. No answer. The long shape of the yard spilled in front of me, a darkening mass. I felt a swell, a vinegary yearning. It was as though at any moment I might go upstairs and pack a bag, and walk out into the black, dewy grass.

"Mom," I said. "Do you think he really left?"

"I guess so," she said, her voice frightened. "I wish he wouldn't drive at night."

My mother touched the cut on the back of her hand. I thought of him in the white car. It had become his car, filled with crap: a haze of crumbs and nickels and hair. Asphalt, breezing past. He'd get really tired. Maybe he'd nod off for a nanosecond. He'd pull over at a rest stop, drink a Dr Pepper, shake it off. Get back on the road, roll the windows down so it'd be cold and he'd be awake, awake, awake, and his heart would race. Having just missed death.

"Mom, do you want to maybe go out? We could go to the mall. We could get a coffee and go for a walk in the mall."

"Katie, it's so late. We already went out."

"Mom," I said.

"What? What's the matter?"

"Can't we go out? Don't you want to get out of this house?"

All of a sudden she snapped at me, her thin neck straining.

"Katie, can't we just stay in? Why do you have to do everything? Can't you just be happy?"

She flicked her finger in the air, in a sort of ampersand.

"Fine," I said. "I'm putting the pizza away."

I bundled the slices into sharp squares of tin foil. I wiped the counters with the dish towel. A burning lump formed in my throat, and I went upstairs.

In Danny's room, a gloaming drifted through the windows—he'd left one open. I felt hollow. I thought of my father, jangling the keys in his pockets, the change, the Swiss Army knife. I was still clutching the dish towel. I stood in the mess, the milkshake cup still there. I raised it, smelled the rotten mess inside. Danny was gone, not here with this, not folding the dish towel. I wanted to scream at him. A thought went through my mind: If he dies, there will barely be any of us left.

But somehow, I knew he'd be fine. And he was. It is not that far, he'd said, in one of those moments when I could see his logic. Flawed though it was, it pulled him along, untrammeled. I sat in his room, craving the same for myself, craving more than a half night of freedom.

Then, I heard a thump. I went downstairs. My mother stood at the bottom of the stairs.

"How strange," she said. She was holding the clock. It had fallen again.

In my mind, I heard something. Call it a radio signal. It was one of the few times I have ever felt her—my sister—and him, my father, together. I began to cry.

"What's wrong, Sweetheart?" my mother said, her cheeks sunken, her brown eyes soft.

"Where are all the photos?" I said. "How could you throw them away?"

"Oh, Sweetheart," she said. Her face white. She stood and hugged me. She didn't ask what I meant. She seemed to know.

"I didn't throw them away," she said, her small shoulder touching my chin. "I'll give them back to you someday. But I just can't look at them now. I can't see anything."

All at once I knew what would happen next. Danny would leave, and then I would, leaving my mother, who couldn't take care of herself. But I saw it wasn't true. She could. Only, not with us here. She said it again, quietly: "Can't you just be happy?"

Perhaps I had to let her ask me that question. Even though trying to answer it frightened me to the bone. Can't you?

We sat in the living room. Danny didn't call. I sat and cried a while longer. Then it was just us with the quiet of the television. Silence like a sentry. After a while I watched too. But it felt like getting a stitch without a painkiller.

Sometimes, when I'm putting the dishes away, or sliding a letter into an envelope, or when I click on my turn signal, about to glide onto an exit ramp, when I'm doing some normal, gentle thing, I think, maybe she's mailed me the photos. They haven't showed up yet. But maybe one day they will.

GUIDANCE & CONTROL

One summer, after my sister died, I went to music camp in Western Maryland, one state over. By then I was eleven. Maybe my parents let me go to camp that summer because they felt sorry for me, or they wanted to be rid of me, wanted to be alone with their grief. I'd never gone to camp before. That year, my brother would grab his fork at dinner and eat only three frantic bites. He was twelve and a half. One night, he carved a hole in the wall in his closet, and slid things into it. He cut off all his eyelashes with a pair of kitchen scissors. He destroyed a bike. He would scream insults down the hall at my father and mother but at neither of them, at *it*, at the hallway, the linen closet, the brown carpet, at nowhere, at everywhere. His voice high-pitched, damaged. My father would yell back, roaring, and I would see delirium. On a snow day, my brother threw a clump of ice at a boy from the neighborhood. The boy threw one back, and my brother got four stitches. It was a double deal. At night, he sometimes would wake, and vomit in a panic. Then he would apologize. I have a theory. I have a theory now that he was trying to show us that it was impossible to die. He was trying to prove that, despite our best efforts, we will survive to see the ruin.

If I wanted to disappear, he wanted to cut himself to pieces.

The morning they drove me to camp, my father was almost jovial. Lying in the back seat, watching the stream of a telephone wire passing overhead, I had the sense that I could be the new girl. Someone would say the name of my school as though it was an exotic word. My father's mood persisted, with my brother next to me, headphones on his ears, until we were on the road, and a pickup wouldn't move as he tried to merge onto the highway.

"Jackass," he said.

Then it was as it usually was, and he was sullen, he and my mother, staring silently out the windshield.

At the camp, there were kids who had been there for two, three weeks already. We drove up a hill past the pool, past tennis courts with sagging nets. My mother went with me to register, into the building like a barn with translucent panels for a ceiling letting in a shallow daylight that seemed to pool everywhere. There was a main room like a gymnasium, and a dining hall. A counselor showed us upstairs to the bunk room. A room with almost forty beds. Then my mother planted a kiss on the part of my hair, and left. The bunks had all been pushed together, into two longs sets, making what felt like a couple of train boxcars. I had a top bunk on an end, near the door, far from the windows. The one least desired. The girl next to me had pink sheets and bunions on her feet and was a foot taller than I was.

I climbed into my bunk and set my sleeping bag down, accidentally stepping on the pink sheets.

"Your mattress is kinda stiff," I said to her.

"I like it that way," she said. "I had yours before but I hated it."

She lay back with one hand on her forehead like she had a fever. The feeling of potential I'd held in the car, even as my father gripped the steering wheel, evaporated. A weight descended on the place like a thunderstorm about to roll through. I went into the bathroom at the end of the long room. There were no lights in the showers, hung with thick blue curtains. A brown stain covered one corner.

At dinner that night, I waited in line holding a plastic cafeteria tray the color of sour milk; the girl with the bunions stood ahead of me. I sat with her even though she hadn't looked at me. Another girl sat next to me, her bangs forming an arch on her forehead.

"Nora got a letter today!" she said. I realized she was talking about herself. "You're too new to get letters," she said to me. "What instrument do you play? I play sax."

"I wrote Matt a letter," the girl with the bunions said.

Nora leaned to me and quietly said, "One of the other boys has a crush on Sabrina, but she likes Matt."

"Wow," I said, although I didn't know any of them. "I play clarinet. I like the sax."

That night Nora taught me to play a card game where you had to slap all the jacks. She was tiny, but already her hips formed a bell on the bench as we sat, moths batting the fluorescent tubes overhead. I heard one of the female counselors say to one of the male counselors, I can't make myself love you, I just don't love you.

For some, it was that summer. That summer he had his arm around your waist and you walked in the dark with the breeze and he whispered. That summer you all fell asleep in the afternoon before dinner, that languid hour with the smell of grass drying, your swimsuits on. That summer it rained and got your towels wet on the clothesline. For me it was that summer of those girls. I have no memory of the boys at that place. They were a forest of skinny legs and battered saxophones, electric guitars, lacrosse sticks. I remember only the one counselor, so blond and tan that he glowed, untouchably, unreally handsome. I remember a bricolage of objects and surfaces. The polished concrete floor in that half-warehouse, half-barn building where everything was spilled—pipe cleaners, an entire bucket of beads one afternoon. The cheap ice cream, strawberry a medicinal pink, sheet music from the band practice that took place every afternoon, folding music stands. The girls were not the band kids I knew from home. Those kids wore shirts with music jokes printed on them. They were overweight, or impossibly skinny. These girls were fashionable, they had sunglasses and cover-ups that matched their swimsuits. They were twelve, or thirteen. The only one who resembled the kids from home was Becky, one of the counselors, who had a triangular bob and wore heavy brown sandals. She admired my clarinet. She couldn't have been more than sixteen. She gave me the private lessons the camp fee entitled me to.

At the end of the week there would be band performances and a recital. Becky picked a duet by Fauré that I would play at the recital, even though all the music there was not that sort of music. It was "Red River Valley," or the theme from *Superman*. At home, I was last chair. On Tuesday the band director, that man who ran the camp and had long white hair that flopped when he waved his baton, moved me to the front. When he counted rest measures, he laid his arms across his belly. The great American composer, John Williams, he said.

Later, at the pool, I lingered by Nora. Sabrina shrieked at me from the water. "Get off my towel!" she said. I scooted farther away, up the pebbled grassy hill. Nora looked over her shoulder at me.

"I wasn't on her towel," I said.

"She's just mad about Matt again," Nora said, and ran and jumped in the pool, and I did, too. She drifted away to the diving board, but I was too scared, and got out. At night, in the bunk's bathroom, brushing our teeth, she said, "You got a tan!" I poked my shoulders with my fingers. I could never become the golden color that she was. We looked at each other in the mirror, sat in the bunks until lights out, Nora picking at her toes. "I'll be thirteen next month," she said. "Then my mom will let me shave my legs."

The next day I played the Fauré duet with Becky outside, under some trees, our feet on pine needles. "More!" she said. She sang along as I played my part. When we were finished, she said, "Good, very good. Just watch your control. So who did you ask to play the other part in the recital?"

I just stared at her, the sound of drums being played wafting out of the main building. I squeezed the tips of my fingers into the holes in my clarinet.

"You didn't ask anyone to play the other part?"

I said, "There isn't anyone to ask."

She let a long trail of air out of her mouth, exhaling, like a practice breath.

"I could skip it," I said.

She raised her flute, resting it against her chin, like it belonged there. I didn't really want to skip it. I wanted to show the other kids that I was the best one there. At least I would have that.

"I'll play it," she said, and she sighed, this time a loose, sloppy breath. I wanted to hug her, even though she didn't want to play it, and I stared into the music stand so she wouldn't see my face.

On the picnic table, before dinner, Nora and I played cards. When I won, she said, You *cheat*, and kicked her heels at the mulch.

The last night, Friday, arrived. The next day was the recital. After dinner, as the sun slipped behind the tops of the trees, a cloud bank the color of ash rolled in. They were calling for rain. At the end of dinner, tables cleared, noise of clattering dishes drifting from the kitchen, the director stood and presented some awards. Most improved woodwind, most improved brass. The girls screamed, working themselves into a frenzy. The counselors cheered. He said how proud he was, how well he was sure everyone would do at the performances the next day. Some of the girls began to sniffle. In the air hung the smells of the meal. Browned beef. Bread, melted cheese, spaghetti sauce. When everyone clapped, I clapped, but I felt silly doing it. The girls were all either upset or ecstatic.

The director patted his hands toward the floor, asking for the applause to die down.

"Now," he said. "They're calling for rain. We planned to show the movie tonight outside on the hill. Do we want to cancel?"

Everyone screamed, *No.*

"Okay," he said. "But if there is lightning, and if there is pouring rain, everyone has to be back in here the minute we say so. That's the deal. No buts!" And he waved his hand, index finger pointed at the ceiling.

The blond counselor came in, wearing a windbreaker and carrying a flashlight.

After the speeches, a ruckus broke out. Some of the boys ran around the balcony by the bunk rooms. The doors to the outside opened, slammed, opened, slammed. I walked around looking for anyone, maybe Becky. I went to the bunk room and most of the girls were there, fussing with clothes, makeup. The counselors were gone. The sky had darkened, the trees turned to a black abyss. I lingered near my bunk, packing.

I went to the bathroom. Girls were looking in the mirrors, doing their faces, their hair.

"Aren't you going to do your hair, Katie?" somebody said.

"Should I do my hair?" I said.

"That's what we always do on the last night," a blonde girl said. "You want to look good on the last night."

I caught my reflection in the mirror. My hair, with its wave gone puffy from the heat, was so long that it often caught under my arms. In the fluorescent light, it looked inky. The girls peered at themselves in the mirror. They looked angry. My chin had a crease, a thin cleft that bumped at the bottom. For a moment I saw my father's chin, brushed in black stubble. So I had his chin, I realized.

"I wasn't going to do my hair," I said.

The girl glared at me. "I was just *asking*," she said.

"I could get my hairbrush," I said.

It was silent, except for brushing, the tapping of bobby pins against the sink edge. I didn't know how to do my hair. I used a barrette. That was how my mother did it. I took the barrette out, felt the shift in my scalp. It had been in my hair all day. I gathered it back up in its tight mass. I had never noticed my chin before. But now I did. For the first time I saw it—I began looking at my face the way they looked at theirs. Its bump, that crease, and I saw something ugly.

I went to the stall, locked the door behind me. They could all hear, hear the sound of me urinating. When I was finished, I went to the sink at the end, where no one was using the mirrors, and washed my hands with the slimy bar of soap, squeezing my wrists.

As I left, someone slammed the door ahead of me, and although I pulled my hand away, the tips of my fingers were caught. A stab of pain ran up my hand, my arm. I tried to be silent, but I yelped anyway. A flash of heat rose to my face, and although I didn't turn around, I knew they were all staring at me. I pulled the door open and Nora was there. She wore a windbreaker five sizes too big for her, so it covered her shorts. I held my hand with my other hand. She had slammed the door. She snapped her head away, ponytail flipping, flashed me a look.

I caught a glimpse in her eye, like remorse. Although I couldn't have named it then. It was something that would become remorse later. She'd only have my face to think of when she thought of that moment, later in her life, only me to witness that she hadn't apologized.

Someone said, The movie's starting! The girls all ran out, clattering down the wooden staircase, and I followed. Outside, the kids were assembling on the hill, jumping in front of the screen, their shadows Rorschach blots. I stood near the doorway, the light from the main building shining outward behind me, my shadow on the ground. The projector sat at the top of a wooden staircase above me, one of the counselors fiddling with it. With a wobbling blare the film began, the sound bouncing around the trees. The kids hooted. The girls sat in clusters on the grass, their ponytails sticking up.

Becky came up behind me. "Aren't you going to watch?" she said.

"I guess so," I said.

She wandered down and I followed. We sat near the top of the hill, I on her left. I felt better; I was watching the movie with someone. The floodlights over the tennis courts switched off. I could hear the switches flip, a powerful mechanical sound that echoed over the movie. One by one, the floodlights went off, the tennis court disappearing into the black. Then we were all lit by the flickering of the movie, shining around every blade of grass. Over the sound of the movie, still, was the sound of insects devouring the darkness.

We watched for a while. On the screen, the characters walked through a cornfield with a setting sun overhead. Then Becky got up and left, without a word. I saw Nora ahead of me, gazing down the hill, not watching the movie. The blond counselor stood near the row of hedges that bordered the trees. He still carried the flashlight. The pine needles felt like a stiff carpet under my legs.

He took a few steps from where he was standing, and sat in the grass. Then Nora got up, her back to me, and sat next to him.

A gust of wind blew, which I heard before I felt, the sounds of leaves moving as though in waves. I shivered. On the screen, there were baseball players in uniforms, carrying bats.

The tune of the duet began to run through my head, and I thought of my father's hands, gripping the steering wheel, and although the melody was almost playful, the sound of it in my mind made me feel afraid. That gust of wind that seemed to last forever blew the darkness around. I stared into the branches moving in the darkness beyond the flickering screen.

When I looked back, the blond counselor—Mark, his name was Mark, I remember it now—was lying on his back. His knees were bent, his feet on the grass. Nora was reclining next to him, resting her head on her hand, leaning on her elbow. She was touching his tan thigh, above the hem of his shorts. She was stroking the hair on his leg. Running it through the tips of her fingers. He lay, hand pressed across his eyes. It lasted for what seemed like hours.

"Do you want me to stop?" I heard Nora say. She asked like it was a serious question. Maybe she thought he was in pain. He might have looked like he was. Under his hand, in the flickering light, I could see he was wincing.

"No," he said.

"I could stop if you wanted me to," she said.

He shook his head.

There was no one behind me. No one could see. The door to the main building was closed. When I looked back, I saw him lift his other hand, and slide it beneath his belt. He let his knees fall slightly open, his one hand pasted against his face, the other working at whatever was there.

I was sitting so close to them. It was as though I was invisible.

I felt tears start to well. I got up and opened the door to the barn. I squinted in the bright light, at the empty room. I wanted to find Becky. I went upstairs to the bunk room.

The light was off. Maybe someone was asleep in there—but no, I thought, they're all at the movie. I couldn't find the light switch.

All of a sudden I felt something move on the floor. Like a shaft of air. But something else. Like someone's hair, passing through the air, pricking my legs. I froze. On the wall, between two windows, was a shadow. In it was a face, almost perfectly formed. A man, bearded, hooded, the shapes of leaves all around him, as though in a forest. The two eyes black, from corner to corner.

My breath caught in my throat. The face seemed to move, twist. The air in my lungs released. I felt my limbs unfreeze, and I ran back to the main room and outside again.

The glare from the movie was almost entirely white, the crowd still. A ball player swung at a pitch, and a crack sounded. There was a hammering in my chest. I searched through the crowd. Nora and the counselor were gone. I found Sabrina sitting with the other girls.

And although they hated me, although they wished I was not there, I went to them and sat, the sound of the movie washing over me. Sabrina turned and stared at me. I guess I must have half-smiled. Her face didn't move, a halo of light from the film around her head.

I would have done anything for someone to simply look at me and let me see their face change into anything other than a mask. I stayed until the movie ended, and we all filed inside. I wasn't going back inside the bunk room unless the lights were on. Unless someone was with me. Back inside, everyone lingered around the main room for a long time. All the counselors seemed to be gone. I sat on a bench, shivering, my hands jammed in my pockets. I was freezing. The door to the outside was open, and the wind rose and fell. A counselor appeared, began shouting at everyone to get to bed.

At last they went to the bunk. I followed, only after seeing that the light was on. Inside there was noise, pillows being thrown, laughing. I sat on my bunk with all my clothes, my jacket on. In the spot where the shadow had been, there was nothing.

"What's wrong with you," Sabrina said.

"Nothing," I said.

"Why are you sitting there like that?"

I opened my mouth to speak, but she began talking to someone else. I felt in my face that I had turned my mouth into the false smile I had worn all week.

Nora came in. She looked perfectly normal. She was wagging her arms by her sides, the sleeves of the jacket dangling over her hands. She tilted her head to one side, and there was none of the meanness of earlier, only a sleepy, wavering look on her face. I almost said hi, like nothing was wrong, and nearly began to cry.

At last Becky came in, telling everyone to go to sleep.

"No more talking," she said.

I rolled myself into the sleeping bag, tried to close my eyes and not open them again. Although I had to go to the bathroom, I just lay there, clenched. Through my closed lids, I saw the light change—Becky had turned off the lights.

"Lights *off*," she said. "Don't make me explain one more time what that means."

For a long while, there was murmuring in the darkness. I tried to listen to it, I tried to hold on to that sound.

"Girls," Becky said.

The talking stopped and there was only the sound of breathing. In the night, I heard the long, low roll of thunder. Slowly, it came closer. Beneath the thunder I thought I heard the sound of an object hitting something, glass, breaking. Of footsteps. As though someone were going quickly, about to break into a run. The sound was under me, not from outside, but not from inside. As though from the space in the floorboards. Perhaps it was only in my mind. The wind moved through the trees, and at last, it rained, and somehow, at last, although I do not know how, I fell asleep.

What do I remember about that morning? It was cold. The sort of cold where you'd freeze in a shadow. The clarinet case. The sheet music, its cover the green of a still river. I try to get my memory to start in a particular spot. It seemed that someone was missing. Maybe someone had gone home early, skipped the recital. That wasn't the point, anyway. The counselors were on edge, maybe it was only that the parents would arrive today, everyone under scrutiny, the kids sad to leave.

I start here: a vinegary taste in my mouth, a reed with a chip in its feathery edge. I had to hold a new one under my tongue, although it never seemed to soften, waiting for my turn to play. I was tucked in the crowd, assembled on the tennis court in the thin sun. I kept watching the hillside for my parents to appear. Kids, holding brass saxophones, guitars. There must have been a dozen short songs played by others, but I do not remember them. The quilt of people shifted on the hillside, some hidden by the chipping green chain-link fence, the links obscuring their faces. Dozens of happy adults in windbreakers. My father would want to stay near the back. My mother would dig in her purse for her lipstick, which she could touch up without a mirror. They didn't make a fuss over things. They were punctual.

But they were not there.

Becky came up to me, dashing across the tennis court during a round of applause.

"Up next," she said.

Then I was fastening the reed in the clarinet's ligature, and I was in front, the green sheet music cover staring back at me. The crowd was a fidgeting mass. We stood for some long seconds. Becky was waiting for me to open the sheet music.

I thought if I waited just one more moment, they would arrive. My mother would see me, would even lift one hand from the strap of her purse to wave, and I would know that they were listening. But I could only hold the clarinet, hold that vinegary taste in my mouth, my fingers on the keys, touching them all at once, as though they held in some secret, trapping it inside.

I saw Becky's soft, pasty arm reach to open the music. She began to tap her foot, hard, loudly. She counted. Two, and, three, and. I could feel my fingers unfreeze, we both breathed in, and we began.

And although it lasted only a moment, I played it perfectly. That was the time, that one time it occurred effortlessly. As though gliding on ice. I barely needed the music. Becky left her line, momentarily, to flip the page, and I heard the sound of my solitary playing rise up into the trees, and I wished it would hang there forever.

It was over. I was among the first to get all my things down from the bunk. I did not need to wait for my parents to converse with the counselors, or the director, who came up to me as the recital finished and said, Well done. Will we see you next year? You have to come for three weeks next year! I didn't linger and say goodbye to the other kids or write any addresses on scraps of paper. Nora left with her parents; that was the last time I saw her. I sat on the picnic table outside the main hall, with all my things, waiting. The day grew warmer as I waited, watching the cars reverse and turn around in the gravel parking lot, the sound of stone being crushed under the tires, people running up and down the wooden staircase slowly dwindling until I was last.

As I sat, I grew angry. I squeezed my wrists and pressed my arms into my stomach. I wanted to crack something. Tiny quivering magnets caught at the ends of my fingers. I stared at my shoes, my white sneakers with bright blue laces. They were too loose. They were foolish.

I don't remember being the last one for very long. One of the counselors must have talked to me, something friendly, perhaps asking me if I wanted to call my parents. But she made me uneasy. I wanted Becky, but even she was gone.

When they arrived, my mother got out of the car without her purse; this meant that we were not staying. She was wearing culottes and she'd clipped her hair up on the back of her head. My father had a crease in the side of his mouth that I recognized, one that formed when all the muscles in his face became pinched from whatever was searing inside his mind. My brother was in the back seat. I could see his sandy hair, the color of my mother's, mashed against the window. My father stood with the driver's door open, waiting for my brother. He was waiting for him to get out, waiting to click the automatic door locks. He didn't turn. I could see only the back of his head, his hair black as iron.

He would want me to stand up and bring my things, but I sat, watching them, waiting for them to come to me. My mother waved to me and smiled.

My brother got out. He was holding a model rocket. He wasn't much older than I was, only one grade ahead of me in school. At times, I looked at him and saw so much of myself that I was frightened.

"Dad," he said. "What about down there?" He pointed at the small open field beyond the parking lot. For a moment, I thought my father would transform into a person he was sometimes. My father could be a bright spool of ribbon, unfurling. When he clenched the back of our bikes and ran with us, down the hill of our street. When he did cannonballs into the local pool, splashing us. He was squirrelly. For a moment I thought he would be that excitable person who would tramp into a field to set up Daniel's rocket.

"Too many trees," was all he said, putting the keys into his pocket and rattling the change that was in there, his arm stiffly against his side.

My brother raised the rocket aloft, mocking its blastoff. "Power systems—on!" he called.

They walked slowly toward the picnic table. I knew it was worse that they had arrived so late. If they had arrived earlier, when more of the other parents were around, they could have disappeared into the crowd. But now one or two of the counselors seemed to descend from nowhere, like vultures, squawking at my parents. My mother was nice to the counselor, cheerful.

"We had a little mishap at home," she said. Then I saw—something had come loose and she was pretending nothing was amiss.

"Did you have a good time?" my mother said, smiling at me flatly, her cheeks powdery from the makeup she always wore.

"Did you have a good time?" the counselor asked. Even then I knew to behave like a child. My father cast a glance at the counselor, his face in a kind of rictus. His thin arms were tan. I wish I could have acted not like a child. I didn't feel like a child; I wish I could have acted instead without that falseness.

"Yes I did!" I replied.

My father paced away, back toward the car.

"Ready to go?" my mother said.

I got my things and my father unlocked the trunk. He wouldn't let me put them inside myself: he took each and put it inside in his own way, even though the trunk was empty and clean. Wispy dark hairs on his hands brushed the bottoms of his knuckles, his fingers, stretched open to reach for the handles of my bags.

The counselor said, "Is this your dad, Katie?"

Beyond the car, my brother was shuffling the rocks under his feet, holding the rocket behind his back. He looked listlessly out into the field, into the sky, as if imagining how it would appear, breaking into a cloud of orange. I caught his eye, and his look threw scissors at me. His eyes a hollow green brown, like the bottom of a stream.

His look said, Say something, you dumb mule.

Before I could answer, my mother said, "This is my husband, Bill."

My father nodded, lifted his hand, shook it, resembling a wave. "We should be going," he said to my mother.

The counselor said a farewell to my mother, and we were all slamming doors and fidgeting with the seatbelts, and it was though we were hermetically sealed inside, and the three of them and the car, with its brown stain in the back seat from a spilled drink, felt unfamiliar. My father drove down the road quickly.

As I watched the trees drift by, a feeling nagged at me. As it occurred to me what it was, I thought for a long time about whether to say something and make us turn around. I almost said nothing. We almost did not turn around. By then we were on the main road, back to pavement.

"Dad," I said. "Dad."

My mother turned around.

"What is it, Katie."

"I forgot my sleeping bag."

She exhaled gently and said to my father, "I guess we better stop."

My father drove for a few moments before he, too, let air out of his nose, until finally he stopped in the middle of the road, shifted to reverse and began turning around.

"Bill," my mother said. "Bill."

He stopped making the turn to answer her.

"What?" he said.

"Someone could hit us. Couldn't you turn around on the shoulder?" Her voice was panicked.

"What shoulder?" he said. "There's no shoulder. I'm already half turned. What do you want me to do? I can't stop in the middle, can I?"

She sat back in her seat. My brother was leaning his head on the heel of his hand, his elbow on the ledge of the back seat window. The carry of his shoulders was hunched.

My father finished the turn, very slowly, it seemed. We returned to the building, where he stopped the car and left the engine running.

"Can you go get it?" my mother said.

We could not have been gone long, but it was as though the place had been abandoned. Under the canopy of the trees and inside the building, the light was dappled. A piece of sheet music lay on the ground, trampled.

The wind blew and the sun disappeared. Without warning, it was gray. I turned the corner around the side of the building. On the gray flagstones, sunken into the grass, was a bird. I startled, and it rose; I heard the tips of its wings, its claws, against the stone. The sound evaporated.

Inside, the cavern of a room was empty, the doors of the far entrance thrown open. The chairs were stacked in corners, the tables and benches gone. As a stiff breeze blew, the sun suddenly returned. Through the translucent panels in the ceiling a crisp light shone in a rectangle onto the concrete floor, as though it had stepped down from above and placed its foot there—living.

Something was in the room with me. I couldn't move. A scraping sound came from somewhere, as though a piece of paper were being dangled, gently, from string, against a brick. A gust of wind blew through the doors, the sound of leaves so loud I thought it would deafen me. Then it was still once again.

I thought of them in the car. I felt afraid that something was hurting them. But I couldn't move. I am not sure how, but I took one step, and heard a voice. I am certain I did. I felt something I could only describe as a pressure. Like someone was blowing a steady breath against my temple.

I heard a car door opening and closing. The sound made me able to move again. I saw the sleeping bag at the base of the stairs. I snatched it, ran out.

On the path leading back to the parking lot, my father was walking toward me. He always walked with a buoyant touch, as though he had no weight. I caught a hint of the kindness that he showed at times. An empty, gentle look on his face, his mouth an *o*, one he'd used when we were too little to tie our own shoes, and he had to do it for us. I wanted him to run and pick me up. But then his face changed, his mouth flattened and the crease on the side of his face appeared. He took a step backward, his heel catching a loose stone, and he kicked it away. He held the car keys, twisting them in his hand. I wanted to say, please help me.

"What are you waiting for, Katie?" he said, waving his arm. "We've been running late all day." He waved his arm. "Come on."

I saw his chin—my chin—the cleft like the border drawn on a map, and it was my sister's chin too, and I had to swallow the tears that had puddled in my throat. He waited for me to walk ahead, a coldness coming off of him as I passed, his breathing, angry.

By the car, under the trees, my mother stood. "You ready?" she said. "You want to put that in the trunk?"

I shook my head, got in the car and slammed the door.

My father already had his knuckles wrapped around the steering wheel. "Is there anything else?" he said.

"Can we go?" my mother said to me.

I was still too stunned to take in that I had to reply, and that the stopping, the starting, the turning, was my fault.

"Yes," I said. "We can go."

Moments later we were again on the back road that reversed us to the highway. I looked into those dark hollows, those shadowed patches under the canopy of branches. We got back on the highway, the white line on the dark pavement ticking by, coolly. My father's fingers seemed to uncoil a little. He was behind the wheel of the car, operating a machine, a comfortable machine, and between my brother's feet on the rubbery floor mat, the model rocket lay, and I could almost feel him waiting for the moment he could watch it explode into the sky.

But then we stopped. Maybe my mother had to go to the bathroom, or was too hungry to wait until we got home.

We stopped in a pizza place. We ate something. It must have been okay. I don't remember the food, or the table. I remember my father shaking the last of the ice out of his glass. He liked iced tea. The ring of a cash register. A cold stream of condensation on the window that looked out into the parking lot. The asphalt, so hot as to practically bubble under our sneakers.

On the way out, as he was exiting, my father crossed the path of a woman. We were all in front of him. He would often shoo us in front of him. I can imagine what expression must have crossed his face to make her erupt. Perhaps she'd tried to hold the door for him. Perhaps she'd made him feel beholden to her for her gesture of holding the door. It would have been a look of pity and fury and pridefulness. *No one asked you.* That's what his look would have said to her. *Don't you look at me like I need you to hold the door for me.* He'd stalked through the door. Then she was yelling at him.

"You are a nasty, old man," she shrieked.

I saw my father wave at her, a pinched grin on his face, his skin the color of a fire engine. He twisted his jangly watch on his wrist, and unlocked the car.

My brother was still holding the model rocket. He'd brought it into the pizza place. All of a sudden he dropped it. It rattled on the asphalt, danced, like it was trying to get away. I saw Daniel's feet in his black sneakers and his white socks with the stripes around the ankles. He was trying to get it. He scurried. But my father got to it first.

In his thin hands, which were already gnarled from whatever was creeping inside, my father picked it up, and snapped it in two.

We descended from the arid hills, the damp lawns unrolling around us. Curbs, mailboxes. The sky a muddy color in the late afternoon. The house seemed dark, although the sun still drilled the meadow behind it. My mother opened the window over the kitchen sink. I heard my brother run up the stairs to his room, two at a time. The white bowl that usually held apples and the oranges my father peeled over the trash can was gone. The fruit was piled on the counter—I understood that this broken object was the earlier mishap. The kitchen window overlooked a deck my father built. He pulled the fifth chair away from the kitchen table, that round kitchen table with its nicked wood. He set it in the corner and sat, his arms folded across his chest, clenching the car keys, and stared out, the line around his mouth turned to stone. Maybe he was willing himself to return to himself, to return to us. The sun was disintegrating, the lawn becoming engulfed in evening. He didn't get up.

I left them. I went upstairs to my room. My mother had cleaned, and the shades were down except for a crack. I passed the closed door of the fourth bedroom. There'd been one for each of us. The upstairs smelled completely different, a smell I didn't recognize, like pine needles. I sat on my bed and I heard my parents' voices. Their quiet talking could have been anything, about dinner, about it being stuffy in the house, but they never seemed to discuss things that happened. I wanted it to not be this silent time of day. Then his voice rose, hers, his again. Through the floor, they sounded like whips.

The thought of the night coming flooded me. I wanted desperately for it to be daytime. I went to the bottom of the stairs. Again they were silent. I heard my mother rustling at the counter.

"Katie?" she said.

"Yeah?" I said.

She walked through the foyer to where I sat, curving her neck around the banister.

"Don't sit there," she said. "We're going to eat soon."

Before I could look at her face, she had turned and I stood, clinging to the banister. As I returned to the kitchen, my father rose, hung his car keys on the hooks by the telephone, and walked out, through the garage.

"I'm going for a walk," he said.

But he didn't go for a walk, really. I heard the garage door open, his great heave as he threw it upward.

"Katie, get the hamburger rolls," my mother said.

I did, and she moved slowly through the kitchen. She peeled potatoes, the peeler rattling with each of her strokes. The clip that held her hair had slipped, the bundle at the back of her head nearly undone. She boiled water in a steel pot. I wanted to ask what had happened to the bowl, how that could possibly be enough for them to miss the recital. But I answered every one of my own questions in my mind.

"What's Dad doing?" I said.

"He's going for a walk," she said. "That's all, he's just going for a walk."

"He's doing something in the yard."

She lifted her head. She took a long breath, a breath that made my rib cage tighter.

He was crouched on one knee, scraping in the yard. In one hand he cradled a couple of bricks. Even from inside, I could see his movements were harsh, as though he was in a spasm. He set the bricks in the spot he had worked at. He stood, a silhouette in the last of the light. He ran the back of his hand across his mouth, brushing away sweat. In his other hand was a tool I couldn't see, a trowel or a spade. He gripped it like a staff, a lone figure in an empty field. I wanted to call out to him. I wanted my mother to run after him, to say, What's wrong. But she just stood there. She looked at the chair that he'd pushed into the corner. She put her hand on it, and pushed it gently. But she didn't move it back.

My father turned and walked in slow steps and only after he had walked the length of the yard did he raise his head, but he didn't look to the kitchen where my mother and I stood, she with unwashed lettuce in a bowl under her hands. He looked up to the windows above.

"Daniel," I heard him call, his voice a cry like a bird's.

"Daniel," he called again.

Upstairs my brother moved. I heard his steps.

"Katie," my mother said. "Go get your brother."

I felt the urge to tell her to go get him herself. A strand of hair had tumbled from the clip, lapped at her shoulder. Her hair was fair brown, but her eyes were dark, exotic, and in the gloom they were blacker than ever, saying to me, *go*. A choking feeling rose in my throat.

I went upstairs, the hallway in shadow. My brother sat on his bed. His arms were under his back and he sat motionless, staring at the wooden shutters over his window.

"Did you hear him calling?" I said.

"I heard him," he said.

"Aren't you going to go down there?" I said, a bite in my voice like I was twisting the link of a chain. "Mom wants you to go downstairs."

"Why can't you stop talking, Katie," he said. "You think I'm listening to you but I'm not listening to you."

He got up, knocking things off the nightstand as he did. I followed him.

"Daniel, wait," I said.

Something made me stop. I was in the hallway alone. The air was cold; I was next to the closed door. All of a sudden there was a shadow on the wall. And I felt it again. Something taking a step. Breathing. But it was also saying something.

It was like a hate. But it wasn't a hate that wanted to hurt you. It was a hate that wanted to warn you. As though it was saying, Go on, get out. Daniel, I wanted to say. But I couldn't say anything.

Then my father called again, the house felt like it was moving. "Daniel?" he said.

And I heard it, and I could move again, and I heard myself say, Please. I felt something hunting me, a feeling that didn't leave me for a long time.

I went downstairs. Daniel hadn't gone outside. He stood at the window in the kitchen, looking, and through the balustrades of the deck's railing, we three saw my father. He waved, looking at my brother.

Daniel went outside. I heard his feet on the dry grass and saw his figure a ways from my father.

I had to see whatever was about to happen. I went to the yard. As I got closer, I saw that it was not a trowel my father had in his hand, but the rocket, repaired. What he had built was a launch pad. A square of grass, ripped away, layered with a row of bricks.

"It's getting dark," my father said.

They set up the rocket. My brother kneeling in the grass, stretching the red cord out. He was scrambling, arranging. He stuck his hand in the air, pointing. The white of the underside of his arm glowed in the dwindling light.

"It's supposed to go four hundred feet," he said. "Northeast, right?"

"Seems so," my father said.

My father seemed to be panting, squatting in his bare feet in the grass, which had turned damp. He was pressing his lips across his teeth, a grimace.

"Dad," my brother said. "Can I light it?"

"It's too dangerous," my father said.

"But I wanted to do it. You said I could do it."

"I said it's too dangerous," he said. "Stand back."

I kept waiting for my mother to switch on a lamp. I wanted to return inside and have the night be gone. Please, I thought. But we were outside, and inside I could see only my mother's face at the window, a white, waning moon.

"Stand back," my father said again.

"But why can't I do it?" my brother said.

"Just stand back."

He had a box of matches in his hand, the long, thick ones he used at the barbecue grill. My brother's face had gone red, he stared at the ground, his eyes practically shut. He pinned his arms behind his back, a gesture he often made. The grass was sharp on my feet, yet it held something damp, alive.

My father had the match in his hand. He looked in my direction.

"No," he said. "Katie, go over there." And he waved, his whole arm, as though swatting a wasp.

I didn't take another step away. It can't get me, I thought. I heard my brother breathing, though, a gnawing sound. He was about to cry.

My father had that match in his hand, between the tips of his fingers, about to strike it. But then he gripped it in his fist. He lowered himself to his knees. He reached for my brother, hugging him tightly. I could see them both, some vapor trail releasing into the air.

The landscape of the yard where I'd spent my whole life then became foreign to me, a wild heath, coated in vines and dark. The yard sloped away, downward, into a meadow that I knew was filled only with the backyards of other houses. My mother was inside the house, I was outside. No one could see me. The moon was rising over the ridge beyond. A shiver tunneled its way down my limbs.

My father, in his bare feet. Digging. All of us, our family, like a machine to him, something that had gone out of control. A tractor, plowing a field, rolling uncontrollably toward the leg of a small animal. I think of that day now and half of it has the flatness of looking into a television, a projection. The other half has the roundness, sharpness, of looking through a telescope. The tune of the duet returned to my mind. It was so beautiful.

"Listen," I said, but they never turned. I went closer to them. But I could not touch them; it was as though they were hot pans on a stove. I could not see my father's face. His back was turned. I could see only the top of my brother's head, and it was shaking, terrified.

I looked up at that moon. I heard the noise of the match my father struck before I saw it. The rocket's ignition cord was a moving candle in the grass. It exploded, shot up into the night sky, going so high for so small a rocket, a glimmering sparkler on its tail, shining onto all of us.

Inside, something shattered. My mother, startled. Another dish breaking into pieces.

A fizzing, a crackling. My brother stared up in awe. He raised his arm and pointed. Then he brought his arm down, his hand in a fist, in triumph. The noise was so loud for something so small.

"Guidance systems—on!" he said.

In the flash, my father's face was covered in lines, as though his face had been coated in dust and splashed with water, and I could see he was laughing.

When the noise faded, he was still laughing. It was a frightening, maniacal laugh, a laugh that bled out into the air like smoke.

"Boom," he said, and another kind of brittle grieving had begun.

SCENIC OVERLOOK

Like this: roads, tarry black. White lines ticking along, a winsome drop of rain on the windshield. A storm about to break. Coffee, coffee, coffee, spaghetti and meatballs. Motels advertising the free breakfast buffet. Parking lots, one streetlight growing out of some tindery bushes. Dead buck on the road's shoulder.

I was at the beginning of a long trip I took when I was twenty-one. I had a square, brown car that I'd bought with the money I'd saved from waitressing. I was filled with some angular, frozen need to throw everything out the window. Some untouchable thing hurtling me forward. The car was terrible and I loved it. The thought of the money I had running out rattled me. I had told my mother I would come home someday, but I would never go home. At least I thought so at the time.

I'd been driving for a few weeks, from town to town, eating in the family dining establishments near motels. I'd stand

and skim a free real estate circular, houses for sale, ranches on dry plots of grass. The waitress would bring my food to go, wrapped in many layers of plastic. I'd see a bit of my ponytail dangling, reflected in some shiny surface. A few times I slept in my car, in parking lots or campgrounds, I had the sense that a timer was ticking, telling me that I had to land somewhere.

One day I stayed at the back side of a storm, under a green sky, all afternoon. I ended up in a motel in Idaho. I had one tall can of beer, the glare of the television. There was no free breakfast, no brochures by the desk; people in lightless rooms in the afternoon with the TV on, the door open. Families, half-families, hiding out. The squeal of I-84 nearby.

I flipped on the TV. I thought about taking a shower, which I hadn't done in a couple of days, but my clothes, hairbrush, underwear, all of it, was in the car. Then I flipped past some unscrambled porn.

The girl on the screen, with several more giggling in the background, had round hips, and was on her knees on a stage bed, a wiry, black G-string stretching to the hollow between her legs. The cameraman aimed at her from ridiculous angles. The absence of a man made it seem like the preamble to some sporting event. She was running her hands underneath her breasts, cupping.

Lick your nipple, another girl said, off camera.

I watched her lift her breast, and stretch her tongue into another shape all together, the cameraman now remarkably still, the laughter continuing in the background, her cow's eyes looking flatly at the lens.

I switched it off. Through the thin walls, I heard the show continue. Whoever was in the next room over was also watching. The room became scummy, I became scummy, like a thin layer of dust or metal or linoleum had settled over everything.

I set down the remote. I could still hear it in the room next door, sounding now like a video game. I had to get out of there. I took the keys and went outside, where it was growing dark, walked to the car and opened the trunk. There was a bag of clothes, a backpack, my boots, a container of motor oil, some windshield cleaning fluid, a few books. A waxy green canvas backpack with dozens of pockets that I'd taken from my brother's closet. I'd also taken a rolled-up map of the desert. I thought maybe I would end up there. I would pass a place—a meadow shaded by trees, a ravine lit by stars—and I would want to stay. To wear a sweater at night. I would want horses and water. I would stop at the side of the road, take some steps down into the land. But then the car keys in my hand would burn my palm. The one ravine, the meadow, it was never enough. I'd think of someone snatching the keys from me, and a power line would blow up my arm and I'd want the road and I'd run back to the car.

I smoked a cigarette sitting in the open hatch, and a woman walked by, also smoking, two small girls by her sides, pleading for something, and she said, no, no, no. They were dressed like it wasn't cold outside—they were from here. In the horizon was a line of black trees, as though they were paper affixed to a wall. I heard a trunk slam, a voice rise. I thought of what they'd do that evening—order pizza or make a PB&J. The kids would drink from juice boxes. I waved to her as they walked back from their car. But she only looked at me, and led them upstairs. A truck blew by on the highway, the Jake Brake grumbling a dangerous sound.

I drove to the gas station just at the line of the trees, bought one more beer, thought about drinking it in the shower. I carried my things for a shower into the room.

The tub had chalky corners and sulfur-smelling water. I lay on the bed in the stiff towel and drank some of the beer. The sound of the TV next door buzzed over the quiet of the room.

Since I'd begun driving, the place I was from had receded into an idea of someone I had once known. All that remained was a gusty loneliness. I was grateful for the loneliness, in a way. Like I had a bird in the cage with me. Somewhere a door slammed, and I drifted off. I often had dreams around that time of an imagined person, a man. He resembled someone I know now that I would later meet.

That night I dreamt he had a chipped tooth and a broad back, and he was angry with me. He was in a bathroom, slamming his hand against a faucet, and it bled. I awoke, I was cold, and when I blinked, I saw his bleeding hand. The towel was dry and I had the beer clutched on my chest. I dressed, and the light seemed blue.

The phone rang.

The ringing cast an urgency around the room, demanding an answer. But there was no reason for the phone to ring. No one knew I was there. Soon, whoever it was would hang up and be gone into the ether. Perhaps it was a wrong number. Or the front desk, calling to convey some information. Perhaps it was, strangely, the woman from the parking lot. I thought of letting it ring as though I did not exist. Waiting for the silence that comes in the wake of a ringing phone. The realization that whoever was there is gone. The prospect of the silence frightened me. So I answered.

"Hello," I said.

A pause, then a high-pitched voice, though I was sure it was male.

"Hey, how's it going?"

"Who's this?" I said. In all likelihood this was a wrong number, in all likelihood my question sounded like a casual inquiry.

"Do you know where you can buy a bike around here? Like a dirt bike?" The voice was slurring.

I said I didn't know anything about whatever he was talking about. "You got the wrong number."

"I just thought if you were from around here you might know where to get a dirt bike."

"I'm hanging up now."

"No, no, wait."

"What?" I said. The pause that hung seemed endless. I hunched over the phone, about to drop it into its cradle, but I did not. I kept listening.

"Are you the girl I saw in the parking lot?"

Something dark and hazy passed across my vision, a strap seemed to tighten across my chest. My eye fixed, strangely, on the dresser, and the indentation it made into the thin carpet.

"I'm hanging up now," I said, and put the phone down.

There were no other lights to turn on in the room. I checked the door to be certain it was locked. The dead bolt shimmied, as though loose. There was no other lock. I needed something to cut the frightening silence. I turned the TV back on at a low volume, so I could hear if something came. The way I'd watch horror movies as a child. The local news came on, discussing weather in another town.

The phone rang three more times. Each time I jumped. Each time I stopped breathing until the silence rose. The space under my shoulder blades burned as I sat against the flat pillow, listening to my own breath in my ears and listening for something other than the muffled stream of the highway.

I thought about making a call to someone. I told myself it was just a teenager. Somebody's idiot son. They probably just wanted to get high, wanted to party. They were far from anywhere, there was nothing to do. Like all people stranded between squares of concrete. They were lost. Like me. Maybe they were nice. It was an odd thing to think. And maybe I looked interesting. Even while afraid of the man I imagined on the end of the line, I wanted someone to think that I looked interesting. But maybe their variety of being lost was wholly different from mine. Maybe I only looked foreign. I tried to decide that I wasn't frightened. But the phone rang. Once more.

Leave me the hell alone, I said into the air, and took the phone off the hook, the tone changing to a muffled alarm.

I fell asleep. When I woke the TV was boiling in static. I'd slept crookedly, and a dullness burned in my shoulder as though I had a fever. It must have been three o'clock in the morning. I went to the toilet, my insides shifting.

As I left the bathroom, I heard a click. Like the key of a cash register being depressed. In the strip of light that bled from between the curtains, a shadow passed.

I heard a winnowing high voice. It asked a question. I froze. The sound of someone's shoe on the gravelly concrete. I reached for the light nearest me, but my hand hovered over the switch. Whoever was outside would surely see the light, would know I was still inside, would know I hadn't fled the room. The lamp in the other corner shone weakly.

The doorknob twitched—like someone had brushed it with a heavy cloth. A sliver of orange-black dark glinted around the edge of the door.

I imagined a man in the room. A crooked tooth protruding over one lip like a fang. I imagined him stalking toward me as I backed away, him grabbing one of my wrists, then the other, me kicking, him gripping my shoulder, pressing.

Someone pounded on the door, three times.

I heard a voice through the thin door.

"Hey," it said. "Hey, how's it going."

The doorknob turned against its lock.

The wind blew right through me.

Then, somehow, it was silent again, and from far away I heard another voice call. I heard boots on the ground, grinding the concrete. Water had welled up in my eyes. A shadow, another, passed in front of the window outside. Something hit low on the wall outside, like a rock being thrown.

They were gone.

I heard something again, and there was a tapping at the door.

"Girl," someone said.

It was a woman's voice.

"Hey, miss," she said.

Slowly, I went to the window. In the shadows of the room I tipped the curtain away. A figured was silhouetted; an edge of a hip, a glide of a ponytail, in a ray of orange light. I put my hand on the doorknob, and slowly opened the door.

It was the woman from the parking lot.

"They know you?"

She had perfect teeth. She was not any taller than I was. The question was like she knew the answer herself, knew that I was foreign.

"No," I said. "They kept calling my room. You see them?"

"Heard that pounding," she said. "They ran when I opened my door."

I turned from her and found my wallet and car keys. She followed me into the room.

"Where you from?" she said. She was barefoot.

"Delaware," I said. "Are they gone?"

"Probably," she said.

"Thank you," I said.

She nodded once. I was unsure if I was really thanking her for scaring them off, or for reminding me that I was not in my own territory. She wore a sweatshirt unzipped at the top, showing a triangle of ivory skin. She looked unconcerned, almost. Somehow this scared me more. A tremor ran up my arm.

"Probably just chickenshit boys." She took a breath like dragging from a cigarette. "Probably got daddies far worse than they are."

She walked away, and I leaned out the doorway. Her bare feet lapped the concrete. At a room two doors down, in a final glance, her eyes said to me, You better get on. Her kids were in there. The vending machine made a whining sound. A puddle of water had gathered on the ground.

I thought of going to the front desk. Maybe someone was there. But from the shadow beyond the streetlight, the darkness seemed to come at me like an animal, and I ran across the parking lot, the highway gone quiet. A paper bag blew by in the wind, pebbles flicked across the asphalt. I turned, one last time. The office was dark.

I had a sense that they would find me and a poltergeist blew through me like an open door. And something else waiting for me to arrive, asking me an urgent question, a question and an answer at the same moment, snapping in the darkness.

I searched my pockets and the room key was not there. Fear thrummed at the base of my neck. I had to go. I spun the car around and drove. The thrumming became the empty highway flying by.

I became aware of my foot on the pedal pressing as far as it would go, of a piercing cold, and I saw that I was barefoot. I twisted my head around and my brother's backpack on the backseat floor. Whatever else I'd left behind—I wouldn't go back for it.

I drove until the trees petered out and the ground contained wisps of brown and a trickle of sunrise shone on the horizon, the headlights of the scant other cars seeming to dim. I stopped at a gas station near the Utah border.

In a patch of grass near the air hose, I tipped over and threw up everything in my stomach.

It was a long time before I could remember this much about that night.

I still can't recall the name of the town.

I DROVE SLOWLY SOUTHWARD. Stayed on the highways and ate food from drive-throughs and mini-marts. I slept in my car at a rest station. In a day I was near the Great Salt Lake. It snowed and was cold. I became very cold. I worried about my dwindling money and hazily thought to find a supermarket and stop wasting cash. The grocery store had been boarded up, but I found a Walmart so bright it could be seen from space.

As I exited, two people walked a short way ahead of me in the parking lot. The guy had dark curls and carried a six-pack of beer next to a pale woman wearing a colorful knit hat. They waved at a man in a pickup near me with a smiling red face, and got inside. They reminded me of the soft people I'd gone to college with. They were a pair of colorful flags flapping. As they pulled away, I followed them. They did not get on the interstate. He flipped on his turn signal and I felt my hand go toward mine.

I stayed with them for miles, distantly tailing the pickup, until the snow abated and became red rock and the sky seemed low and flat. The road emerged in a tourist town full of stores selling camping gear. I had dropped out of hinterlands to where the air held a different cold: pungent, blooming. A ways outside town, the pickup's blinker flashed. I saw a sign for a hostel. Backcountry hikers, it said, and I turned in, too, as if that was where I had been going all along.

It was a large country house at the top of a steep drive backing into a ridge of threadbare trees. There were a few adobe outbuildings and muddy cars. The air had gone dry and the fuchsia sky gave way to blue as it drifted toward night. The pickup was gone and the couple—I assumed they were a couple—weren't there. A man with glasses sliding down his nose rented me a bunk, said, Hike at your own risk, you're in bear country, and pointed at a red sign taped to the desk. In the upstairs hallway, another sign read, *Men and women must sleep in their designated dorms—absolutely no cohabitating.* In the room full of bunks, I dropped the backpack on a bed. I could already see stars. Inside, it smelled of cafeteria and cedar.

Later, I went downstairs and caught the smell of someone's dinner wafting from the kitchen. The couple was there. Under the hat her hair was spiked red, and he had golden skin and a large head that reminded me of an adorned Buddha. The sun had gone down and it felt like fall in Delaware, that hour when the last of the sun dies and a cold sets in that feels warm. I could see the valley beyond, a white space.

She rested her hand on his back as he watched a burner. I picked up a box of macaroni, from a shelf marked "free."

The man said hello. His eyebrows were two sharp points that nearly touched in the center. "Ashim," he said with an English accent.

"Katie," I said. For a moment there was only the hissing of the stove's burners. I wanted to say something more, but a lid had been set down on my throat. How absurd it was that I had come here. I set the box back down.

But as I turned to leave, without introducing herself, the woman, also English, said, cheerfully, "So where did you come from?"

"Delaware," I said.

"Long way!" she said.

"We're heading east," Ashim said. "Sharon, would you like to do the rice? This is ready." He pointed at a bubbling pot.

"So, what's in Delaware? Aren't there some islands?" she said to me, overlooking his impatience. "Have some," she added, nodding toward the pot of rice.

"There's a famous island that was written about in these children's books about horses," I said. "Chincoteague."

Their faces spread and lightened in recognition, and I went on about the strip of land that jutted into the Chesapeake Bay, the smell of brine, the flat sky, the horses that swam. I was standing by the shelf just talking. I must have been awkward.

"But I only went there as a kid," I said. "And that's not where I'm from."

"Where were you before?" Ashim said. Sharon got bowls from the cluttered cabinet.

"I was waitressing."

"No, I meant if that was a while ago, have you been traveling since then?"

I wanted to answer yes. But it had been drifting, an icicle sliding on a frozen pond. And the strangeness of how I'd come upon this place had the weight of a deception.

"Pretty much," I said. I began spooning rice into my bowl.

"We were working at a surf shop in San Diego," Sharon said.

"Too easy to spend all the money on rent and beer," Ashim said.

"But it was fun," Sharon said.

I said I had an old friend from high school who was working at a ski shop in Colorado, maybe it was similar? But he didn't hear. "I don't know what we'll do next," he said. "Friends of mine had their whole gap years planned out down to the week but I never did that."

"We met at college," Sharon said. She sat at the rickety table and began to eat.

A few others came in and out. A kid who couldn't have been more than seventeen. He was a strawberry blond with a red, wrinkled face, and was so thin that I was startled. Ashim asked him where he'd been. He'd left Spokane a month ago, said he, and was biking to New Orleans. He hadn't slept inside in two weeks.

An hour later I drifted to the porch to smoke. It was barely above freezing. Sharon joined me.

"That boy is astonishing," she said. "I'd be too scared to sleep outside alone all that time."

"I've done it," I said. "I was scared."

"Outside?"

"Mostly in the car. I was still scared."

Ashim joined us, and rolled two cigarettes, one for himself and another for Sharon.

"We're thinking of doing a hike near Green River," Sharon said. "Why don't you join?"

Her face seemed to beam in my direction, her glance silently grasping my hand. The thought of hiking in green mountains with them was almost luxurious.

"Sure," I said.

"We were thinking of going farther," Ashim said. "But I couldn't work out how to get there without a car."

I realized then the other man and the pickup were not here, that they must have gotten a lift.

"How far is it?" I said. "I could drive." He grinned, and then she did grasp my hand.

"How brilliant," she said.

Inside, the cyclist sat on the couch wrapped in a blanket, taking huge bites of whatever was in the bowl he held under his chin.

"Boy's going to waste away," Ashim said.

That night, Sharon was the only other person sleeping in the women's bunk room, one rack over. I drifted off, feeling like I was in a tunnel, the moonlight an exit to an open field. I heard a sound, and was afraid before I woke up fully.

"I'm sorry I woke you," she whispered. She was climbing out of the bunk. "Don't tell."

"I won't," I said, and she quietly opened the door, certainly sneaking to Ashim's bunk. As I drifted to sleep, the thought that stayed with me was how nice it had been to tell someone that I was scared.

The next day fast-moving, rippled clouds had rolled in, turning the sky a steely white, shafts of sunlight zooming through. Ashim sat in front as I drove. He had a crisp state park map.

"We haven't been able to go this far yet," he said, his voice a flurry of excitement, pointing to a hazy yellow line at the edge of the map that led into green scrim. "This valley," he said, "You can go far into here, off park land. Streams in the desert."

"I haven't seen water in too long," Sharon said.

We traversed a bluff on a twisting, pebbled road. As we rounded a bend, a deep yellow-green valley came into view and I felt the cold sun enter the car. We were breathless. We parked on a gravel drive on the edge of the park land. We jumped a fence, hiked through shrubs and golden dirt. Sharon wore a blue scarf and gave me a black canvas hat, fraying at the edges, to wear. Compared to them, I was small and winded. His father was Pakistani, his mother was English; he was refusing to accept their offers of money. Sharon wanted to own a shop, to dress its windows. We'd all watched the same comedy and Sharon quoted a line I could not recall, and as we climbed, we repeated the same catchphrase, and I did not know if I laughed because it was funny or if I was laughing only to laugh.

I no longer remember which film it was. The wind cooled us and the sun dappled the forest floor. Sharon's laugh was up in the trees, and Ashim took her hand.

We followed a trail to the top of a hill that overlooked a meadow of straight grass.

"Let's sit here," Ashim said, and we sat on soft ground, as though the spot had been tended. Ashim wandered off and picked up a long birch branch as a walking stick.

"Ashim and I met in a place like this," she said, staring out at the meadow.

The red spikes of her hair peeked out from behind the blue scarf. It reminded me of a sunset.

Before I could ask her more, she asked, "So how long will you stay here?"

"Maybe a little while," I said.

She touched my arm and said almost tenderly, "Do stay. We can take some trips together."

I wish I could remember what else made me feel so close to her. Not much remains: the two of them, in a glade of fluttering grass, the sun glassy and bright, his black curls waving on his elegant head. I pictured a window dresser, someone who artfully places things in a glowing case. She probably asked me why I'd left Delaware. But I couldn't have answered. She said, of him, "Now I know he's my family."

Nearby Ashim scanned the meadow, holding the stick as though it was a broken object.

"Let's follow this trail," he said, and we moved on, down the hill.

We paused to stare at a wide paw print—surely a bear. Soon, a stream emerged with its quiet trickle.

"Look!" he said, and his curls seemed to jangle. We were gleeful. The stream grew stronger. Ashim said, let's cross, and we found a path of white branches to traverse. They went ahead of me, stumbling, laughing, droplets of cold water splashing around their ankles. I followed.

Ashim pointed. Ahead was a dam made of sticks and branches holding back a deep pool of water. Water gently flowed over the top of the dam. A tiny brown creature splashed above it, wood in its mouth.

"Look at its teeth!" Sharon said.

"It's so small," I said. It seemed to spy us. Although it was small, it seemed impervious. I imagined a pool of small fish behind the dam, all for the taking. It would never go hungry.

"I'm glad you left," Sharon said abruptly. "Now you're a stray, so we could find you."

In my mind is a picture of their boots on white branches. Of her hand, lilting across the blue, wispy cotton of her scarf. I thought I would be lifted up into that endless sky, that air filled with damp, the scent of mineral and pine.

We drove back, stopping in a strip mall with a supermarket and a liquor store, where we bought cheap red wine. The windy feeling of nighttime and dinner approached. We drank and cooked.

"Come on, eat," Ashim said, laughing. "Just eat some bloody rice." He shoved a bowl at me, and I ate.

As we sat on the cold porch again, Sharon said, "Tomorrow, let's go do Looking Glass Rock. It's a long drive but let's do it."

I said, "You find it on the map, and I'll take us there."

"What a wonderful idea," Ashim said, his brow lifting. He rose to go up to bed and said, "You'll have to come see us in Vancouver when you get there." Which struck me as odd because we'd see each other tomorrow. I said I would.

"Are you coming, Sharon?" he said.

"Be there soon, my love," and his hand drifted away from hers.

"That is, if we ever get back to Vancouver," she said, and we sat giggling about nothing for some minutes, finishing our cigarettes.

That night, in the bunk, I awoke to her getting out of bed again. I imagined me with the two of them, in another city, a chilly, sunny place, in a bar with a pool table and more of their friends, then we'd drink a bottle of wine in someone's cluttered apartment. We'd eat amid a dozen candles and leave the dishes until morning. Being with them had sparked a yearning in me that, once it was there, felt immutable. Something that had no connection to the past, to the gray shopping centers of Delaware. The TV. The lawns. I thought, I'm going to tell them. About that motel. The woman in the sweatshirt, her perfect teeth.

The ringing phone.

I SLEPT WITH A PICTURE in mind like a snowed television. I awoke and it was as though the channel had abruptly returned. Downstairs, the proprietor stood cleaning his glasses.

The cyclist sat on the carpet. "Got to rest up for one more day," he said, stretching. I asked if he'd seen Ashim and Sharon.

"Saw them leave real early this morning," he said. "I can't sleep past sunrise. I think they're gone."

I was sure they'd turn up. They'd gone out, maybe for an early hike. I made a piece of toast and ate it in the kitchen, and the morning passed.

When I hadn't seen them at noon, I went to ask the proprietor, but he wasn't there. I put on my jacket and in the tepid cold walked down the long drive and back as the golden afternoon settled.

When I returned the man was at the desk.

"Excuse me," I said. "Have you seen Ashim and Sharon?"

"Who?" he said.

"The couple," I said. "He's English?"

"Right," he said. "Haven't seem 'em. Must be gone."

I asked him if he was certain.

"They're paid up, so can't say I care much," he said, clicking the dusty keyboard of his computer.

A feeling settled around me, the gray of a melting ice cube. I returned upstairs; my twisted sheets lay in the bunk. Sharon's was empty. I hadn't even noticed, somehow, that her things were gone. From the room's one window, my gazed landed on the strip of muddy land where cars parked.

It was then that I saw that the brown car—my car—was not there.

Thick air flooded me, a chest pain grew. I clawed through my things. The car key. It was not there. I threw my jacket on the ground. Pressed its pockets. Shook it. Nothing. I'd hidden the meager amount of money I had left in the backpack, inside a plastic soap dish. I began to gasp for breath, they'd probably taken that, too. I tried to take inventory of everything I had left. I stuck my hands in every pocket—nearly crying when I found a ticket stub from a metal show my brother'd gone to with his idiot friends, until, at last, I found the money.

I ran back to the manager's desk. He was on his way out, a bundle of papers under his arm.

"Wait," I said. "I think those people stole my car."

He kept walking, I followed him out to the porch. I stammered—yesterday—today—all day—now they're gone.

He flicked his eyes at me, serious.

"Well, shit, missy," he said. He squeezed the bundle of papers. "We can call the sheriff. Trouble is he's up with most of the law in the county at that bridge site. Collapsed yesterday."

He shuffled back to the desk, wrote down a number. Said there wasn't any 911 here but they'd been trying to get it.

I called it, there was no answer.

That night, someone turned on a movie. Some others had arrived. It had turned icy outside, flurries spinning in the air, but inside was dry and hot from the snapping radiators. I had gone hollow inside, and could only sit, burrowed into the couch cushions. The cyclist fell asleep almost immediately, looking like a corpse.

The film was a period drama about slave ships in the nineteenth century. A man with a whip. A woman digging at the nail that fixed her shackles to the wall. I wanted it all to stop.

When it ended, the others got up as though they were satisfied with the happy, inspiring ending. But I felt ill, I could not talk. The darkness sluiced around the house.

A voice called from the foyer. "Missy," the manager said to me, holding out the phone's receiver. "Got the sheriff on the phone."

The sheriff took down the details. I could almost hear him scratching laboriously with a sharp pencil. When I gave him the car's year, he repeated it back to me. Incredulous at its age.

"Now, you sure about this?" he said. "You see them? Anyone see them?"

I exhaled, the sound reverberating into the phone. I told him I hadn't seen them, that it'd been at dawn.

He apologized for what little he could do. Said he'd put it out there in case anyone spotted them. I whispered back, thank you, and hung up.

Fine, I thought. Fine, fine, that's fine. I sunk into the direness of my situation, like sliding into a pool. I was stuck here. Only that thinning wad of cash hidden in a soap dish. Everything, everything else gone. How I would get anywhere, where I would go, nothing came to me. I needed help. There was no one to ask. The image—candles, messy plates—was so foolish, so false. Ashim, his finger flying off the edge of the map. I thought of me showing up in Vancouver. They wouldn't even know me. I had walked around all day like a little fool, thinking they'd return. And a part of me didn't want to believe it had been them. I could have begged the sheriff to help me. But I couldn't believe it would make a difference.

Some inchoate urge came over me to talk to someone who knew me. Please, I said, please help me. There was only one person to call. I picked up the receiver, the dial tone swirling in my ear.

I thought of my mother on the other end. With one hand I squeezed my left index finger. You haven't called, she'd say. I stopped wondering where you were. If your father were still alive, you know he'd be wondering. But you never believed that, so, what do you care.

I could hear her small, hard voice. You always have to try so hard to *do* everything.

I dialed anyway. I would have taken it. Maybe, maybe she would send me some money. Or maybe, she would just talk to me, not about these things, maybe for once she would be a version of herself that I needed, or at least, give me an image of something I recognized, something that meant we were family.

She did not answer. The machine picked up. The mechanical voice narrated the number. I had removed my father's voice from the recorded message. She had never replaced it with her own.

―――――

I AWOKE THE NEXT DAY knowing I had to leave that place and never come back, and with only one idea of where to go. To Looking Glass Rock, where we planned to hike. I asked the proprietor—could he give me a lift? But he only glared at me over the glasses, his mustache twitching, and shoved a bus schedule and a trail map at me.

He disappeared into his office. I caught a glimpse of the cyclist. He wore a yellow rain slicker and tight pants; he was packing up. He climbed the stairs to the bunk rooms. On the porch was his gear. The contraption he towed on his bike sat open. On my way out, after I'd grabbed my things, I peered up the stairs. The cyclist was still in the bunk room. I stuck my hand inside his bag, pulled out the first thing I touched.

It was a tent, rolled into a neat column.

I'm sorry, I whispered, then I was gone.

Perhaps I made an effort to go to Looking Glass Rock. I did get on a bus, following the long tourist road out of the state park. I watched the brilliant sun atop a ridge, a monumental rock, blistering red. I counted the rest of the money. I had $182 and the rest of the groceries we'd bought; they'd left those. A highway sign read Colorado. I was tired of the snow. I wanted to go where it was warm, where there would be heat and green. But my old friend was there, working in that ski town. We were back on the highway. A Cracker Barrel, advertised by a mile-high sign. I was hungry. I thought of a burger and fries, the greasy lull that followed. The memory of that taste made me feel, for a moment, almost as if I were on vacation. And so I got off the bus, hills spilling out around me. Car dealership, dingy flags flapping.

I walked across the street to a diner. A waitress brought me a plastic menu. I ordered, the sound of my voice strange. I was tense—I should have saved the money. But I wanted to be inside. The waitress returned with my drink. I wondered what people could have thought of me, if I looked scared or terrible. Out the window, cars screamed down the access road, filling the highway.

Two men sat at the booth adjacent to mine. They were bald and wore warm coats. The man with his back to me was much larger than the other. He was asking his companion question after question. The other man answered in gestures—a shrug, a twitch of the eye, as if to say, I won't even answer you with words. The smaller man stood and walked away, nearly colliding with the waitress, who was bringing my food.

"Pardon," she said, and he didn't answer. "Bring you some ketchup?" she said to me.

"Yes, please," I said.

The larger man in the booth leaned over. "You can use this one, here, use this one," he said.

The waitress gave it to me.

"Thanks," I said, and stopped.

His face had a bloated piece, running around one eye and into his forehead, the skin with a waxed quality, as though it had been removed and replaced. I was alarmed, felt my face flush; it was rude to stare. When he spoke again it was fast, like he had water in his cheeks.

"Where you headed? You headed to the canyon? Never been there."

"Which canyon?" I said.

"People ride their bikes in the canyons. Why you by yourself?"

The flush deepened. "Don't know," I said.

He twisted his head over his shoulder, peering out the window.

Then a reel of words came.

"Ride your bike. Isn't that free? Isn't that freeing? Isn't it freeing to be a girl? You got a map? You know what that map is telling you? That no one gives a fuck where you land. Better eat that over some eggs and coffee and get out there. World's waiting."

The sentences tumbled from his mouth—babbling, childish, exuberant. As he spoke, though, the damaged piece of his face seemed to grow redder, as though inside he was aflame, and it might snap off and flare at me in warning. Then, somehow, the speechless question I'd heard in my head for days had a name. Perhaps, as I sped away from the motel, this warped message was what had been waiting for me. The taste of the food in my mouth changed. It turned metallic, hot, rich, like rare veal, and I tasted blood.

He was silent again, only breathing loud enough to be heard from where I sat. I reached for a napkin.

Then my clumsy hand knocked over the drink. A wash of cold liquid spilled over the table, hitting the floor in a brown stream.

"Oop!" he said, and stood, his frame hulking, and pawed up a pile of napkins, slapped them into the puddle, wetting his hands.

"That's okay," he said. "Happens to everybody!"

The smaller man returned and shooed the larger man away and out, and the waitress came with a damp rag, flitting about how it was all okay. The smaller man stalked out in front, leading the larger man to the parking lot.

I watched them out the window. The flush had yet to recede. The smaller man opened the passenger door, gesturing to say *get in*. The sun was on its way down, sending an orange rivulet down the gully of that access road. Somehow the bright sun made it seem colder. The big man stood. He was staring out, he did not get in.

I knew what he was looking at. He was looking at the distant sun.

All at once the smaller man seemed to be angered by the big man. To him, the big man was deformed. Because of his face, or not. He grabbed the big man. Shoved him. I could see his lips say, Get in the car. The big man flinched. And though I couldn't hear it, the small man was screaming, the rage kicking off of him like a lightning bolt.

I GOT ON ANOTHER BUS. On the highway, an 18-wheeler cruised up next to me, a car carrier. It hovered there for miles, blocking the sun, drifting, for so long that I could see each car: a red truck, a vintage hunter green coupe, a blue Honda, and last, a beige sedan. It was filled with personal items—a blanket, a sunshade for the dashboard. I watched the cars being pulled along, unable to get free.

A sign emerged that read Lookout, and the bus stopped.

Clouds sat, dipped in purple, seeming to touch the red earth. There were a few other cars there, people snapping pictures. There were two men nearby in hats and fleeces. I was jolted by the fact that I recognized one. Or I thought I did.

He was a boy I'd gone to high school with—played trombone in the band, wore a Miami Dolphins jacket, he was blade thin and blond, his hair cut as though for the army. He raised a camera. The flash went off. He turned, and his rectangular jaw cut the air. The smell of chalk rose in my memory, the smell of humid rain in the school parking lot, of burned lunch in a cafeteria. He'd gotten a job as a waiter. I remembered a white uniform shirt open at the collar, the creamy, hairless skin of young men. I remembered his in particular, recalled a spring of adolescent desire. What had happened to that boy? Was he standing at an overlook, on vacation, snapping photos? It was only a figment.

All of a sudden, I wanted no more of those memories, I wanted to flip them over like a bedspread. He turned, and even more resembled this boy, a grown version of him, so much that I blinked, and had to look away. He raised his head—a flash of recognition? Something in me grew charged and hot, like shame. It wouldn't have been him. Or anyone. No one I knew. I walked back to the bus.

"Katie," I heard a voice say.

Right then, I was sure. It was him. But I ignored it. I couldn't bear for someone to see me as I was right then. And I feared that if I turned to him, I'd never escape that past, that place.

I got on the bus, it pulled away. I pulled my coat over me and slept.

When I awoke, we were stopped again. A minivan was parked next to the bus, a man in khaki shorts wiping the feet of a tiny child.

It took me some time to settle on my next destination. Before I did, I think I finally did go on a hike near that Looking Glass Rock, but far off the map. I'm not sure I could find it now.

I stopped to wash up in a park restroom, my sneakers on the muddy concrete floor. I looked in the mirror and my mouth had begun to appear to me like a dark gaping hole. When I walked again, my legs felt hard and thick as fence rails. The sky was the color of ash floating up from a campfire. I rose to the top of a hill and found I was walking on another road, chinked yellow line in the pebbled, cracked asphalt.

The words of the man in the diner arose, like a seer's vision. They weren't his. They were mine. Had he even said them?

The truth of what the map is telling you is that no one gives a fuck where you land. Look at that! Now you're free. So eat *that* over eggs and coffee and get out there.

I lay down in the road, cheek to the asphalt. The tilted mountains in my vision. A car could come—I swallowed that feeling, sweet and brown, like a cold drink. I stood and clambered into some brush.

I was as alone as I've ever been.

What a gift no one's going to tie you down. Gift like a good beating, I suppose. Get out there, world's waiting.

I heard a rustle. A bear emerged from the brush. I locked eyes with it, its nose twitching, its breath gasping, about to roar. And then it did roar, as loud as a truck barreling down a hill. But I was no longer afraid. I got down into a stance as though I were about to fight it. I was ready.

NOE VALLEY

When I spin the globe of my youth, this is where my finger lands, always here, in a snowy desert. I was in Arizona. It was January and I was traveling around with a backpack that I had taken from my brother. I was sure he'd want it back someday, so I felt like a renter. I was twenty-one. Already I had a line frozen between my eyebrows, a future frown, a present frown. Now that I am older, I see this crease and think maybe I always had it.

I was taking a long bus ride to Breckenridge, where a friend of mine was working and maybe I could get some work. Katie, she had said, You have to come here.

At the bus station, near some dusty railroad tracks, it was freezing and the sky turned purple. A woman arrived, a sleeping baby on her back. For a while it was just the three of us, until a guy arrived and harassed me endlessly for change, his blond hair matted into coils, his eyes a blue that made me think of cleaning fluid. Maybe he was a lost hippie, a military school dropout, or a kid who'd grown up singing hymns, writing notes in the back of the liturgy manual, like me. Like me, he was burning something up. I finally gave him some change and he disappeared. He did not get on the bus and I was glad.

At last we departed, the sky turning orange and the tires rumbling. I sat in back, where it was warm. I couldn't keep my eyes open on the of pages my book; I fell asleep.

What was I doing out there? On a bus, leaving a small town bounded by braised dirt and a yellowing lake, near the foot of the Artillery Mountains? My mother had forwarded a letter to me from my college: The deadline to reenroll approached, it said. It was stuffed into my pack, ignored. I wanted only to listen to the quiet noise in my head with no one remotely close. I was in a fury to be anywhere other than the bricked and landscaped sprawl where I was from, anywhere where there was a mountain and a rain cloud forming. I had felt the cave of my family closing around me. Finally, I had become aware of their tolerating me. It wasn't that they wanted me to leave—but when I did leave at last, they slid away from me. I couldn't blame them. All of us, we were unwell.

My father had died when vascular disease had thickened his veins. His lungs had failed far sooner than anyone's should. Sometimes, sentences my father had said near the end walked through my mind. *I can't eat this.* And the same sentence translated into the harsh, over-correct French he spent half his life teaching. He was squirrely, had a wry humor laced with a bitterness that I sensed even as a child. As he became sick, the blistering rage that had always rattled through him spread into all of us and sunk. He became helpless, demanding. The week he died, I arrived at the hospital and he'd raised his head at me, looking then like a bird in a nest, his beak opening to ask, "Why aren't you in class?" So I had gone to class, driving the two hours down there, stumbling in late through the half-empty hallways and listening to a lecture I can no longer remember. In the hours I was gone, he died.

By that January, that day I fell asleep on the bus, it had been a year. I was thin from eating next to nothing, my hair had grown to my waist in a mess of broken ends, and I had a scar on the pinnacle of one cheekbone that I often touched like it itched.

When I woke, there was someone sitting across the aisle from me, reading. The bus had stopped—I'd slept through it. His eyes were brown, as though I was staring into the hollow of a tree. For a moment they fixed on me. He turned back to his book. Outside we were passing orange rocks. When I looked again, he was sleeping.

He was thin, but curved, like he was strong; his hair was variegated black. His chest rose and fell. I heard the baby I'd seen in the early morning at the station fuss softly, caught a glimpse of its mother rocking it. The two of them, him and the baby, I held them in my mind for a moment, with the quiet sound of tires. The thought was oddly tender. But after a few weeks of traveling, I'd had enough bad run-ins with strangers that a wariness had crept in.

The rhythm had changed; we were on a new road.

I heard him stir, begin to turn the pages again. Then he spoke to me; I ignored him, but he said it louder.

"What are you reading?" he said.

"Henry Miller," I answered without looking up.

"Do you like it?"

The way he said it was like he had thrown a small pebble at me. A motorcycle roared by, the rider's black helmet glinting in the sun.

"He's in Paris. Drinking. And begging his American friends for money," I said. "I assume you read it."

"I read it, yeah," he said. "When I was drinking and begging my friends for money."

I laughed, despite myself, closed the book, losing my place. He moved like a bird, twitchy, scanning the horizon. He seemed to be awaiting an answer, his face twisted into a smile.

"All right then," I said, opened it again.

"I'm reading Chekhov," he said. His voice was almost nasal. But not so much that I minded. He showed me the cover, as though he was embarrassed by it. *Selected Stories*, a painting of a woman on a pier. He turned it toward himself, like it would tell him something.

"Strange cover," I said.

A billboard passed outside the window; we were slipping toward the city.

"So, where you going?"

"Colorado. Got a friend in Breckenridge."

"Right on," he said, nodded like he knew it. A feeling arose as though I was reading a book for the second time. Like I was in the backyard of my old friend's house on the shore, a thousand miles away in a humid August, the two of us in a hammock, the sound of the ocean nearby. A part of him reminded me of that place.

I didn't trust it, though, so when the bus stopped in Albuquerque, where I had to change buses, he said good luck getting to your friend, and I let him disappear into the hazy building, its floor like a sooty beach. I didn't bother to ask where he was going.

Outside, under the blade of an awning, I called my friend Melissa from a pay phone coated in dust. She shared a condo with six people. She was teaching herself to snowboard and working behind the counter at a resort. I'd shared a lab table with her in tenth grade. We'd snuck out to the gravelly parking lot to listen to a tape of punk rock. When I said I would come to Colorado and get a job, she'd said, Good luck! But you can sleep on the love seat. I imagined a trail of muddy boots and a pile of skis. The voicemail picked up.

I had a feeling she wasn't there anymore. When I spoke, I sounded like some odd, old thing.

"I'll be aiming for much later tonight," I said.

A wave of stale air passed over me as I returned inside, where it smelled of floor wax and vinegar and a TV blared. I sat on a green plastic chair. A woman across from me looked at me warily, uncrossed her ankles, stood, and walked away. I went outside and tried Melissa again.

This time the machine didn't pick up, a man speaking their number over a hissing sound, as though snow were falling. Where I was, there was nothing but asphalt baking. I didn't know what I would do if I didn't go to Breckenridge. Or if I went, what I would do if she wasn't there. I could idle around looking for a job. But sleep where, I wondered. It was an expensive resort town. And too cold to sleep outside. I'd done that; it wasn't good. I'd thought I would settle there with Melissa for a while.

But I didn't want to settle. I wanted to be moving. There was that letter, stuffed into my bag—I could go back. I thought of the mountains I'd seen, purple rusted in orange. A feeling dropped, and I returned to the living room with my mother in the gray light, her inching into the space my father had taken up on the couch. It was still too soon. I couldn't answer that letter. I clenched the receiver, silently asking it what I should do.

No answer came except one. I would get on the bus.

"Bus 86," the announcer said, through a sandstorm of static.

But then, as I filed onto the crowded bus, I saw the boy climb on. He was there again. He sat in the row across from mine.

The bus pulled away through a tumble of buildings, giving way to an exit ramp and dry grass, towering clouds blackened beneath. The noise was a clamor of muffled voices. It had turned cold. The boy abruptly said, "Were those guys hassling you?"

I recalled the shaky man who'd asked me for change at dawn. Wait, I said to myself. Had he been there too?

"Who?" I said.

"In the bus station. Two guys bugging me for change," he said. "Said they had bags stuck in a locker. I thought that had to be a lie, but I finally gave in. And then of course they went right to a locker."

His shirt was speckled with tiny holes, soft and frayed around the edges. He worried them with his fingers.

"Funny," I said. "That happened to me this morning. I gave a guy change. For a second I thought you were talking about the same person."

"Same everywhere," he said. I said I guessed so. He turned to the window and rubbed his socked foot. He'd taken off his boots. His hands were wide, the veins thick and ridged, his thumbnail perfectly straight and sharp, as though he'd cut it with a ruler.

"Was he harmless?" he said, turning back. "The guy who asked you for change?"

"Don't know," I said. "But he sure thought I was an easy mark." As he smiled his top lip turned to the shape of an archer's bow and had the swell of a bee sting. I went back to ignoring him.

I read in the shifting afternoon light; he did too, curled into his seat. Hours went by, and the bus climbed into low hills with trees thick with needles. By then it had grown too dark to read, having slipped to that impossible hour when the light has not gone but the world is obscured in bluish white. We entered the mountains on a wide highway with snaking curves. The moon was beginning to rise. You'll go blind, I wanted to tell him.

The next thing I saw was the pages of his book shaking. Then there was the noise—a crunch like the trunk of a tree shattering. Someone shrieked in front of us, the bus wavered from side to side, voices shouting, and the tires rolled over something thick—one, two. A dark liquid hit the edge of the windshield and the bus was sliding. A heavy object hit the underside of the bus and the floor vibrated, debris clattering its way down, under our feet. My limbs felt full of cold vapor. I felt the bus might tip as people gasped. In the moon dark, the bus was sliding off into the ravine between the roads. I screamed. But then the tail of the bus moved, the engine roared, and it was turning toward the other direction. There was a great hiss of steam and a snap—the sound of a log cracking in fire coming from the undercarriage. Then we were at rest. We had stopped.

When I was able to blink again, what I saw first was his hand, reaching across the aisle, gripping the armrest of the seat in my row. I followed his arm upward and he was looking at me, urgently, his eyes seeming to wait for an answer, his chest heaving.

Seconds passed with only the hissing sound in the air, until people began speaking in frightened tones. The driver stood at the head of the aisle. His face was gray under a blue knit cap, which he took off, hands shaking. He spoke in a choked voice.

"Is anyone hurt?"

Around me, thirty or so sets of eyes peered over the backs of seats, heads shaking.

"All right, we've hit an animal. Everyone needs to get off and go to the left side of the road. Leave your things. Do not cross the highway, stand on that side." He jerked his thumb to the dark ravine. He opened the door and raised the handset of the radio.

Despite what the driver had said, the boy got his bag.

"You'll never see this bus again," he said. He pulled mine down, the muscle in his forearm clenching, and handed it to me.

Outside was an icy metallic cold. We crossed the gravel of the road's shoulder in a strange parade. The front passenger side of the bus was coated in liquid, a spidery crack in the windshield. Down the road a long ways was a black streak; at its end, a shrouded object interrupted the white ticked line. Beyond it, where the road disappeared into a curve, a car's headlights glowed bigger, and as it approached, it slowed and maneuvered around the animal.

As I stared at the car's taillights, the boy stood near my elbow. My arms felt unsteady. He put on a sweatshirt and a brown canvas coat. The driver exited the bus, stalking towards us, his face ghostly.

"Everybody needs to move another fifty yards that way," he said, gesturing. A state trooper was ten minutes away, he said. The bus company was sending another bus.

"It'll take you as far as Durango," he said.

"Shit," I said.

"What the hell are we supposed to do in Durango?" a man said.

"My medicine is in my bag," a woman said.

"Where'd you say you were trying to get again?" the boy asked me.

"Breckenridge," I said. "Now that I think about it, I don't really know how I would have made the other bus anyway."

He shoved one hand in the pocket of his jeans, his shoulder rising.

"I'm going to California," he said. "Eventually. About now I feel like I could use a beer."

He laughed, and it had a distant, windblown sound. He stamped his feet, a searching look in his eye, so much voltage in that lanky body that I thought he might run off into the forest.

"I got this friend near Durango. He has a place but it's his mom's, or someone's. Might call him when we get to the next stop. Bet he'd take one more. If you want to come. Figure it out in the morning."

Soon all the light would be gone from the sky and we'd be standing under the moon.

I said, "What's your name again?"

"Wes."

On the next bus, we sat in two adjacent seats as headlights carved a rhombus into the distance. He said he knew the friend with the house from Minneapolis, where he lived for a while, but he was from Wisconsin. His family were farmers. He had worked at a ski resort a few winters in Granite Peak, halfway to Minneapolis. He lost his last job in Cimarron working at the farm supply store, and then had no place to live, but he was enjoying it. He did an impression of his former boss, buttoning his jacket to the top, which made me laugh, made my stomach loosen some. It seemed fair, he said, that'd he'd been the one to go, since he had only worked there half a year.

"Seemed like a lifetime," he said.

At the Durango bus station, wooden and warmed with space heaters, I watched him call a number he knew by heart. I hadn't said yes to his offer. A cold whistle went through my head saying that I could figure out some other place to sleep if I'd wanted, I could spend a chunk of my money on a motel. Or I could sleep on the wooden benches.

"He's leaving now," he said when he hung up. "You coming?" He shoved a bunched hand into his pocket, his shoulder rising again.

I was trying to fix on the image of me on another bus in snowy mountains. I could do it. I'd find Melissa somehow. But right then, it didn't seem possible. The station door opened and a blast of cold air came in, a frustrated passenger winging his cigarette into the gutter. I'd had some bad times up until then. But then the air hit my face, full of an icy, wintery scent, and I wanted to jump. I wanted to see this house, in a town I'd probably never see again.

I said, "I guess I could do with not sleeping on these benches."

We waited, gazing onto a stripe of asphalt lit by streetlights. A ripped-up BMW churned slowly into the light and a kid got out, skinny, in a black baseball hat, and a football jersey draped beneath an unzipped sweatshirt. Wes raised a hand, said, "Dude," and they clamped each other on the back while the car shuddered.

"Joey," the friend said to me, putting a slack hand in mine, his face grinning and pale. "Get the hell in," he said. "Wes, you drive."

The house was a small ranch with a sprawling lawn darkened by low trees. Inside was cold and the lights were off except for one halogen in the kitchen. Joey pulled three beers from the fridge and then opened a sliding door to the backyard.

Outside there was a patio with a clay stove, still shimmering orange. Joey handed us each a beer. He rolled a joint, hands steady as a jeweler. Wes touched his beer bottle to mine.

"You made it to the best house in Durango," he said as he took the joint from Joey and inhaled.

"Whose house is this?" I asked.

Joey sucked on his beer and slouched forward against the cold. "I think it's mine now," he said.

"You think?" I said.

He pondered and then his slack face grinned. "My mom took off with her boyfriend, and a month later he came over.

Found him sitting in the kitchen in the dark. Thought he was going to punch me. But he threw an envelope at me with ten grand in it, and they haven't been back."

"Fuck," I said.

"Spent it and made it back three times," he said. "Best thing she ever did for me. That and taking that asshole with her." We all laughed, theirs in amusement, mine in a kind of relief. Wes's face was wet and he wiped the damp away with the tips of his fingers.

Back inside, the house seemed colder than outside.

"Give y'all a ride to Breckenridge tomorrow, if you want," Joey said. "I'll get some runs in."

"Sounds good. You can have the bed," Wes said to me, putting down his bottle and lying down on the couch.

Joey said, "You got him after the manners upgrade."

I stood there thinking how I'd missed a step. Was Wes also going to Breckenridge? Already I was sleepy and nervous from the beer.

"You can take that one," Joey said, pointing down the dark hallway. "Night."

In the bedroom, the lamp was broken. Lying in the bed, I almost could hear Wes turning, a gentle creak seeping through the wall. I grew warm; I took off my shirt, my jeans. A crack of light shone from beneath the door. It was so quiet that I was certain I could hear the sound of snow melt on the roof, trickling. Look where you are now, I thought. A brief hoofprint of fear hit my chest. The blunt object on the highway's edge flashed in my mind.

There was a chair near the door. I got up and fished around in the dresser drawers, until I found something, a shirt, I guessed, and tied it from the doorknob to the chair, sure to make a noise if the door was opened.

When I woke, light seeped in. The bed was covered in a rumpled floral comforter. In the front room, Wes stood on the spotted tan carpet, drinking from a mug, lifting a slat of blind with one finger, observing the suburban street. He wore a clean white undershirt.

"Think he'd mind if I showered?" I said. "Been on a bus for two days."

"You can go first," he said.

I showered and combed my hair into a square knot at the back of my head, drank handful after handful of cold water from the tap. When I emerged, Joey returned up the front drive, looking sobered up.

"Mom's bed treat you okay?" he asked.

"Fine," I said. "Thanks for letting me stay. Can I get to town somehow? Figure out this bus mess."

"Think I'm driving," Joey said.

"That's nice of you," I said. "But I don't mean to put you out."

"I think we're going," Wes said. "Are we going?" he said to Joey.

"Am now," he said, shrugged.

I looked at Wes. "I thought you said you were going to California."

"Sorry," Wes said. "You showed up and now he and I both got snowboarding stuck in our brains. Sorry we're latchin' on to your plan. He knows this place where he always stays, I kinda always wanted to go there."

I thought, I should go on without these two. Wes was smiling, that voltage returned, like he was plotting. Like underneath he was saying, Fuck it. My declining money, plus the thought of yet another bus ride overtook whatever I was trying to talk myself out of.

"Well," I said. "I guess that suits me."

Then it was like they were doing something they'd always done, packing up the car like two boys building a fort. They threw boots in the trunk and I sat in the back with two snowboards. When we were on the highway Joey rolled a joint and passed it, but I declined. Power lines rolled overhead, the wet highway boiling down to a two-lane road. We passed a river, fuzzy with whitecaps. Soon the evergreens were dusted in snow. We stopped for gas. "I got twenty bucks," Wes said, and went inside to pay. He ambled back, boots crunching the salty parking lot. He walked on the balls of his feet. Like some quick waltz was hidden under each step.

The road became white with new snow. Houses trickled in at the side of the road, until, at the base of the next mountain, we arrived in town. Joey said, "Where we takin' you?"

I told him the address, and he seemed to know it. As he drove we passed people strolling in ski gear. Maybe Melissa would be at the condo. Or her roommates.

The condo was down a steep hill, one skinny path plowed that looked like it would soon be filled with snow.

Joey stopped the car. "Might not make it down there," he said.

"I can walk," I said. "It's 3C."

"You get her on the phone?" Wes said, tipping the seat forward to let me out.

"Nah, but I think her roommates are there." I turned to go. "Nice meeting you all."

Wes gripped the door, squinting into the wall of cold. "Okay," he said.

I caught a searching look on his face, same as when that bus had roared to a stop.

"Bye," I said, and turned. I heard the engine roar and the door slam. I began to walk, my boots sinking.

I was halfway down the hill when I heard Wes call.

"Hey," he yelled. He waved, motioning for me to come back. He said something else to suggest I come with them, use the phone wherever they were going. Perhaps he said, we can call her from there. But I don't remember the precise words. I remember the sweep of his hand beckoning toward the open car door. I heard the we, I heard it ring in my ears, and it made me turn and begin climbing the hill. I remember my answer as I got back into the car.

"I forgot to give you guys gas money," I said.

The place Joey took us to was buried down a hilly gravel lane deep in evergreens, a long building of amber planks with a high porch and dozens of parked cars.

"What is this place?" I said. "Is it like a hostel?"

"Sort of," Joey said. "More like a camp. Or like a compound."

"A compound?" I said. "Are you guys in a cult? Are you Branch Davidians?"

They both laughed as we got out.

"No, it's okay," Joey said. "It's run by this Aussie. Lots of staff who work at the resorts. Or people competing, or training. It's not in any guidebooks. No phone number."

Wes said, "You might be able to find some work if you ask around."

"Good idea," I said.

We climbed a short staircase to the entry of a great room, filled with couches, a stone fireplace reaching the ceiling, open with rafters, with a balcony leading to another hallway. A vast window overlooked the mountains. Joey and Wes each paid eight dollars, and the guy at the desk handed over some keys. I took note of how far eight dollars a night would go.

"You might could catch a ride into town with somebody," Wes said over his shoulder.

"Thanks," I said. "See you."

I waited around all afternoon, kept trying Melissa from a payphone. Outside, a pile of skis leaned on a railing, and the sky was unchanging and silvery. After the sun went down, I tried her one last time, and she answered.

"Katie," she said. "They turned our phone off. We went to the grocery store five days ago and paid the bill and now it's finally on again. Where you at?"

I told her I'd gotten a ride and she said, "That hippie snowboarder place? Good girl." There was a long pause and she sniffed. She said she had finally gotten a job teaching actual skiing, but it was in Snowmass, and someone'd taken her room. Said she had a ride up there tomorrow.

"Oh," I said.

There was a fuzz in the line. "Shit," she said, "You're all the way here now. I'm really sorry. I'm such a fuckup."

"No, you're not," I said. "I should have found you somehow."

Another long pause, and she said, "Yeah," and sniffed.

"So, what do you think you're going to do?" she said.

I sat and watched the fire waving like pieces of cloth.

Before we hung up, she told me that my mother had mailed her a postcard. It said that my brother had moved to Baltimore, and she asked would I tell her not to send any more postcards?

It was too late to go anywhere else. I went to the desk and paid for a bunk.

The dorm room was vacant except for dark and I climbed into the bed. A hard anger descended on me. But it lasted only a moment, and in its place came a luxurious, blooming appetite, and I was glad Melissa hadn't asked me to come. The window was coated in stars.

The next day I decided I should look for work. I took a bus into town, felt out of place in my black jacket and boots. The cafés and stores and bars were all lighted like living rooms. I peered in a beauty salon, where ladies in white parkas lingered over magazines. From the knees down I was misted over with mud. I walked away. Down an alley, near a dumpster, a man in an apron was breaking down boxes, slashing the corners with a knife.

At one of the resorts, I found some people setting up for a festival of some kind. Bands, a chili cook-off. I spotted a guy with a clipboard behind a table, sunglasses on top of his ball cap, who, when I asked, said they could use one more person. The next day, I showed up at the crack of dawn, spent the next two days serving hot apple cider in Styrofoam cups. The last afternoon, the guy with the sunglasses gave me three hundred-dollar bills. Nice hustle, he said. I bought a sack of groceries, enjoying the feeling of paying without wincing, took the bus back to the camp with the rest of the tired staff.

When I returned, the gravel lane for cars seemed empty. I scanned for the busted BMW. I didn't see it. They'd taken off. Melting ice dripped off the porch railing, and the sky was blacker than I'd ever seen, the air thin as a slip.

But the next day as I made my way to town again to see what I could find, a stripe of blue sky appeared and Wes turned up. He was walking out of a board shop. He saw me coming.

"Find your friend?" he said.

"Nope," I said. "She's on her way to Snowmass for a job, we missed each other."

"Sucks," he said, sinking one hand into his jacket pocket. "Kinda happened to me too. Thought I might know a guy in there, but he doesn't work there anymore."

We began walking down the sidewalk, the mountain with its strips of white ahead. "Not so great working at resorts," he said. "Spend all this time on other people's fun."

"Did that all day," I said, and told him where I'd worked.

"Damn," he said. "I shoulda done that."

He was twisting something in his hand. I had an impulse to grasp it, as when my brother had something of mine. Before I could stop myself, I took it from him.

"Isn't that the ugliest thing you ever saw?" he said. It was a zippo encased in blue plastic, a skull on it, blue flames in its eyes.

"Agree," I said.

"My people are rednecks," Wes said. "I got six uncles and sixteen cousins. They all got cars in their yards. Except for my dad."

He said he guessed that was all from his grandmother. The farmhouse he'd lived in in Wisconsin was his grandparents'. He said she must have gotten so sick of his granddad being a quiet old fuck that she had to fling herself all over the place with possessions. She found a thing she liked, and stuck it on the wall. His mother had left when he was in the fifth grade. He said the uncles were all as big as Babe the Ox. But his dad was small, couldn't tolerate the disorder.

"Man used to iron his Wranglers. Bought one thing a year and it was always expensive. When they died and that farmhouse was ours, my dad ripped all the shit down. I didn't know what redneck meant till I went to college."

He said it and—that letter in my bag. A moment of nerves passed through me, like someone was waiting for me. But it subsided almost as soon as it arrived.

"Where'd you do that?" I said.

"Community college, until I realized I was getting high every day and still getting As. Then I transferred. Started applying for scholarships until I got one."

He bit his thumbnail, snared it in his teeth, until he dropped his hand abruptly, as though trying to break a bad habit.

"Thing was, I could never picture myself doing the jobs they say you're supposed to want after you finish. So, maybe I don't know what the point of it was."

"I did the same thing—transferred. And then—"

I remember telling him, in a sentence or two, my leaving after my father died, but I stopped before he could react. "Now I got thirty grand in student loans."

Wes laughed, shook his head, in consolation, it seemed. "You just took that right out of my hand, didn't you?" he said.

I gave the lighter back, and the tips of his fingers brushed the inside of my palm.

We found our way into a giant hotel, scammed a bunch of leftover sandwiches from a catered lunch, and ate two apiece while tramping through the snow, cars spraying salted slush on us. My boot caught on something, and I tripped, falling into a pile of snow, and we laughed. The day had unspooled into a strange, bright dream.

The sun was dipping, and I said I might head back.

"Think I will too," he said.

The trees on the road had grown dense, clouds soldered to the skyline.

"Where you going next?" he said. "I mean if you don't stay here." He pinched a handful of pine needles off a tree, the snow shaking down.

"I don't know," I said. "I feel like I should know but I don't."

"Can't think about it, can't ignore it," he said.

"Exactly," I said. He began breaking the needles into millimeters, dropping pieces.

"Now I just think how it could be over in two seconds," he said. "Like a car could come right now and hit us, and if I'd been thinking about what to do with my life, instead of just walking. I don't know, maybe that would be too sad."

I listened to our boots on the ground. I laughed.

"What?"

"I just thought of the deer. That sound."

"Sorry—didn't mean to put that in your head." He clenched his packet of needles. He ordered their tips, arranging them like wildflowers.

A quiet that didn't feel like quiet descended. A sort of hoop around us, a space. Like he had let me in it, momentarily. I wanted to grab on. We'd heard the same sound—a puncturing, the crushing of bone. We'd seen the same fear on each other's face. That sound would now never belong only to me, or to him.

I see, now, that I had been surrounded by a slow-moving fog of grief. The kind you can't see when you're in it. As he and I walked with the ghostly sound in our imaginations, this was the moment when the fog was punctured. I was thinking not of my father, but of that animal. Its death that could let me feel a sadness, a fear, that had purity, cleanness.

He frowned. On the bridge of his nose was a wine-colored birthmark, like a spot of dried blood. He was close enough for me to see this. His frown changed, imperceptibly, a mere lift in his brow. But there it was. Like honey, flowing off a spoon.

That night there was a big dinner in the kitchen. People were saying it would be the last real snow of the season. Joey returned. New people had arrived who seemed like they had money. One of them was a red-faced stocky guy, drinking a tall boy. Eating around the couches, it felt like church youth group, except there was a snarl in the air. They sat with Wes and Joey and me and started talking ski injuries. Wes lifted up his pant leg to reveal a pink snake of a scar, not from skiing, from a baler, and a whirl of anger, the reason for which I couldn't see, undid itself on his face and he pulled hard at his beer.

"You know this place is haunted?" the red-faced guy said to me.

"That so?" I said. "No shit."

"No shit," he said. "You snowboard? You look too cute to snowboard."

"I'm too broke to snowboard."

"You got a boyfriend?"

"Nah," I said.

Wes stood and walked off, disappearing into the hallways.

The guy carried on for a while longer, until someone passed around a container of white powder. I took my beer and went outside.

The hillside behind the building was a glittering tundra. There was a swing set, the swings like sculptures, under perfect rectangles of snow.

I heard footsteps and Wes's shape emerged from the light off the house. Down the ridge, at the far mountain, the ski runs were lit in hazy white. He came and stood by me.

"Guess you'll be headed to California," I said.

"My cousin's got this house in San Francisco," he said. "Going to housesit while he's in Thailand for a few months. Thought I'd hang out here till he cleared out."

He drank from his beer. "Pretty back here."

"Yeah," I said.

"More dudes hassling you," he said.

"Decided to clear out for a bit, rather than tell him to fuck off," I said.

I took a few steps and rocked one of the swings so its snow began to teeter.

"Look at that, you ruined it," he said, and held the chain still.

"I didn't ruin it. That's ridiculous. We should both just sit on them. Here, I'll do it," I said, and shook the chain. Droplets fell, making black buttonholes on the pristine white below.

"See? I ruined it for you. Now you can sit," I said, and I did.

He seemed frozen, but some heat was rising from him. At last he sat, and the chains creaked.

"How'd you get that scar on your face?" he said. "Fall into a snowbank?"

His mouth was in a thin-lipped smile, the corners curled to his eyes, like they'd been drawn with a pen. I felt my hackles rise.

"God, I hate being teased," I said. "What are you even doing down here?"

The swing's chain rattled as I stood. I stalked down the hill toward where the snowy brush began.

He reached for my arm.

"Katie," he said. "I was only fucking around."

It dawned on me that some other current was coming from him toward me. A petulant question pounded in my head, *What am I doing*, my boots destroying the snow. He followed me, touched my sleeve. He was breathing like something had come undone.

"What's wrong now?" I said, and the sound of my own voice startled me, it sounded new.

He didn't answer. He kissed me. Slowly, yet with a tautness, so much that I thought he might dart away. Like it might crack us in two.

When he pulled away, the cold air was filled with snow.

Then, he pulled my hand sharply and led me up the hill and inside, through the crowd toward his room. I had the urge to not be pulled, but to push, a part of myself that emerged for the first time right then. A part I recognize clearly now, a part that wishes to possess a risky thing. In the hallway I yanked on his hand so he turned back, his face now full of the beauty that I had managed for days to ignore. This way, I said, stepping in front, and pulled him the other way, to my room.

My room was empty, the bright moon shone on the whiteness below. I remember the sinews of the backs of his hands, one on each of my hips, the sound of my own breathing, sped up so I thought my heart would collapse on itself. And then him taking my hand, roughly, to his cock, simultaneously hard and soft, like the skin of a lamb's ear. I couldn't stop myself from calling out.

At that moment he lifted me, turned me, and I felt I was being carried.

Afterward, we lay facing each other. "I'm sorry I teased you," he said. "I only said all that because I was curious."

"I never answered your question," I said. "I threw a snowball at my brother. He threw one back. It was filled with gravel."

Wes turned away, facing the ceiling. "My dad, after he pulled me away from that baler, he kicked my ass. Never been hit so hard. Said if I ever got close to that thing again, he'd kill me."

"I'm sorry," I whispered, and he leaned to kiss my eye, my ear, the hollow of my throat.

"I am so curious about you that I can hardly stand it," he said.

With an instinct I wasn't aware of I lowered my hand to the mist of hair on his stomach, lower and lower, until he shuddered. Suddenly he grabbed my hand, and said, "Hang on a second."

He held my face. "Will you come to San Francisco with me?"

In the hallway someone's boots squeaked on wet linoleum.

"You want me to come with you? Why?"

"I lied before. My cousin already left. I'm supposed to be there soon, to house-sit for him," he said. "If you don't come, I'll feel like I been kicked in the chest."

I heard his plaintive tone and I forgot myself completely, that same sensation arising: *Look where you got yourself now.* It was interrupted only by his taking my hand, resting it on the ripple of his chest. There were so many reasons to say I wouldn't go, but I could not name them. They floated through my head like ash.

"Are you afraid?" he said.

"No," I said.

"Were you afraid that day the bus hit that deer?"

I shook my head yes.

"You know what I'm afraid of?" I said.

"What?" he said.

"Ghosts."

A day or two later, we left. Different weather came, rain that made every car that passed sound like a geyser. Joey came to the deck as we left, thumped Wes on the back once. His cracked grin faded as he said to me, "Take care of yourself."

Wes took my arm, the birthmark on his nose twitching as he smiled. We hitched a ride to the train station. He told me what kind of people to look for who would stop. "They gotta look like they want to do something dangerous, but not too dangerous," he said.

At the train station, Wes handed me a forged rail pass. "Don't tell," he said. He seemed like he'd done it before and I guessed that he had. We listened to the rails churning in snow, and in my imagination we were in a Russian novel. He pulled his canvas coat over us, and there were only the two of us, watching the arrivals and departures.

THE TRAIN ARRIVED IN SAN FRANCISCO in midafternoon. We trudged up buckling sidewalks lined with deep green trees, past houses with steep staircases. The house was in Noe Valley. Wes said the cousin who owned it used to sit in the basement dicking around with a computer, then went to Silicon Valley. Now he was loaded. The house was ivory, with a filigreed iron gate in front of a purple door. We opened everything up like children. A bay window with a view like the lookout from a cliff, a bedroom with a red carpet. Later we went out and bought some groceries. Wes carried the plastic bag across his back, shivering, San Francisco's chill far colder than the snow we'd just come from.

But we didn't eat any of it. We came home wet from the mist. He caught me by the hip. He picked me up and carried me to the bedroom. On the bed I lifted his shirt, my fingers on the skin above his belt, his hips so slight it seemed I should be the one to carry him, his breathing against my ear, his hand finding a spot between my legs that throbbed, and I held one knee against the wall. He gripped the beam of the headboard, pulling until it cracked, biting the top of his knuckle, as though to keep from calling out. When we rose, the tiniest streak of blood had seeped onto the blanket.

We spent the next day and those that followed in a sort of languorous river. From the back corner of the house, we saw new shapes in the landscape every day. I felt we were floating over a mossy island, amid a sunset streaked with fuchsia. Not even the totality of the San Francisco gray, or the gray I'd left behind, could cut through this feeling. We opened drawers and found take-out menus, birthday candles, matches. We went to the hardware store and had a second set of keys made, and I sent the house's address to my mother on a postcard.

The day we had keys made, Wes looked at the inside of his wallet. "I'll lay this out," he said. "I'm just about totally out of money." Worry passed over his face briefly, but then he found a guitar and made me laugh with his terrible singing as I lay on the couch.

"You're going to give me the boot if I keep doing that," he said.

It was in that time, one of those evenings, when Wes told me that his father, too, had died. His mother—they weren't in touch. He didn't elaborate, and I didn't. I wanted instead to hear him talk about Wisconsin, as he did sometimes. Dirt bikes, a pond. Summer air gone chilly at the end of the day, light hitting a river of grass, swirling in bugs.

I thought of where I was from, nothing but a flat grid of curb and traffic lights that swung in rain. He fell into a soft sleep, his arm around me so tightly that I could feel him breathe.

With almost no trouble Wes found a job at a bar in the Mission, a place with red brocaded walls and an old phonograph. "It's so easy," he said. "Half the time you just open beers and then you have another dollar." Eventually I found a job as a waitress, at a bar near Dolores Park. Wes sometimes came in before his shift at the bar and sat at the counter drinking coffee. He and the owner, Lewis—who wore a stubbly, trimmed beard, described himself as an *old queen*, and charmed everyone who came in—became friends and I loved it. Wes was unkempt compared to the tony customers, but he lingered there like he was cooler than all of them. Maybe he was. His hair had grown long. "He looks just like my ex-boyfriend," Lewis whispered to me. I loved how obvious Wes was, doing nothing but watching me rush around with chicken salads and espressos. Each week we reveled in the money we were accumulating. I put away some for me, thinking I'd buy myself something, and a time passed that was months but felt like weeks. The house became ours—we filled it with things that were ours: a pair of potholders, a cheap radio. My brother's backpack stopped feeling like it contained everything I owned. One day as I was slipping a little cash into it I saw the letter from the office of student affairs and it didn't rattle me. I merely set it back inside. I saw myself in the mirror and my face was round and pink as if I was growing new skin.

In April, big patches of warmth began passing through. The bougainvillea on the house burst into magenta overnight. On a rare Saturday we both had free, Wes woke and said "Let's go look at the tide pools."

We went to the beach on the Headlands and clamored over rocks adorned with algae, brilliant and iridescent.

We spread our blanket on the sand. On a cliffside, we spied a brown clapboard house, a lone figure standing on its deck.

In an offhand, almost sleepy way, he said, "Cousin's going to come back soon."

"How soon?"

"Not sure," he said, and began talking about where to go next. Mendocino, maybe, closer to the forest, or Oregon, up the coast, where there were sailboats, logging towns, vineyards.

In my head I asked, What's wrong with here?

"I'd have to quit my job," I said. "You'd have to quit yours."

"Wouldn't be the first time," he laughed.

In the distance, the figure was gone. Wes offered me his hands and pulled me up. He looked at me and it was as if I could see everything unknowable in him. It was a thought that almost had mass. And then, with so much mischievousness in his voice that I nearly laughed, Wes said we should stop by the café, and the thought of leaving dissipated.

We stumbled into the café bringing the salty air with us. Lewis squeezed my hand and winked at Wes and put two golden-colored pints of beer on the bar for us.

"Taste. Made from hops grown in my hometown. Near my folks' farm in Michigan."

"You grew up on a farm?" Wes said. "Me too. Wisconsin."

"I knew there was a reason I let you hang out here," Lewis said. "What do they grow?"

Wes swallowed his mouthful of beer, clacked the glass down. "Nothing," he said, with a bitter laugh. "Bank took it."

Wes wiped his lips on his sleeve, abruptly got up and headed for the bathroom. Lewis put two refills on the bar. "His is on the house, sweetheart."

I hadn't pressed him to tell me the story, hadn't wanted to be pressed myself. But suddenly I wanted to know. When he returned, Wes seemed to sense this, and as he spoke he slowly raised his eyes. After the bank took the farm, his father got a job at Home Depot, in the sprawl that had cropped up a hundred miles down the freeway. One day, when he hadn't been working more than an hour, he had a heart attack and died.

"Got up at 4:30 in the morning," Wes said, picking at the holes in his shirt's collar. "Drove two hours. All he did that day was tell some lady what aisle the lightbulbs were in."

I put my arm through his, and the bustle of the café filtered incongruously around us. I thought of the two-hour drive I'd made to class. Like a fluorescent bulb flickering to life, I heard my father's question: Why aren't you in class? I could almost hear what he would have said to me now: And look. You dropped out anyway.

There was a siren in the air as we walked home that night. I wanted those memories, his and mine both, to fall away into abstraction. I wanted to stay right here. I felt this was what Wes wanted, too. I was convinced he did.

A lush undoing, a sadness, pooled alongside the gorgeous fog of that day. A kind of happiness that arises, even now, every time I tell anyone how my father died. Every time I tell it, the details fuse with that spring day, that night. In the morning, we talked about the tide pools, about our hangovers, and about how, soon, his cousin would return.

Some weeks later a long string of days without clouds arrived. I remember it was a Monday; the café was closed so I had to pick up my check at Lewis's.

Lewis, at his desk in the back office in a pink tie, said, "You and that man of yours come by later. Having a little staff party. My friend from Sonoma's coming in with new reds. A few"—he wiggled his eyebrows over the rim of his glasses—"free samples."

There was so much amusement in his voice that I felt like giggling as I strolled home in the sun. Wes would love it.

"Lewis wants us to come over tonight," I said, when I found him in the garage, sweeping the floor. "His friend is bringing wine from Sonoma."

"Sonoma," he said, like he was thinking. He laid the broom aside, held up a postcard. "From my cousin. We have two weeks," he said. "And this came for you."

He handed me a letter. From my mother. *Someone from the college called again*, she wrote. They were sending some piece of paperwork. These must be reenrollment papers, I thought. *Will forward when it arrives, whenever that is.* I could picture her as she wrote in her looped, blue handwriting, pictured my father, winding and unwinding the cord of his wheezing breathing machine around his hand. In that moment I felt pulled, stretched, like that cord. Two weeks. I tried to fix on what would happen then.

"Let's go," Wes said.

"Where?" I practically snapped.

"To the party," he laughed, and turned to flip on the radio.

That evening the usual rhythm of Lewis's place was replaced by raucous laughter and movement that reflected in the rain-soaked windows. Lewis's friend opened bottle after bottle until

I could smell it all around us. Wes grew more and more inquisitive about the vineyard and listened to the man talk about the Russian River. I could almost picture a stone building with barrels, yellowing hills, a pebbled path leading into vines. As Wes listened, the image spread from him in a way that I could almost see, like a wake in water.

"Here's our number," the man said to us. "Call me up if you ever make it up that way." Wes took the napkin he'd written it on and slipped it, almost secretively, into his jacket pocket.

Lewis shooed everyone out before the night decayed. Wes and I walked home, and he talked, in a way he usually didn't, spinning notion after notion about going to the Russian River Valley. We shed our wet things inside.

Then, Wes went down to lock the garage. Amid his things, he'd set his bag down. It was open. My eye landed on something—a bottle of wine jammed inside. A feeling struck me as if I'd watched a can being shot with a rifle off a fencepost.

I stepped in front of Wes as he climbed up the stairs. "Did you take this?" I said. He must have heard the wither in my voice.

"It was there to be took," he said, flashing his arms out in front of him. "They were for everyone."

"He's my *boss*," I yelled.

"But we're not even going to be here soon."

"So what?"

We argued in a way we never had, in a way that felt hard and twisted, even though what he'd done was no worse than things I'd done. "God, you can have such a stick up your ass," he said.

And then he hit the bathroom door with his fist. A dent appeared. He cowered, holding his hand. "Fuck," he said.

Somehow, the heated air between us melted. But I still didn't reach for him. We stood in the dim hallway.

"I'm sorry I said that," he said.

I turned from him and threw myself into the chair by the window.

He followed me. Then he knelt by me and leaned his temple on mine, a lock of his long hair brushing my eyebrow. "Sweetheart," he said.

"Is that what you think about me?" I said.

He raised his head, his face alarmed.

"I don't want to go anywhere without you," he said. "Since that bus killed that deer. Don't stick a knife in my heart. Say it's all right."

The unnamable thing we shared stretched between us again. And so I did, I did tell him it was all right, I let him kiss me, his hands on my cheeks.

Suddenly he grabbed my hand, that lightning in his body. "We could go now. We could go tomorrow." He said he would call that guy from Sonoma, start looking for work for us.

I was filled with a stupid, delirious happiness. One that I almost couldn't contain. But I pointed out to him, we had no way to get up there.

"Let's keep working until our days are up here. We'll need the money."

"You're right. We will," he said, and lay his forehead to mine.

That night, we curled into bed, and Wes fell asleep, one hand on my pillow. But I could not sleep. A little needle pushed at the limit of my skin, about to prick me. It said that maybe there was no place for me here—or anywhere—and maybe if I turned over a stone in me there'd be nothing but dirt. It said, *This isn't my house.* But I wanted it to be, I wanted to have this place with him. Maybe if I stayed with him, it could be. I believed it so fully.

The job at Lewis's wasn't the first I quit for stupid reasons. Nor the last. The day I told Lewis, I found him in the kitchen cooking. As I spoke, he looked down at a rack of ribs that he carefully flipped. When I'd said what I had to say, he paused, and gave me a heavy look. Something in my chest froze. He'd known all along.

"Off you go," he said, the tongs in his hand looking menacing.

And just like that, our days in that house ended. Before we could figure out the next thing. The details got away from us. Like a prescription we failed to fill. Wes's cousin, a huge man in a baggy black blazer with curling hair that touched his shoulders, returned from Thailand. We threw what we'd accumulated into our bags—scorched earth. At the last moment, Wes grabbed a few pieces of mail.

"Did you drink all the Pellegrino?" Wes's cousin said, as we were walking out to the sidewalk. "There was a case of Pellegrino in the garage."

Wes shook his head. He called after his cousin, but he'd gone inside. Wes's eyebrows raised and sank, and the purple door slipped shut.

INSTEAD, WE STAYED in an apartment in the Mission that belonged to of one of the skinny art kids Wes had tended bar with. On the corner above a gas station and a convenience store that sold almost nothing and had a bell that chimed day and night. A shower with a glass block panel, a bare bulb over the sink. One night Wes cut his hair into it. A layer of brick settled on me when we got there.

We couldn't have been there more than a few days when one day Wes was gone for hours, until he called up to me from the gas station parking lot, calling my name until I came to the window. He motioned for me to come down. He had something, he said. The asphalt was slick underfoot. Wes had a set of keys. He led us to a black Volvo, not new, but not old. He unlocked the door.

"Where'd you get this?" I said.

"Don't worry about it," he said, smiling.

"What does that mean?"

"It means don't worry about it." He opened the passenger door. "Get in," he said, teasing. He left the door winging open. I hesitated. With the laughter in his voice gone he said, "I'm waiting."

And so I did get in. But I felt like a thumbtack was pushing at me. Wes drove out of the Mission.

"Why can't you say where it's from?"

"Katie," he said. "We can go now."

I didn't answer. He drove and we sat in silence.

In my memory, sometimes I stay in the car.

What I did do: As Wes slowed at a light, I got out. Wes drove next to me as I walked on the sidewalk, horns blowing behind him, and called to me, Katie. Katie.

Until he stepped on the gas and drove away.

How many more days did we pass together? In that apartment in the Mission? Did we return to *us*? Somehow, we must have. One night, on our way to bed, I saw him, the bathroom door opened a crack. He was leaning so closely to the mirror, scanning his face with a look of such anger that I took a step away. Suddenly he reared his arm back—as though to crack the mirror with his fist. But instead, he punched the faucet with one painful crack. I heard his gasp. I wanted to wrap my arms around him, but I couldn't witness it. I let him be.

Then one night he left and didn't come home until seven in the morning. He had chipped his front tooth. He came to bed, I tried to get him to tell me what happened. But he didn't, he only slid on top of me, his breathing like an engine, his teeth clenched. When he rolled away I said, "Wes—" but he fell asleep, his mouth open. I saw the chipped tooth and for a moment he looked like a wolf.

Did we ask each other, Are we going? Did we ask, When? Maybe it was the next day that, on the kitchen table, I found the stack of mail Wes brought from Noe Valley, and in it a letter from my mother.

She was sending the documents from my college. Her note read: *I don't know what you'll want to do with these. But here they are.* It was only a brief letter. *We are sorry to have to report that the extension period on your reenrollment application has passed.*

The bulb overhead felt too bright. I didn't know what to do with the documents. As I lay them down, he came home. He wore this striped shirt I remember, blocked blue and white, like a sailboat flag.

"Where were you all day?" I said, but he didn't answer.

"Remember my friend Joey?"

I looked at him. "Of course!"

How could he forget? There was an electricity in me, like static.

"Heard from him. He moved to Mendocino," he said.

A simmering feeling that had lain there all day began to boil. Wes's fingers had found a soft, worn notch in the table, which he pressed, again and again, with his thumb.

"Mendocino," I said. My voice sounded hard. I waited for what was between us to become unfrozen. But his face was angled downward in such a way that I knew it wouldn't. His face, even at that angle, I could see, contained the same stare he'd given to his own face in the mirror. I wanted him to look at me. But he did not.

When he spoke, it was in a quiet voice.

"Picked up a shift at the bar. For cash," he said. "I gotta go."

I heard the door close behind him.

Eventually, I thought, his shift would end. I waited that whole day for him to return, the light changing from one gray to another. It became evening.

Through the haze, as though a bolt had shot through me, I stood and snatched the letter from the counter.

Why aren't you in class?

I hadn't done the one thing he wanted me to do. But what did it matter? It was nothing enough money and energy couldn't undo, and it was done. It was over. And suddenly I was angry, deliriously angry. And I tore the letter into hundreds of tiny scraps. I was angry at my father for leaving before we could heal, and leaving my brother, my mother, me—we'd have to do it on our own. And who could say if that would ever come. I was left with the realization that the thing that was our family had crumbled to bits. And it had been made wrong all along. But I couldn't have said all this in that moment—I didn't know it then. I was only twenty-one. I only watched the scraps fall to the ugly carpet like snow.

The apartment changed to a frightening cage. Before I could stop it, I was crying. Everything: poison. What a fool I was. I took the blanket from the bed and clenched it so tightly my knuckles turned purple-white with pain. I sat, until, slowly, the crying ceased.

The bell rang in the store below. Someone had entered. Through the blinds, up the hill, I saw it. The black Volvo.

A line had formed in my chest and started winding its way through me. A kicking, biting feeling. My eye fixed on the dresser.

On top, in a dish, were the car keys.

I began putting my things into my brother's backpack.

I knew Wes had caught me at a terrible time in my life, when I didn't know how to seek out something that wasn't broken. I often think of myself on that snowy hill, Wes calling for me to climb back up the slope. Sometimes I wonder what fate would have befallen me if I'd stayed in the car when Wes had asked me to. If the hurt would have been slower. Like the long, helpless decline of my father. Maybe I needed it to hurt hard, heal quicker.

Turns out, there's not much of a difference. Not a day passes that I don't say, Wait. Just let me see the gold stitches in your eyes, one last time. Not a day passes that I'm not in desirous need of that house. Its bougainvillea in rain.

I drove away and knew Wes was imprinted on me, much the same as my father, a specter, frightening and beloved, a thing I wished I could jettison but would pull like a boat. We two were fixed as we were right then, as though in glass. Sometimes, this fuses with the image of a man, collapsed on the floor of the lightbulb aisle.

But as I drove away that day, I was throwing a net into the air—that was the moment before it lands. Before it had caught anything. When it was splayed in the air, utterly free. Even as I drove away, with no map, I began to feel it.

Sacramento. Fresno, Eureka, Klamath. I-5. The 101.

SCHOOL FOR
THE DEAF

1.

When I first had the stolen car, I sped as though I was being chased. As though I was escaping the person who'd stolen it. But as the miles accumulated between us, I slowed down. I couldn't think of myself as having stolen it from him—I'd *taken* it from him. Behind him was the car's unseen owner. Even as I slowed, maybe pulled over at a lookout off the highway, thinking I'd eat a PB&J, have a cigarette, take in the view, I braced myself for every passing car to screech to a halt, tires squealing, its driver yelling *That's my car, thief!* I wanted to get to a town, somewhere where I could stay put and park the car until I figured out what to do with it, but I had no money to buy another one.

I drove around the desert for a few weeks, sleeping in campsites and parking lots, until I found an ad for a rooming house on the bulletin board at a truck stop near the New Mexico border. This was before everything was connected by the tubes of the internet, when bulletin boards could send you places. *Housing, long-term and short. Available for group meetings or retreats*, the ad said.

The place was formerly a school—so the woman who ran it told me, as she handed me a blanket and keys to room 106—and had once housed scores of deaf high schoolers from all around the state.

Pay by the week, she said.

On the lawn a swing set dangled in sunlight and shadows, like an image from a fading, blackening postcard. Three tall, narrow, alpine dormitory buildings nestled in a copse of birches. That place: formerly of oak doors, whitewashed walls, and floors of burnished planks. Now coated in tan paint and brown carpet.

Room 106 was on the first floor at the end of an endless hallway. Every door was open, and each room was filled with furniture in disarray. A black mark on one putty-colored cinder block wall. A mattress, propped pornographically against a bedframe. A reel of plastic blinds clapped against an open window. There was an ancient, oily darkness in all that place's blankets. Everywhere the smell of antiseptic and instant soup mix. The entire floor was uninhabited except for me—the few others staying there had rooms in other buildings, or on the top floor, where there was a shared kitchen. My room had two skinny beds that I slid together like pushing continents on a map. At night I pushed free the rock that someone'd propped open the door with and the door closed.

By then I was on the back side of a bad time, and found a job bussing tables at a banquet hall. But one shift, all of us crammed into the dish room, the manager laid us off. It didn't seem to land very hard on most of the people in the room. One lady just took off the black vest they made us wear and calmly retied her ponytail. In that desert town, a scorched touristy place, jobs never lasted long.

During the days I went into town, past bars and restaurants, the smell of green chile and frying bread in the air, past the Hotel St. Francis where vacationers sleepily lounged on a columned porch. Often, I'd sit and read at the putrid coffee shop, where communal computers could be rented by the half hour, and customers who were often barefoot and clad in hemp waited to use them. But its patio had a view of the mountains, flecked with white aspen trees. One afternoon, while I was there, I found a want ad for summer day camp counselors on the bulletin board. It was a county-run program in the rec center in town. By then I could pass for respectable. Like I could pass for an acceptable babysitter. I drove over to fill out an application, the gas gauge hovering perilously low.

In the nights, I went to the bar I liked. An ancient silver spruce grew through the center of the deck and had a bottle opener nailed to it.

Back in room 106, in bed after some drinks, I thought too much about the man I'd unwisely followed for a while, about being in love. I'd felt turned inside out by it. I would lose myself in dour brooding, in the thousand lives ghosted upon the place I'd landed. Silent, gesticulating versions of myself, without the terror of adulthood and all the noise. Love affairs between eighteen-year-olds conducted in silence. Someone sneaking in and out of the window with a note. Footsteps like tiny earthquakes. At last, I would fall asleep, but badly, and often I woke afraid, as though being startled awake by silence.

I was inhabiting an in-between when the girl showed up. It was the day after one of these nights of bad sleep. I'd gone out and when I returned, she was on the payphone just inside the door, its glass panels shot through with security wire. She wore combat boots and her round face had a wary look as she held the receiver, not talking, as though it was just ringing and ringing. She saw me and the look shifted to surprise.

Back in my room I thought she was probably lost. Or she had taken one look at the place and was calling to make other plans. I thought of wretched Frank, always making some kind of fried meat on the one hot plate in the upstairs kitchen, or Delton, the Rasta guy who said he was writing a book and was always at the picnic table outside, who told me that the school was haunted.

I turned to close my door—the girl's face was in the doorway and I jumped. She leaned around the doorjamb, her hand in a wave.

She laughed and grabbed her mouth as if to prevent its escape.

"I'm sorry," she said. She carried a backpack, seemed younger than I was. "I just moved in. Down the hall. You the only one here?"

"Mostly," I said. She smiled, cheekbones rising so high that they almost seemed to glint in the light. A crown of short blonde hair hid newer growth underneath that was nearly black. She glanced around the room at one thing, then another, my meager possessions.

"You looking for something?"

"No, no, it's just so nice and cool in here. How long you been here?"

"A month or so."

"Where'd you come from?"

"West," I said, after a pause. "California. I was traveling around. You?"

"College. In Ohio. I skipped all my finals. There's one class I could still pass if I write a paper. I guess I could go to the library."

I thought about telling her I'd also skipped a few finals, that technically, I'd dropped out, that my father had died, that I'd missed all the deadlines to reenroll. But that had been a year and a half ago, and was fading into one of my errors in life, rather than a problem that needed to be solved.

"See you round," she said, walking away. "Sorry I startled you!" She laughed at something, I wasn't sure what. Her laugh was the sound of a bird set free, splashing its wings on a pond with a sky full of squawks. It was a laugh that left a mark on the walls. A laugh, that, for her whole life, people had been telling her was too loud.

After that I didn't see her for a while. On a Monday—the town became even sleepier on Mondays, the weekenders having gone back to Denver or Albuquerque—I returned to my room where, incredibly, a note was taped to my door. It said the people from the day camp had called. I ran to the payphone and called them back. An exasperated woman answered.

"Can you be here Wednesday at 8:15?" she said. "Six days a week."

Absolutely, I told her.

"One more thing." Papers rustled in the background. "Have you ever been convicted of a felony? Coffee got spilled on the form and that checkbox is all blurry."

I had not, I told her.

After I got off the phone I went out and bought eight dollars worth of gas, picked up a can of beer and some of the good tacos from Felipe's, and ate on the tailgate of the car as the sun drifted down. I decided it was time to make a phone call.

At the payphone, I dialed, and she answered.

"Mom," I said.

"Katie?" she said. "It's so late here."

"Sorry," I said. "I forgot about the time change."

She cleared her throat. I pictured her at home, in her nightgown, one light on in the den, the glare of the TV shining at her.

"You doing okay?" I said.

"I'm fine," she said. She sniffed. "It's been so long since I've heard from you."

In the pause that followed I wanted to say, I'm sorry.

"What are you going to do?" she said. "Not come home? You're too spoiled to be drifting around like that."

I started to speak and my voice choked in the back of my throat, like I'd eaten a bug.

"Well," I finally said. "I got a job."

"That's something," she said.

"I guess it is," I said.

I thought about elaborating. It was a program for at-risk youth, I could say. Or that they aimed to not hire convicted felons.

"So," she said. "Where are you?"

"What does it matter?"

"Katie," she said. In her tone, I could picture her face, simultaneously displeased and sad, her eyes black marbles. "Really." She said it again. "Where are you?"

I didn't elaborate. But I said she could call me. I gave her the phone number to the pay phone of the rooming house. That was more than I'd said in months. After my father had died, we needed to be apart, a signal she'd sent me in not so many words, and that was where we still were.

"It's really very late," she said, and then we said goodbye, which, for us, means I love you.

I didn't want to be in that building of empty rooms and their decades. I walked across the clearing between the buildings where a cracked Adirondack chair sat, down to the little copse of birches. I lay in the crackly grass. Half an hour of sunset went by, everything a glowing maple color. The heat of the day had lifted and the air had become crisp and layered with the scent of charred firewood. The stars began knocking the sun out of the sky. A feeling swelled over me, like rain slowly collecting on a windshield. She was right. What *was* I doing? My mother's voice pinching my ear. I had slid down a mine shaft.

Back inside, at the far end of the hallway, the girl was there, pushing a rock into place to prop open the door. I thought about telling her she shouldn't do that, that it wasn't safe. But I just watched her fumble. I wasn't in the mood to talk, but there she was.

"Hey there!" she said. "I heard you on the phone—you found a job? Cool!"

I hadn't seen her, but she'd been there. Her expression was filled with an updraft of happiness.

"Oh sorry," she said. "I didn't mean to eavesdrop. I was sitting on the wall outside having a cigarette. I keep trying to quit."

I pictured her wrestling with a pack of cigarettes, flushing them one at a time down the toilet, flinging them like flower petals. The contrast made me laugh. She asked where the job was. When I told her, her face twisted into utter surprise. She asked where I'd found it.

"A flyer in the coffee shop," I said. "You know that place on Laredo?"

I went inside and dug around until I found the slip of paper where I'd written the number.

"You could probably call."

She grinned, white teeth shining, like she never smoked at all. Then she threw her arms around my neck.

"Thank you!" she said, into my shoulder.

I stood stiffly. "No prob," I said, stepping back.

"Wait!" she said. "What's your name?"

"Kate."

"Yahlie," she said. She stuck out her hand, and we shook. Which was weird, considering she'd just hugged me. As I closed the door, she waved.

After a while I went to bed. Distantly I heard a door close. I lay in bed reading. *It was generally agreed in New York that the Countess Olenska had lost her looks.* Had I pushed the rock away from where she'd left it propped against the outer door? I rose and stuck my head into the hallway—the door was closed. I cracked the window and the curtain waved in the breeze. *A few days later the bolt fell.* I fell asleep at last.

I woke to a sound. Not the silence that usually interrupted the blackness of my sleep when I awoke in the dead of night. It was a sound I felt more than heard. But when I came fully awake, I heard nothing. A different silence, a ghostly silence. I imagined mute, frightened teenagers in every empty room. Then I heard the sound again. It was someone walking.

A bright light suddenly shone through my window, its beam the shape of a sword. I jumped.

The beam moved slightly and I heard someone. It was a flashlight. In my head I shouted at whoever might be out there lurking, but nothing came out.

The beam switched off and the footsteps retreated. I sat up in bed, blood pounding.

I picked up the book, held it. I turned on the lamp to read, but I found that I could not return to Newland Archer. I felt as though there was a bottle on a table, rattling. I wondered if that girl had seen the light too, and if we were sharing the jittery feeling.

The evening before the job was to start, I found a note on my door. It had been typed, on a typewriter, on a thin filler paper.

Dear Kate, I'm writing you this note because you told me about your new job. I called the number you gave me, and they gave me a job there too. I went to Uptown Grind on Laredo just like you said. It's not good coffee. But I like the patio. So now we're going to be coworkers! I'll try not to bother you too much. I'm typing this on the typewriter at the antique store. The key for the period was broken but I fixed it. The comma key is still broken. I have to go now because they want me to stop. Anyway I owe you a beer. Do you ever go by Katie? Katherine? Or maybe it's with a C.

—Yahlie.

I thought, Who spells it with a *C*? And then, Well, you hugged me, for Christ's sake. I'll get a beer with you.

I went to the hallway and there was her face again. Almost hovering—I jumped.

"Jesus Christ," I said.

She laughed that laugh. That breathless, screeching laugh. "I did it again!" she said.

In one hand she held a sewing machine by its handle. She fumbled with keys to the room right next to mine.

"You move down here?" I said.

"The lady moved me. Something about a leak. She said she could put me in the other building, but there's only one guy there. It was creepy. So, I told her to put me here."

She opened the door and her room had more stuff in it than I had to my name. Colorful candles with pictures of the Virgin of Guadalupe, a journal open to a page filled with miniscule writing, a turquoise T-shirt on the bed, a pack of cigarettes, wadded up pieces of paper. A basketball, a guitar.

"Oh, by the way," I said. "You shouldn't prop the door open. It isn't safe. I saw you doing that the other night."

"Oh," she said, her face turning concerned.

"I mean," I said. "I'm sure it's okay during the day."

She nodded. "What are you doing with that?" I said, pointing at the sewing machine.

"I was going to teach myself to use it, but I can't find the manual. So I was going to go to the library. Do you know where the library is?"

"Sure," I said. "Could show you if you wanted."

"Really? Thanks!"

"Well, all right," I said. "Guess I could take you up on that beer."

We drove in the hot night and sat at the picnic table at Felipe's, with two cans of Tecate and tacos. A crowd of schoolkids in uniforms were speaking Spanish.

"So, where're you from?" she said. "Did you say California?"

"I was there for a while, but I'm from the East Coast. Delaware."

We had laid out an array of salsa in crumply white containers.

"So, aren't you still in college?" I said. "That final?"

"Actually," she said, looking down. "I just dropped out."

"Well hot dog," I said. "Good for you. Me too. Where from?"

Amherst, she said. She was from Pennsylvania. Her parents were Israeli and wanted her to transfer to school in Israel. She didn't want to; said she'd had a boyfriend she didn't want to leave. Her parents hated him because he was Catholic, but he wasn't, she told them, he was an atheist. But they didn't believe her, and somehow they found his phone number and called him, got him to admit that he wasn't an atheist, that he believed. Then they'd broken up anyway, and she'd left before junior year finals. But she and the boyfriend were still talking, sometimes. Now they were in a period of not talking.

"This stuff is so stupid," she said. "It's like we're in the medieval age. I'm sure he'll call me and it'll start again. I bet it will always go on."

She chose the greenest salsa and dripped it slowly on her paper plate.

"Sometimes when we're talking, I feel like I'm watching a beautiful sunrise," she said. "Like I might die if he hung up. And then it always changes, and he says something that makes me feel like we're all broken. Like I'm all broken. Then as soon as we hang up, I want to be back on the phone with him."

I wiped my hands on a paper napkin, my fingers rusty from spices. She ate a tiny bite of her taco, one bean at a time, like she was trying to perfect the balance of onion and pinto. She drank her beer and gazed into the distance behind my head, into the blue mountains. She had a calm look, but it wasn't only calm, it was like she was rubbing a lamp, deciding what to ask for. The light hit her chin. I thought of the man I'd followed and thought of telling her about him. But, it was her story, and I realized, I wanted to hear it. When I would get to know her better, I would realize how uncommon this moment of silence was, how often she filled silence with a kind of talking that felt to me like a foreign language, about sewing machines, electrical outlets, plants, basketballs, the wars in the Middle East.

"So how long has it been since you talked to this guy?" I asked.

"I was about to dial his number on the payphone the day I got here," she said. "But then I heard the door open, so I never called."

She took out her wallet, the bills crumpled, and got up to get one more taco.

"You're eating those all wrong," I said, when she returned. "You gotta get it with your hands and just have at it."

When we got back to the rooming house, the three buildings cast tall shadows that seemed to swallow the ground, so dark that we felt blind as we approached our door. Inside, there were notes delicately fixed to each of our doorknobs.

Be advised, it said. *Temporary residents will occupy the remainder of this floor beginning Saturday.*

2.

The job turned out to be primarily babysitting, herding fifth-graders, mostly girls, back and forth across a heath of cacti and yellow-white leaves and a chilly gym with a dusty floor. Lula, twice as big as the other kids, with braids the color of sand, always humming. Gabby, with coal-fire irises and an untied shoe, always mumbling and making bracelets from plastic string, complaining of a headache and holding a wrinkled drawing. That Yahlie and I had been put in charge of these beauties seemed both foolish and incredibly wise. That first day, one of the other counselors taught yoga, telling us to find our centers. My hands in the prickly grass, I thought, Why? Yahlie was also grimacing. We laughed silently.

Immediately I loved being with those kids. I wanted to show them something new. As if there was even one thing I could teach them while making lanyards and bracelets. As if I could ever understand their lives, as if that'd ever be possible. But somehow when I looked at them, I believed that it was.

Later in the week, as we ate orange slices before making prints on construction paper, Gabby said her dad was in jail. She yawned, rubbing her eye with her tiny fist.

On Saturday, at the end of that first week, the residents arrived in the rooming house. I returned to my room and the door across the hall was ajar, the room occupied by a boy in a wheelchair.

I stood with my key out. He made a noise, and it occurred to me he was waving.

The chair filled the whole room and emitted a hissing noise. Abruptly it made a grinding mechanical tilt. The mattress and frame had been tilted against the wall, and the room felt like a cell, the empty spring like a device of torture. A woman was behind the chair, doing something. She wore a blue polo shirt and a black crocheted shawl over her shoulders. She said her name was Crystal, and that this was Micah. He looked at her vaguely, impatiently, like she was his minder, one he didn't need.

"He wants you to come say hi," she said.

I stepped into the doorway. Micah had long hair and a trail of saliva connecting his mouth to the headrest supporting his neck. A flag on the arm of the chair said Praise Jesus, and another on the other arm said Metallica. I waved. "My name's Kate," I said.

"We moved the bed to make more room," Crystal said.

Slowly, through a churn of saliva, Micah said, "I sleep in my chair, I sleep right here."

"Most of the other kids can sleep in regular beds," Crystal said. "Just you and that other girl living here?"

"There are some others, mostly in the other buildings," I said.

A man came in, his bald head as shiny as a roll of copper wire, with pert round glasses, a lanyard, and a clipboard.

"Are you our neighbor? Hi!" he practically shouted at me. "I'm Nabil, I'm the program director." To Crystal, he said, businesslike, "We've got a round of med service at 4:30, and dinner at 6:15," and he was gone.

"My boss," Crystal said.

Micah spoke, partially coming out as a wheeze. "He's," he said, "boring."

I laughed, but then felt stupid as I did. Crystal said, "You got that right." She sat on a stool, working at the boxes and gears and tubes loaded onto the back of the chair.

Micah gave me a willful look, like he wanted to ask me something.

"So, what's your story, Micah? What are you into?" I said. A dumb question; I could have guessed from looking at the flags. His eyes were a pair of cut turnips in his head, his skin nearly colorless. He seemed big, like if he were standing he'd be a linebacker. When his features stopped their twisting, he said, in his airy, milky speech, "Ultimate fighting. But there's no goddamn TV in here."

"Nope. No TV," Crystal said. "You're all set, buddy."

"Sounds cool," I said. "See you round."

As I left, Crystal said, "Hey, you got any cigarettes?"

I gave her one. She gave me a squinty, friendly wink, and walked off like she had somewhere to be.

A mirthful laugh rang. I didn't go to my room. I walked down the hallway feeling like an intruder. Half the doors were open. A blond boy in a squat chair was tossing a foam basketball into a hoop suction-cupped to the door, making every shot. He swiveled; I saw he had no legs. Nabil was in another room with a tall boy with a neatly trimmed afro, strapped into a chair with tiny wheels. His limbs were causing him havoc. A girl, not in a wheelchair, but more a stool with wheels, scooted out of her room, backward. Her face was flattened on both sides. She was all nose, her eyes buried deep into their sockets, the size of beans. Her hair had been tied in the half ponytail of a darling child, but her face betrayed her. She pushed with one sneakered foot, the other hanging, her hips round as apples, filing the entire seat of the stool.

Yahlie came trudging back, a bag of groceries in each hand. She looked tired because she'd gotten a second job waiting tables. Probably I should have done the same, but I hadn't. I took a bag of groceries.

"What's with that look on your face?" she said. "You look perturbed."

"All these people."

"Oh," she said. "Right. I guess these are the residents?"

I was envious right then of her being able to view things as they should have been, not as strange. Or, if not that, to ignore things that were right in front of her. It was stupid that I was perturbed by them. She opened her door and set down the bags.

"Look what I got," she said. One bag was filled with maybe three dozen dinner rolls.

It was a sunny moment, thinking of all the sandwiches we could make. We went upstairs to the kitchen and put two into the toaster oven covered in crumbs.

On the way back to our rooms, a girl, three feet tall, on crutches, her elbow a gnarled pumpkin, smiled at us.

One morning at the rec center, Gabby yawned so hard that I thought her head might split into two. She was, it turned out, the daughter of a man who'd refused to inform on drug cartel uppers and was now—as she called him—a permanent jailbird. Later, at lunch, I watched four of the girls huddled in a shady grassy patch, away from the others. A leafless aspen stood drying in the sun. I heard their high-pitched giggles and saw Gabby's hair streaming in the wind. Yahlie came and stood by me.

"They're like a circle of witches," she said.

After lunch we covered plastic letters in finger paint and pressed them onto construction paper. Yahlie insisted it was in fact printmaking. She kept saying they were limited editions.

"Do you need help?" she asked timid April, not yet sprouted, who every afternoon ran to meet her father, who was about my age. April was trying to fix a letter in place.

"I don't know how to do it," April said.

I watched, Yahlie suddenly flustered. I could see she wanted me to help, their twin sets of brown eyes staring up at me. I took the plastic *A* in my hands, watched April's twig fingers move it, saying, Let's just take a little piece of tape. When we were done, Yahlie laughed a hollow laugh.

"These kids love you," she said. "I always say the wrong thing. It looks so easy for you."

That can't be true, I thought.

At the next table Gabby yawned.

"You are still yawning," I said to her. "Why are we tired?"

"My grandmother lives with us now," she said. "My uncle gave her my bed and I sleep on the floor next to her. I can't sleep with her snoring."

She jabbed at a piece of felt with her blunted scissors. Yahlie and I exchanged a glance. It was the first time I could tell we shared the same sense in our hearts, of helplessness. I took Gabby's scissors and said, "Let's cut out a *G*."

When I got home, I spent the late afternoon in the cracked Adirondack chair, reading and drinking beers. *All I want is to listen to you.* During the day the residents were so joyful—they laughed all the time. I let their sounds sink in and make me feel peaceful. Someone was calling, Hey, hey, hey, over and over again. There was sun in them that I just couldn't have, even if someone poured it for me in a glass.

I went back inside, and Micah's door was open.

"Hey there," I said. "You have a good day?"

"Whatever," he said, his face obscuring his smile in hitches and ticks. He flicked his eyes at the two bottles clenched in my fingertips.

"Can I have one of those?"

"No way, José."

I had my key out, about to go inside, but I waited for him to answer.

"Screw you," he said.

Down the hallway, the noise of wheels bumping over the doorjamb sounded. Three boys wheeled in, riding low chairs like race cars, speeding. They seemed like babies compared to Micah. One of them, blond, a miniature surfer, screeched to a halt in front of Micah's open door, and the other two followed.

"Hey, *Micah*," the blond boy said. "Praise Jesus!"

I opened my mouth to say something; they sped off.

"He's an asshole," Micah said, and rolled his eyes, swiveled back toward the window. I wished I could slip him one of the beers.

That night I heard him arguing with Crystal.

"Leave the," he said, "door open!" His voice was as loud as a heavy metal singer. When I got up later, heading to the bathroom, his door was open. The chair tilted, that mechanical grind.

After lights-out, Crystal came to our end of the hallway while Yahlie and I were lying around. She sat in my desk chair. We opened the windows and the three of us smoked a spliff Crystal brought. We heard a moan; it persisted for some moments.

"Does that always happen?" Yahlie said.

"Most of the time," Crystal said.

It was true. We'd heard it every night; at night they were less joyful.

"Ever want to know what they're saying under there?" Yahlie said.

Crystal took a long drag. "I know what they're saying. Sometimes I wish I didn't."

Neither of us replied. I couldn't think about it. I wanted to slice off my own arm, I felt so wrong, talking and thinking about them like they were one big monolith.

"Night's a bad time," Crystal said. "So. What do you guys do all day?"

"I waitress, and we both work at the rec center summer camp," Yahlie said. "I made Katie tell me how she got a job there. Then I got hired too."

We passed the spliff around. "How about Gabby and that mattress thing?" I said to Yahlie.

"I know," Yahlie said.

"What thing?" Crystal said, and Yahlie told her.

"You should just give her the mattress in Micah's room," she said, laughing. "He's not using it."

The next afternoon, walking in from my car, I heard happy laughter and saw them all in the narrow yard between buildings, wheels crushing the patchy grass, playing a game with a ball, Nabil with a whistle in his mouth. Crystal stood on the outside with Micah. She wore the crocheted wrap over a flannel shirt, even though it was roasting hot. He twisted his head at me, and said, "Get me out of here." They all heard him and watched me pass.

I didn't reply because maybe it would have embarrassed him. I made a face that said, No can do, buddy.

"We're going for a walk," Crystal said, pushing his chair as Micah fiddled with the joystick. "Micah doesn't want to do the activities today."

His face was leaving him, it was twitching so hard. A tube pinned to his collar, making a sucking noise, touched his cheek.

"She comes too," Micah said, pointing his knuckles at me.

"I think I gotta go," I said.

"Bull," he said, "shit."

"Micah, don't say words like that to people," Crystal said. Her eyes and fading smile suggested she wasn't going to put up a fight.

"All right, all right, I'll go for a walk," I said.

Micah pushed the joystick. It was slow going across the cracked sidewalk in the hot sun. His chair seemed like a rolling amp. We went around the building, to a steep, pebbly cut of asphalt that led to the road's edge.

The flags on Micah's chair rippled in the faint breeze. "Are you into Metallica?" I said.

"Used to be," he said.

"What about Jesus?" I said. "That's what your other flag says."

"My mom," he said, "makes me put that there."

Out of nowhere, from the other direction, the boys in the race car chairs appeared. The blond ringleader froze, then began wheeling toward us.

"Hey, Micah," the blond boy said. "Praise Jesus, faggot!"

He held a stick in one hand, and as he sped by, thwacked it against the wheel of Micah's chair. The stick became stuck in the spokes, cracking loudly, and he let go. It lay broken on the sidewalk.

The tube in the corner of Micah's mouth slurped, but I could hear the words.

"Eat shit," he said. But they were long gone, their wheels rolling on that crappy sidewalk like it was nothing.

"Boys!" Crystal yelled. She took out a cell phone and tried to work the buttons. "I have to call Nabil."

Micah looked at me. He said, "See what I mean?"

I couldn't think of one damn thing to say back to him.

"Listen," he said, slowly, haltingly. "I overheard you. About that mattress. Take it."

A look of amazement must have crossed my face.

"I have," he said, "really good hearing."

"You're like a bat," I said.

"Just take it. Won't tell."

Later, when I relayed this to Yahlie in my room, she laughed her laugh and clapped, and I thought it would bring down the walls.

And so it came that after a shift the next week, I stole a look inside the files to find Gabby's address on her emergency contact form. Late at night, Micah let us in and watched the doorway for Nabil, grinning so hard his face flattened entirely. At the last second Yahlie decided we should shove it out the window, where it got stuck halfway through like a tongue. We unstuck it with Yahlie outside pulling while I stood on the desk and pushed, all the while Micah telling us to hurry up. We drove to Gabby's house with it sticking out of the back window of the Volvo. We carried it wobbling up the driveway to the quiet porch, our feet making noise on the gravel driveway. We rested it against the porch railing. "Come on," Yahlie whispered, giggling. I peeked inside, through the parted curtain—maybe, a figure in the shadows.

3.

That night, Yahlie and I drove straight to the bar. We were triumphant in our ploy. We were like the cartoon *Robin Hood*. By then we'd seen Gabby's last name—her father's name—spray-painted on walls around town. Yahlie and I smoked and talked about our big stupid plans, which had already started to form. Denver, maybe. She had this habit of recovering an abandoned conversation days later, weeks even, and turning it over like a throbbing vein.

A woman with thick brown braids hanging down the front of her shirt sat at the bar, one stool away. Her clothes were beautiful: a soft shirt in sky blue, a long skirt in a barely different shade, beneath which a pair of silver-tipped cowboy boots gleamed. She leaned into Yahlie's shoulder to say, smiling, "You two look like you're scheming something fun."

She had kind, lovely wrinkles. She was curvy and tall and had a crystalline glint in her gray eyes like a wayward nickel.

In all the months I'd come to this bar, I'd never spoken to anyone. Only Yahlie, when we'd come together. I usually went to be more alone than I already was. It felt suddenly delicious to be talking to someone new; it felt right to spend my last ten dollars on beers with lime and salt. She was probably thirty years older than we were. She was on vacation and staying at the Hotel St. Francis, which was too stuffy, she said. So, she'd ended up here.

"Want to hear the best pickup line anyone ever used on me?" she said, pausing, holding a cigarette, lowering her voice, moving her dark, arched eyebrows. "'Can I buy you a drink?'"

We laughed hard. And then she did buy drinks. I tried to give her a five-dollar bill and she waved it away. She asked us many questions, like we were precious jewels. In her eyes, our short life stories became epic. We talked about our big plans: open an antique store, write for magazines about something important, like water shortages, environmental destruction. As we talked about doing those things, the thread between Yahlie and me thickened, like the ideas we had were new and rich and brilliant. But more than that, the ideas were *ours*. Even though we had just met, we could do them together. As we talked, in her eyes, I could almost see the ideas forming, just like the two of us were forming into something right then, as we slowly got drunk.

After a while she said, "Girls, I'm out of cigarettes, and I'm not driving," and asked if we'd go buy her some. So we did. I was driving with a thankless buzz, which felt like an asshole thing to do. We could have walked somewhere.

When we returned, the bar had filled with locals blowing off steam. The bartender turned the music up—rockabilly, with a slap bass and fuzzed-out electric guitar and a delicious, dirty rhythm that made people get up to dance in their boots and dusty jeans or Hawaiian shirts or tank tops. By then I was trying to slow down on the beers she was giving us, watching them sweat. I started to wonder how we'd get back to our rooms. We lit cigarette after cigarette.

The bartender poured the woman in blue a whiskey. A pause occurred in our chatter. Then the music changed, to a hard, slow song, an unruly, dragging guitar playing in time with a deep-throated singer. Something had gone sour in the air, though I couldn't name it.

"Y'all ever been left?" the woman said abruptly.

Her face shifted, like a wire had been cut in the room. Her eyes were filled with tears, but also, something else. Something had crossed. She rubbed her palm with her knuckle, grinding.

We moved our stools toward her, and Yahlie tried to comfort her in the way that women do. It hurt thinking of whatever was in her. Like she could have pulled out her own eyes. A nervous regret ignited in me. Like I could be here for the next forty years and become her. In that instant I began to see that we were vessels for a broiling rage that had been just under the surface, and now, once she'd tenderly pulled us in, she was going to unroll it on us. And she did. She spilled over us her medieval story of hurt and resentment, the details of which I cannot remember. How long did we sit listening? It could have been twenty minutes or an hour. As she told it, she became angrier, sadder, and a deep crease formed on her brow.

Suddenly, she took her purse, an expensive white leather bag, and began taking out photos, tearing them to pieces.

"Me," she yelled. "I been left."

She picked up the empty tumbler in front of her. With one hard crank of her arm, she flung it. The glass crashed into bottles, and liquid began streaming. Yahlie yelped, covered her face. I was too startled to move, like she might turn toward us and fling something else. A crack ran up the bar's mirror.

The bartender lamely attempted to demand that she pay for what she'd broken. But he looked at her state, seemed to give up, and put her in a cab—it took some doing. I guess this happens in bars. You stay too long and smoldering coals go ablaze. The pieces of photos lay on the bar, fragments of smiles, eyes. I couldn't look at the torn faces. The bartender calmly swept up the glass. The jagged edge she'd brought with her still hung over me. I looked over at Yahlie and her eyes were wet.

When we left at last, we'd forgotten where we parked the car.

At first it was funny, an antidote to what had just occurred, as we searched side streets lit by the moon, and Yahlie's half-tears switched to giggles. I became irritated and started to swear.

"Listen to you," Yahlie said, her laugh sounding like keys on a typewriter.

"Damn," I said. "Why don't you quit cackling and help me?"

"Don't get all mad at me," she said.

Then we quit talking and searched for the car, sulking. The incident made me feel like we both were slinking down a tunnel. A thin streetlight shone so we couldn't see the stars. I felt like I'd been transported back to the suburbs, where there was no landscape to lift us, no stratosphere.

"There it is, goddamn it," I said at last.

It looked like a pet we'd tied to a tree.

When we finally got back to the boarding house, we were filthy and cold. It was quiet. We'd passed lights-out for the residents. I felt we were haunting the place. I wanted to tap on Micah's door, tell him, Mission accomplished. But his door was closed. We stood in the pathetic brown bathroom brushing our teeth.

Suddenly, I heard the sound of metal sliding against concrete. Yahlie heard it too. Another noise—a bash, metal hitting metal. Something hitting the floor. A voice called, a delicate scream, like someone being pricked.

We went to the hallway just in time to see the blond boy in his fast wheelchair with his minions. His face contained a mischievous, terrified look. It frightened me. Micah was there—he had fallen. His chair tipped, a scattering of broken parts. A line of blood on the floor. A tire print in it. Yahlie shrieked—a shiver went down my arms.

"Hey!" I yelled after the boys. But they were gone. Crystal appeared, running toward us.

Sometimes, I tried to do the right thing.

I tried to sleep that night, but lay grinding my teeth into my cheek. I tried to read. *Archer hung a moment on a thin thread of memory.* Tried not to think of Micah's soft, broken body on the beige floor. Of his enormous, broken black machine. The only thing in my mind was the commotion—the lights of an ambulance flicking away.

Through the thin walls, I heard Yahlie get up. She scratched her fingernails on my door.

"You awake?"

"Yeah," I said, and let her in.

"Don't laugh. Can I come stay in here with you?"

"I'm not laughing."

She stepped around to the other bed, the one I'd pushed against mine when I'd first arrived. She laughed, this time a hollow sound. "I'm afraid," she said.

"Me too," I said. But what I didn't say is that I was afraid that she'd never get used to this place. That she'd call that boyfriend, go back to college, leave for Israel. Then I'd really be alone. But wasn't I already?

I had a hard, cruel thought: *You little shits.*

I wanted to take that blond kid in his chair and toss it, as hard as I could, and watch it crash in front of a moving truck. I wanted to take a pipe and hit his face until it collapsed.

"I feel sick," I said.

"I do too," she said. "Wait. I have to get up. I didn't check to make sure the outside door isn't propped open."

She jumped from the bed. I heard the sound of the rock scraping concrete as she pushed it away, and the sound of the heavy door closing. But it made us feel no safer.

We fell asleep, our heads under the blanket, the space between full of pinpoints of light.

The last afternoon we worked at the summer camp, it rained. Early in the evening the sky turned unruly pink. Then it cracked into a black mist. Everyone in town watched it rain. No one knew what to do when it rained. The dust turns to mud, but the dust returns.

The last day of camp, I was sad. I could get another cater-waiter job, refilling water glasses and passing out plates of cake. But somehow, when I had that job at the summer camp, I was happy. I had no aspirations, but I had every aspiration. I was going to live outside consumer culture, I was going to eschew traditional norms. I was going to think harder than everyone else. I wasn't doing any of those things right then, but when I had that job, teaching kids to make paper hats, it seemed like I would.

That last day, we went back to the rooming house, now empty, the doors again yawing. The building was full of a different silence. I opened the door to my room and smelled a strange odor. There was a bird on the floor, in a small pool of blood and glass. The window was shattered.

"Yahlie," I said. "Come see."

Her face became a pale mask and she shouted: "Fuck!"

In the story that became Yahlie and me, that bird is the thing we always talk about. When we talk about how we met. How we were living in this weird place and a bird flew into my room. It's always that bird. Even with all the other things that have happened in my life, in hers. But there's this one other thing I've never talked about with her. Although lots of things from that time come up, spilling out like nickels from a paper sleeve.

Maybe I want to keep this one just for me. About when we went out to buy cigarettes for the woman in blue.

We stopped at the gas station near the low bridge overlooking the concrete arroyo. I'd walked to the edge while Yahlie went inside to pay. Down below were eight, maybe ten, skateboarders. They'd fixed up a light, cleared the weeds, had a place to sit. They looked like nobody else I'd seen in town. All dark, wavering angles.

One of them was riding back and forth on the concrete under the bridge, which was shaped like a half-pipe. He kept going. He was a penny, swinging on a length of string. The rest sat, serenely, their heads turning, left, right. Left, right.

At the apex, he was lit by the moon.

Yahlie came and stood next to me. We were reverent. We didn't know what was coming. Sometimes I blink and I am standing there still.

ANSWERING MACHINE

Sometimes I blink, about to return a message from Yahlie, and it's that Saturday again, and she and I are in that borrowed house. Before I can call her back, that day is replaying like an old VHS tape. In that Saturday of my memory, she's just returned from going out early to buy the paper and when she walks in the door, I almost don't recognize her—she'd cut off all the bleached parts of her hair and what remains is the color of a well-done steak. I'd been dropping hints about not dyeing it again, and she'd told me I was a good friend for telling her the truth. We're reading the paper on the patio and she's drinking black coffee and underlining passages from the arts section. The sky is a crystalline blue and the air smells somehow of melting snow, things more or less as perfect as they could be.

But then she says, "So? Did you send the letter?"

"Yahlie," I say. "Already? I just sat down. It's too early. I'm still drinking coffee."

"All right, all right," she says, putting down her pen, and drinks with an exaggerated slurp.

I try to read again but now she's distracted me.

I go inside and to distract myself further, I wash my hair under the tap. The window above the enormous tub looks into the neighbors' backyard, where a cat is lying in the sun, tail oscillating.

We had sublet the house—way up on Aqua Fría Road on a side lot filled with swirling yarrow—from a lawyer, a rich man who only lived there in winter. Besides the sprawling bathroom, it's filled with thousands of dollars of velvet sofas and chairs. We'd saved a little money and were finally out of the rooming house. This is the first time we haven't felt like captives or vagrants. These days we're more like two pioneer women who'd met face-to-face on the Oregon Trail and became traveling companions after losing their wagon trains in a snowstorm.

The house had a mop and a broom and a phone, the number to which I'd sent to my mother. On the steep hill behind the house was an acequia, a rivulet of water that seemed to stop flowing when the sun went behind a cloud. There were so seldom any clouds that when they appeared the water became confused and breathed in ice from the darkest part of the earth and grew itself a frozen heart.

It did not matter that the house would become shitty. Because, right then, on that Saturday, the house felt like ours.

In my bedroom, my hair wrapped in a towel, the letter to Wes sat on the dresser looking at me. I'd managed to actually write it, but couldn't bring myself to mail it. I'd been using the excuse that we needed to buy envelopes. And that I was certain he'd moved on from the only address I had, the one in Noe Valley. Seeing the letter makes my stomach seize. I could just brush it behind the dresser, and never see it again.

Yahlie thinks this letter is about his abrupt departure, but it's about the fact that I am eleven weeks pregnant. I had begun to worry that I could no longer conceal my growing abdomen.

The morning dies, it becomes the afternoon.

I try again to read the paper, this time from the purple velvet couch, a shaft of light on the floor encasing the dance of dust particles in the air. Yahlie comes in gripping her mug.

"The Arts Section has so much about dance," she says.

This is one of her remarks that makes her simultaneously good at conversation and out of sync with the rest of the world. She has a fidgety look, quivering from coffee and grinning. She goes to the corner of the living room where she'd spread the parts of an old typewriter she found in the trash.

She examines a piece of metal, then another, and then says, "Look, it's lunchtime. We should go out."

"What?" I say. "I heard you say something different. I heard you say, 'We should Cobb salad.'"

She laughs a soundless laugh. She has two laughs: one thunderous, and this one. It's larger than normal, and her nostrils flutter, her mouth wide open in breathless, teary pauses. Her laugh is a thing of beauty. Usually, she laughs at what I say far harder than is warranted.

The phone rings. Yahlie gets it before the answering machine picks up. The anachronistic owner of the house still uses one, a beige plastic thing the size of a brick. He can't figure out voicemail. From the way she's talking I can tell it's this guy Gus who works at the free weekly paper. The one time I met him at the bar, he'd sat at our table, swimming in a pair of overalls and eating corn nuts. He had kind, nervous eyes and moved in a lurking sort of way—either shy or serial killer. He and Yahlie met at the coffee shop. It only took ten minutes before they were on the bench out front splitting a cigarette. But that's her. She had this kind of interaction with strangers occasionally—as often as not it would turn to flirting. She gathered up friends and lovers both. Gus was squarely friend.

She hangs up and says, "Gus is going to come over."

I stare at the shelf holding the lawyer's dumb books—*German Shepherds for Dummies*, twenty airport paperback novels. I don't want anyone to come over.

Earlier in the week I'd gone to the clinic.

It was 4:47 when I got there—they were about to close. The receptionist in scrubs working the front desk looked tired.

"How far along are you?" she said, as I handed her the brick of forms I'd just filled out.

"Eleven weeks," I said. "Give or take. Can I come tomorrow?"

"You still have a couple days," she said. "Sleep on it. Do what you have to do. We'll call you. And my system's down, I can't put you in now."

As she'd flipped through my forms, I'd stared at a mug on her desk with a banana peel stuffed inside. She pressed a brochure into my hand, repeated that they'd call me, and I left.

Outside, a leaf scattered on the pavement in front of me. The brochure was printed on shiny, thick paper. *Options*, it read, adorned with a tiny cross.

After that, after the waiting for this phone call began, there wasn't room for anyone else.

"What did you say?" I call out Yahlie.

"He wants to go shoot some arrows," she says.

"Do we have to?" I ask.

"Really? You don't want to learn archery?"

"What is this, summer camp?" I say, but she doesn't answer and says she's hungry.

"Our house needs groceries," she says, and tosses my sneakers at me.

So we go out to the new Albertsons way out on St. Francis, where the scrub pines have been chopped to make way for strip malls and the desert ground looks scorched. We take her car, a white pillbox full of crap in the back seat. The parking lot has been paved in spongy new asphalt. It looks like the suburbs, except the building is covered in trim shaped like little hats, meant to represent, I don't know, Anasazi ruins. Still, even though the store's brand new, there's a teetering, coin-operated rocking horse out front.

The store is icy cold and deserted. We pass a wire cage full of rubber balls. Twenty sponges hanging in a line from the shelf. It feels amusement park-ish. As I wheel the cart around, I bump into a tower of mega-packs of disposable diapers. We buy tortillas, two rectangles of cheese, beans, coffee. In the produce section I get lettuce and tofu and ginger.

"Ginger is gross," Yahlie says. "So stringy."

She gives me the look of disgust and pity she makes when she hates something and wants me to hate it, too. She has filled the cart with stuff we don't need. Baking powder and a can of coconut milk and wasabi peas and an air freshener. She arrived to town with her car full of the same kind of stuff—no boots, no sunscreen, no pillow. But I like it; I am too practical.

Back in the parking lot, Yahlie says, "You know what we forgot to buy? Envelopes."

"Ah," I say.

I open the trunk, and feel squeezed, as though I've been pressed inside it.

"Why do you care so much if I send it?"

I ask even though I know the answer. This Wes had given me a broken heart that turned out to be one I barely survived. Yahlie wanted me to get over it. Possibly this was selfish. She thought I was fun, and she was sick of this heartbreak making me unfun, of putting up with my conspicuous sadness.

"You know what you said about my hair?" she says with a soft grin, like she was trying to stifle a laugh. "I'm telling you the truth. Like a truth you need to hear. You should send it. Tell him whatever you need to."

She doesn't know that the letter contains facts alone: What is and what won't be, by the time that phone call comes.

"Maybe I will," I say. "I mean, I will mail it."

The trunk gapes at us and she starts loading the groceries into it.

"He's not at that address anymore," I say. "I'm sure of it."

We load everything and I look across the hill, across St. Francis, where a racquetball court stands alone in a clearing. Someday there will be a park there. Or, there was a park there once, and all that's left is the racquetball court. Inside, people play handball. Boys hang on the fence surrounding the court, watching. Beyond is the middle school, and beyond that is the rooming house where we used to live. I look over at a woman pushing a cart, a small girl in the seat. She pops the trunk to a minivan and flips her sunglasses to the crown of her head. The girl waves her hands.

For a second, the wooden-trap feeling I've had all day is gone, but just as quickly it returns, and I want to stay in my empty, thoughtless moment, and to hold onto where we are right here, to keep my eyes on Yahlie's hands, lifting the airy plastic bags.

As we pull into our driveway, another car is blocking our driveway, the overgrown elderberry tree brushing its roof.

"Oh hey, Gus is here," Yahlie says, turning off the car. As we get out his head pops up like a gopher's. He's been sitting on the front porch. Yahlie goes over to him and looks back at me as if to say, Look what I did! She takes his elbow and they walk in.

"I was over at the office working on a story," he says. "I left and came here but you weren't here."

I lug all the groceries in myself as Gus looks at everything, aimlessly picking up a pepper grinder, inspecting the microwave, straightening a dish towel. A blond curl is protruding from the newsboy hat he's wearing, and his longish corduroy coat makes him look out of place in the desert, and probably overheated.

"Is *this* your backyard?" he says, peering out at the elegant stones and succulents, his eyes bulging. "Nice." The house is quiet then except for the stirring of the trees. The thought of the afternoon shifting into some pointless excursion and dull chatter makes my heart sink. I don't want to be friendly. I don't want to talk about what I'm doing these days. I stand with my hands on the bags until I unfreeze and spill the groceries on the counter and start to make a turkey sandwich.

Yahlie comes in then. "Is it okay that he's here?" she half-whispers, her hand on my arm.

"Is he going to stay all day?"

"Come on, it'll be fun."

She reaches and picks at the turkey from my sandwich.

"Dude, stop that," I say, swatting her hand. "Make your own."

I go outside and sit sulkily and eat. What I really want to do is have the day this began as. Where I had no thoughts and it was just Yahlie and me, hanging out. On this other, better day, maybe later we'd go out again, maybe exercise, like normal people. We did that one other time. We found a track at a high school. As the sun, blocked by bleachers, slowly lowered, she did Tae Kwon Do in the grass while I ran laps in the moon's orbit. She was strong, had big hips and curvy calf muscles and she refused to shave. Compared to her, I am made of grapevines, and am ashamed of any wispy hair on my body. I heard her calling, *ah-yah*, *ah-yah*. I ran faster. A car rose and descended on the road behind the bleachers. Out of the corner of my eye it seemed like I was passing it. When I got tired, I sat on the edge of the track, its texture like bread pudding in the sun.

When she finished, we lay on the sharp grass of the football field.

"The sun here reminds me of Israel," she said. "It makes me miss my sisters."

I pushed my fingertips into the track and they came away blackened.

"What should we do now?" I said.

"Stay right here," she said.

This day is not that day. I hear them inside as I slouch on the patio, a piece of her laughter flying up into the air, his nasal voice.

"Let's go shoot arrows," she says to my back, as they walk out to the patio. "Gus is gonna show us!"

She comes around, Gus's face over her shoulder.

"You look weird," she says. "Don't scratch your cheek. Your face is all puffy."

As she reaches over and swaps my hand, I realize I've been scratching at the scar on my cheekbone.

"I should probably stay here," I say.

"No!" she says. "And do what? Come with us."

"I don't know," I say, my face resting on my balled fist, my elbow crushing the chair's arm. "I can't."

"How can you say that?" she says, a look of wonder and sadness on her face, like I'm both a child and a wise old woman. She walks closer in little Charlie Chaplin steps, leans down and taps my shoulder, three times, like a cat's paw, and says "I know you would be really, really good at archery."

As usual, her charm cuts through the melancholy that I am felled by, enough to get me out of my chair.

Then I'm in the driveway with the two of them. Gus says to me, "Why don't we take your car? It's so fancy."

"It's a Volvo station wagon," I say.

"That's fancy! And safe! That's what the ads on the TV say."

"We're not taking my car," I say.

"I'm sure it's fine," Yahlie says, brushing off what I'd told her about the stolen car.

I know she's trying to be cheerful, to tell me not to worry, but I shoot her a look. I want to point out that we probably shouldn't take my stolen car to go shoot arrows in a dirt-filled riverbed on a stranger's property. Her face droops and I feel the awful feeling I always have when I've been too harsh. But she gets it, and then we're in Gus's dark economy car, riding down a road so rutted that the tires are rattling and drowning the two of them out.

"Shouldn't we stop and check out that noise? Is something broken?" I say.

"It always does that," Gus says, and I sink lower into the backseat.

We pull up to an arroyo and Gus sets up a target he's pulled from his trunk. Yahlie looks at the target through her fingers, held into a rectangle. I can almost see the frame: a crooked scarecrow and an arrow hanging in the wind. Gus grabs the bow and makes almost all his shots, while carrying on about a story he's writing for the paper.

"Fraudulent antiquities," he says. "I'm going to uncover it. I got a source out in Galisteo."

"Wow," Yahlie says.

He thrusts the bow at me. "Your turn," he says. I take it, lightly, and then he angles me toward the target. Okay, okay, I tell him. He recites various instructions. Keep your elbow in, pull from the shoulder. Yahlie grins. I pull back, and the bowstring flaps and tosses the arrow forward into the dirt. But the next one hits the white circle with a thwack, and on, I don't know, my fifth or sixth, the arrow hits the target's yellow circle. Like piercing a poached egg.

"Ho ho!" Gus yells.

"I was right!" Yahlie calls. "See?"

"That's enough for now," I say, and hand it off to Yahlie. She gets it to fly but misses the target, and Gus resumes, slowly narrating instructions. He takes back the bow to demonstrate. His talking wears on me. Suddenly, a jackrabbit pops its head up from the gulch between us and the target. Gus aims at it, fires.

"Hey," I call, the jackrabbit pouncing away.

"Did I get him?" he says.

"He got away," Yahlie says, laughing, this time, thunderous. "Those things are fast."

My look must have said, *this doesn't seem like you, who squeals when I swack a fly.*

"Can we go now?" I say.

I hear a cracking noise. In the distance a faint plume of smoke rose above where the jackrabbit fled.

"Yahlie," I say, "Do you see that?"

"See what?" Yahlie says without looking. Gus only shrugs.

"I want to leave," I say.

"Okay, okay," she says, tromping to take down the target, and in my mind all I can see is the tip of an arrow piercing the fur of a rabbit, and an image of myself, hands cupped, running vainly to catch the blood before it soaks the dirt.

We go home. The golden hour has descended and the trees and dirt hover in gold. We open some beers and Gus takes his to the patio where he falls asleep in a chair. Yahlie gets in the shower, one of her endless showers where she turns the water off and on many times. I look at my open beer, undrunk, and think of the brochure in my dresser—*Options*—but I take a drink.

I decide to make one of my oddball stir-fries. Every vegetable in the house. Plum sauce, a little crushed red pepper. I start a pot of rice. The phone rings, and for a moment I think—*it's now*. But Yahlie comes out in her towel and answers it.

She talks in Hebrew, its beautiful angles and rumbles echoing through the house. I recognize one of the handful of words she'd taught me—*aba*. I try to call up others. *Ani. Rosh. Avak.*

When they hang up, she comes in holding the cordless phone, I call out the word. "*Aba!* Father?" I say. "Did I get it right?"

"Yes!" she says. "My sister bought a house. She wants me to stay with them. She says I can have their extra bedroom."

Her face is all excitement. I think, I just found you. Now you're leaving?

"Mmm," I say. "I can't imagine having that much money."

She stares out the back window, dripping, takes a loud breath and puts the phone back in its cradle. She comes over and sees the ginger.

"Hey, don't use too much of that."

"I won't use too much. You'll like it, I promise."

The pot sizzles under my hands and I lift the cutting board to gather the diced ginger. I flip it in, one teaspoon at a time.

"Enough," she yells. "Enough!"

"Yahlie, shut it!" I yell back. "Right in my ear. If you scream like that again I'll slap you."

She clacks her tongue at me.

"You know I don't like it, and you did it anyway."

"It's just a little. You won't even taste it. You freak out over nothing, you know that?"

She stomps away to her room, leaving the house quiet. I push the sizzling stuff around. The carrots have become a dull orange. As it cooks, I think, I shouldn't have said that, and pick out a fleck of the ginger that does, indeed, appear fibrous.

"It's ready," I call out.

Yahlie comes back, dressed. We fix our plates and eat on the velvet couch, the matching lamps on the end tables turned on, our legs tucked beneath us. She spills a little on the velvet. I wipe it up with a paper towel.

She takes a bite.

"Can you taste it?" I say.

"Not really," she says. "But you can floss my teeth for me later."

"What about those ears of corn we ate at that fair that time? Those were stringy."

"Those were delicious," she says. "All that butter and spicy stuff on them."

"Sometimes I think there's nothing in the world but food," I say.

She chews and nods. "But isn't it quite a privilege for us to say that? The social forces behind eating delicious things all the time…"

She trails off, not finishing the thread of what was probably a brilliant idea. Usually she returns to it later, whatever it is.

It's dark and I'm running the dishwasher when Gus wanders in from the patio.

"There's food on the stove," Yahlie says. "It has ginger in it."

"Love some," he says.

"Okay," I say. "Enough with the ginger."

She exhales loudly and stands. She picks up a heavy magazine and tosses it onto the coffee table with a slam. "That wasn't an insult," she says. "That was just a statement of fact."

"Well then, you can make your own food next time," I say.

She lifts and drops her shoulders, her hands out like claws.

"You know what?" she huffs. "I've been trying to cheer you up all day."

Before I can say a thing, she goes out the front door. I hear her start walking down Aqua Fría Road, and think of following her, but I let her go.

Gus stands, his hat crooked. I unfold and refold the paper towel I used to dab the couch. I think of all the other unkind things I could have said: That's the last time I waste an hour cooking for you and your bonehead friend. That's the last time I let you bring over some random person you met once. But it feels so mean to have those barbs in my head. Gus straightens the hat and spoons himself a plate. I go to the patio, thinking maybe he'll leave me alone.

Of course, he follows me out. He slouches in the lawyer's green chair, eating with the plate six inches from his face.

"This is delicious," he says. "Where'd you grow up?"

I think, Must he make conversation?

"Delaware," I say. "You?"

"Canada. I'm always jealous of people who can cook."

"You speak French?"

"*Oui*. Not all Canadians speak French, but I do," he says. I think, surprise, a thing in common. The way he says it, it sounds like *way*. I can only think what my father would have said, which is, *Wrong*.

He finishes eating and pulls a pack of cigarettes from his jacket pocket and lights one. He looks like Raggedy Andy smoking. He says something about how water is the next thing. How water's going to be like oil.

"So how do you guys know each other?" he says.

"We met here," I say. "We both lived for a while in that place on Cerrillos, that rooming house."

He asks me if I liked the place and I shrug. He holds the cigarette like a conductor's baton, waiting for me to continue, but I don't answer.

"Maybe you guys will tell me about it someday," he says, standing and taking his plate inside.

He says it as though he'll be back next week. One thing I hate about this town is that you never see someone only once. It's too small. The guy you'll never see again doesn't exist.

I go inside, where Gus has flipped on the kitchen overhead light. The brightness makes me realize how filthy we have let the place become. A muddy streak on the linoleum and dust and footprints everywhere, the stove top littered with vegetable shards and spattered oil. I open the fridge and take out another beer. This time, I don't even pause before taking a drink.

I see on the answering machine that there is a message. A red blip. I don't know when it arrived. How had I missed it?

No, I say to myself. I don't want to hear this message. Not now.

Gus picks at things around the countertops. I pick up a sponge from the sink and start swabbing it around.

"Are you guys, like, a thing?" he asks.

"No," I say. "Don't get that idea. We're more like sisters."

"You argue like sisters," he says.

He wanders toward the bathroom. I follow him, about to snap at him, but then I think, He's not wrong. He starts opening the medicine cabinet.

"You like it out here?" he says.

"I guess so," I say, stunned at his nerve. "Quit nosing around in there."

"You guess so?" But he doesn't close the medicine cabinet, and instead goes into my room.

"Dude. What do you think you're doing? Get outta there."

But he's already picking up my stuff, flipping at things with his fingertips. My books, my stack of prints from the art class at the day camp where Yahlie and I worked. He turns my fan on and off.

"So, what is your story?" he says, and laughs a twitchy laugh. All I can think is, Stop laughing, stop touching.

"Yahlie said she didn't want to go shoot arrows if you didn't come too," he says. "So, I was wondering what your deal is."

I want to say something, but nothing will come out, as though a draft has blown over my throat.

"What's this?" Gus says, touching the folded page on my dresser. "Writing letters?"

"Nothing." I snatch it from under his finger. Some of my beer spills, and the letter gets crumpled.

Just then I hear the door. It's Yahlie. Her eyes have a wet, tumescent look, but she walks in with a prancing step, like nothing happened.

"Hey," she says. "What are you guys doing?"

Gus shrugs, and I just stare, clutching the beer aloft, my tongue momentarily dried out. She eyes the crumpled letter in my hand and strides to the kitchen.

"Where'd you go?" I say, following her, but she doesn't answer. She starts rifling through a drawer. She upends everything; it resembles a drawer I imagine she and I would have in any place we live, a drawer of ragged ends.

With a whish of her hand, she produces a thin, white object.

An envelope.

"Guess what I found?" Before I can answer, she says: "A mailbox."

Suddenly I feel like I'm in a tiny, tight room.

She takes the letter from my hand and uncrumples it, folds it, slides it into the envelope.

"Here's a stamp," she says. Somehow, she has this, too, in her hand.

And so, I write that address, the only one I know for Wes. I affix the stamp. The two of us go outside, down a street I've never walked on, leaving Gus lurking in the house The sky is filled with clouds like haystacks in a snowy field at night. The mailbox sits on a corner, a hulking thing in the blue dark. Below us, a gully, a trickle of water, a fluttering sound.

Yahlie says, "There it is."

The picture of the receptionist at her desk bursts back into my mind. The whir of her computer. One other thing she'd said hung in my mind: *You missed it for today*.

I stare at the mailbox.

"He isn't even there anymore," I say.

She reaches to take it gently from my hand, her hand on one end, mine on the other.

"You're almost there," Yahlie says. "You can do it."

Neither of us will let it go.

"But," I say. "Mailing it won't change what has to happen."

"What are you talking about?"

I see then that I have succeeded in concealing my abdomen and she hasn't even guessed that there is more to this. That she believes what's in the letter is an outpouring of my broken heart, instead of the bare facts it contains.

"Yahlie. I'm pregnant."

It was the first time I'd said the words out loud. It feels incredibly stupid, my being so rude to her about Gus or shooting arrows or about the food. In her tender, still stare, I finally see that she is wounded by my stupid, mean comment, and how, all day, she was trying to care for me. And sees my sadness. She's trying to take it away—even though I couldn't share what it was for. It's my fault, I want to say. All of it.

She doesn't say anything more, only releases her fingers from the envelope. She opens the creaking mailbox door. A gust of cold air seems to blow from inside, and I let go, the white envelope disappearing.

When we get back to the house, Gus has discovered a bottle of tequila.

"I think it's time for margaritas," he says.

"Yes!" Yahlie says, and then I say yes too, because what else is there to do?

But then she looks at me, worried. I shrug, and say, "It's fine." I begin cutting a lime.

"Hey look, there's a message," Yahlie says.

Don't play that, I want to say, but before I can, she hits the button. A beep screams through the room. There's a hissing sound that, for a moment, my mind confuses for the sound of a machine my father had been hooked to as he sat in a chair, near the end.

This is Southwest Women's Choice, a woman says. *We're calling to schedule your appointment.*

"Hey, that's that place," Gus says. "I wrote about those protestors last month. They're always holding those signs showing bloody pictures. Freaky."

He squints as he realizes abruptly what he's saying. In the split second it takes to breathe in, the notion of uttering some fake cover story—just a checkup!—crosses my mind, and dissipates in a gasp. We three know what this appointment is for. Then this person, this Gus, becomes folded into the cone we're in, and I realize I let him in, because the look on his puffy face is one of kindness and confusion, as Yahlie and I have become flushed with embarrassment and shame. He'll never know that what flushed our faces was also my withholding it from her, when she and I both knew that she is the only one who could shepherd me through what is coming.

I try to cut the lime but the knife is dull, and it's like punching a hole through leather.

The woman on the message recites some numbers slowly. But then, she seems to get confused. She has to back up and start again.

Her voice echoes through the kitchen. The broom in the corner casts a shadow, and I think how that's not its usual place. I try again to cut the lime. I think of sentence diagrams my father wrote in French on graph paper; of notes my mother wrote on index cards about her rose bushes in her loopy, mannered handwriting. *Drift rose shrub, spring: No new growth*. The lime becomes destroyed, a creased, useless husk. A ghostly trace of the meal I cooked passes through my nose, my throat, the scent of ginger and lime.

I stop, and see Yahlie's black eyes. The woman is still talking. I feel like we should go do something. Maybe go to the old cemetery. Or to the bar. Or the all-night diner off I-5. But I also feel like there's a crack in the floor and I am slipping in.

Another loud beep sounds and the message ends.

Gus clears his throat. Yahlie and I both gawk at him. He straightens the hat again as he looks at her, then me. "That place is right by my office," he says. "You need a lift or anything, just holler."

Then the phone rings—and we three jump. Gus lurches toward it to answer, but Yahlie and I block his way. I can still feel it, that lunge. And I can hear the chants: *sin, sin, sin*.

CLINIC

I had decided that I would go to the place and do what had to be done. The night before, Yahlie and I are in the bar. The name of that place escapes me. We are always there. It is eating us alive, that bar. It is always her. She and I, we two, as if bored from rock.

We order two plates of huevos, half red sauce, half green—Christmas—and eat out of Styrofoam containers at the picnic table under the tree. Yahlie is curvy and tanned to golden brown and has big feet with the white stripes of tan lines from her sandals. This week she has cut the last of the blonde from her hair, and is letting it grow into its natural dark kink. Yahlie has been all broken up over her sometimes boyfriend who, finally, inexorably, broke up with her. Now she is electric with mania.

I can't remember who sits down first, us or the two brothers. But then they occupy the other end of the table.

I was drinking, drinking.

One of them looks petrified in the '80s, a breezy sort of haircut and three buttons open on his shirt.

"I have the best ever pickup line for you," he says to Yahlie.

"No thanks," Yahlie says.

The corners of his thin lips drop in feigned surprise and he raises his hands. "Okay then," he says. "How about this. My name's Pete. Can I buy you a drink?"

The other one, who has hair in black S-shaped curls, groans and pinches the bridge of his nose like an old man. Even so, he smiles, showing a set of pearly teeth. Both have faces like hawks.

"That was it! That was the line!" Yahlie yells.

"Believe it nor we've heard it before," I say.

"I believe it," says the one with the curls. "This is my brother. My name's Lawrence. Pete here is my brother."

I was in need of another drink myself.

"Does that offer extend just to her?" I say.

Lawrence gives me a look both sharp and desirous. He has a round chest that bulges and long forearms. Me and this Lawrence, we had shared a moment.

"Of course not," he says.

Yahlie says something to Pete and they both laugh like alarm clocks. Finally, a person with a laugh as loud as hers. Another round was produced.

Yahlie asks what they do and Pete says he manages the bar at the Hotel St. Francis. Pointing at Lawrence, he says, "He lives in LA. He's the one who got his life together."

I eat another bite of food and bite my tongue. I touch it with a napkin and a spot of red expands to pink. I take a drink of my beer and it tastes like I've held a nickel in my mouth.

A moment passes, Lawrence says, "Would you two like to go with us to a wedding?"

"That's quite a pickup line," says Yahlie.

Pete laughs, his feathered hair waving, as if to say, this was not part of the plan. "Okay, sure," he says.

"When is it?" I say to Lawrence.

"Now."

"Now?"

"I guess it's not really a wedding," he says. "It's the wedding reception. The wedding happened earlier today."

Yahlie and I exchange a glance. I am slowly ripping off the tab of the Styrofoam food container.

"So, what are you doing here?" I say. "Shouldn't you be there?"

"Taking a break," Lawrence says.

"Whose wedding?"

"Our father's."

They both begin laughing, the sound wafting up into the silver spruce. Yahlie and I are too bewildered to laugh.

"Who's your father marrying?" I say.

"A woman named Katie," Lawrence says.

"That's my name," I say.

"I know that's your name."

Had I told them? A strangeness showers over me, a vacant barrage, a quake. Did these beers contain twilight sleep? Have I forgotten who I am? I have, I did. But there it is, inscribed on me. Like catching a gleam in a certain shape right in the eye.

"You should come," Lawrence says, his face a rounded rectangle beneath his curls.

Pete says, "It'll be fun. Our father owns a ranch, it's pretty big. It's a big party."

Unasked for, in my head, a woman's voice speaks to me. Above the sounds of the bar, above the talking of the brothers and Yahlie. In a brisk voice, the woman is leaving me a message: *We are calling to confirm your appointment for noon tomorrow. If for any reason you need to change this appointment, please call us before 4:30 p.m. today.* The image of the man it belongs to rises in my mind. Like either of these men could be him, strolling back from the bar with more drinks. His peaked eyebrows. The spread of a smile across his face, his chipped tooth a fang. He was a dark wolf.

Then he is with me, and won't go away.

"I can't believe you're inviting us to a wedding!" Yahlie says.

Her face says she wants to say yes, to go somewhere with strangers, to play this game. It's happened a hundred times. I get roped into some idiotic evening when all I want is to sit and crush some beers and laugh with her about nothing.

"No," I say.

"Come on," she says. "It'll be fun."

"Will it?" I say.

Pete talks details, rattling on about where it is. Yahlie's face, her eyes big as dinner plates, says she wants it. She needs me to say yes.

"Sure you don't want to?" she says.

"No thanks," I say. "I'm good."

"I think I'll get a ride with them," she says. In the time it takes for the three of them to stand from their seats, the thought of her leaving me here makes me clench my teeth. I squeeze my beer can, the aluminum crushing under my fingers, until they are all staring at the snapping destruction.

"Fine," I say.

She squeezes my arm, her eyes twinkling.

"You need this," she says to me quietly.

She's talking about tomorrow. About the message, about noon. "Do I?" I say.

So we leave. Yahlie drives, as I always seem to insist she does, since I have yet to figure out what to do with my car. Just then it seems like a joke, like another dumb thing I did and can't fix. Pete says he wants to stop at his house first, and we follow them in their car, a white sports car junker that fumes. They drive with the top down. I put my head in my hands and try to fix my gaze on the moving white bumper. I start to feel ill.

Pete's house is half of a low building, a shed on packed, weedy sand, with a pinyon tree so wide it might engulf the house.

Pete invites us in. In the room, ceilings not much above our heads, is a burgundy carpet, empty cups, crumpled newspapers on the floor. In the next room is an unmade bed, a wood-paneled wall painted black, a dangling calendar.

Lawrence, seeming chagrined at the squalor, says, "Want a drink?"

"Sure," I say.

But then one can't be produced. In the kitchen every surface is covered in dishes. There is no room to wash anything in the sink, the cabinets are all empty.

"Pete, how do you live here?" Lawrence yells.

Pete rummages, finds a different shirt, more or less the same as the last. He peels off the old one—his chest is pinkish, round. Stretch marks like white strings creep up his shoulders. The image of the man—I couldn't even think the word, *father*—arises. Like he's following me. His lean chest, scattered black hairs across its ripples. A shiver runs through me.

"I gotta get this place cleaned up," Pete says. "I need to get my life together." He sits, changing his socks, looks around at the empty walls.

We leave, and drive behind them through the neighborhood of aluminum-sided casitas, until we reach the long, straight road that leads out of town.

"I wonder what happened with their mother," Yahlie says.

"Now they'll have a new mother," I say. "But they're too old to have a new mother."

After the last traffic light Pete hits the gas and we're speeding away from town.

"What the hell are we doing?" Yahlie says, laughing, as she puts her foot on the gas, her mouth ajar in a kind of wonder, and I feel it too, this wave of fearlessness that feels so good I could eat it. I think maybe she was right, I do need this.

The road turns to dirt, and we take dozens of turns over white rock chips and broken pinon needles. I fear Yahlie's car might sink into the dirt. We lose the sky in the dust from the headlights, their bumper nearly invisible, a pair of red taillights. I still taste nickel.

A turquoise post emerges, looking like a totem in the ground. The loose dirt gives way to combed gravel, a driveway lined with cars, some tall and expensive, their doors crushing into the bushes. We approach a house. It stuns me looking at it. In front is a circle like an English manor might have, only with a saguaro in the center. We get out. The house is built from logs, a shined barn door, a vaulted window. The sky returns, blue-black and littered with stars.

"Ladies," Lawrence says.

"Is this where you grew up?" I say.

"Nope," he says, a grin passing over his face. "We were broke."

The grand front door clanks as we enter a salon of brown leather couches and earth-toned geometric pattern rugs and a lofted landing over our heads. A chandelier made from the hoop of a barrel. The house is empty but voices drift in through the open windows.

"I guess the bar's this way," Lawrence says, and we go out back, where people are scattered through a pebbly yard, a tent of thin canvas behind them, lit with strings of amber bulbs. I smell a waft of marijuana.

A woman with polished gray hair emerges from the crowd in a white dress with no sleeves.

"Who are these young ladies?" she says.

"This is the bride," Pete says to Yahlie and me.

"We couldn't come dateless to the reception," Lawrence says.

"Of course!" she says.

A drink has materialized in Lawrence's hand. He introduces us, and Yahlie says, "You look so beautiful!"

The bride says, "It's always easy to look beautiful on your wedding day."

When I take her hand and say my name, she says, "That's my name too!" She has soft, rubbery wrinkles around her eyes.

A man approaches in jeans and cowboy boots and a plaid shirt.

"I was just telling these ladies that it's easy to look beautiful on your wedding day," the bride says to him. "Especially the third time around!"

They both laugh loudly. He is much older and much thinner than the bride. His eyes, rimmed in red, make him look like he's been in front of a campfire. He blinks. It's like they're testing us to see if we're real. I try to make myself look real. Try to look like I know why I'm there or what I'm doing. Like I am a person who occupies space. I know we should ask them some questions. Where will you go on your honeymoon, how did you meet. But everyone else here already knows the answers to those questions. We are the only ones who don't, and nothing feels real.

Then Yahlie says the right thing. "Thank you so much for letting us join Lawrence and Pete. You have a beautiful home."

They effusively thank her. "Make sure you go see the horses," the father says, as they turn off to other, realer guests.

"Let's get you a drink," Lawrence says, and we go to the bar. I get whiskey and I think, this is bad. I think the beers have worn off, but they're still there, in my skin. Then it's like we've forgotten about the bride and groom. We sit under the amber bulbs in the tent. Lawrence asks me a dozen questions. What brought you out here? I give him vague answers: I was in California for a while, then I came here. Where in California? San Francisco. It's clear he likes me. We get up and walk around the yard, back inside, into the room with the chandelier. He keeps bumping my hand with the back of his. He says, how do you two know each other? in a cloying, lurid way.

Then, the predictable game is instantly underway, this game Yahlie wanted, and I flirt as I'm expected to do. And it feels good, like getting high, flinging these bruised thoughts from my head. These two think they're using me, but I'm using them. Then I do a thing that sometimes happens. I lie.

"We went to college together!" I say. "My roommate was her boyfriend, so she was always at my house. They then broke up, but we stayed friends."

A useless lie. I don't know why I say it. Yahlie pinches in her giggling and plays along. But she won't say more. She won't add to the lie. For a second it feels true, that she and I are just temporarily between things, and what ties us together goes further back than this town, that we are reliable and solid. For her sometimes I think it's true. She gets phone calls from her sister. She plays along to Lawrence and Pete, but on her face, a hint of alarm.

A wind passes over us, brief and humid. Too much truth. I'd been in damp wind with its father, him in his black jacket soaking up the rain. Him rolling a glass between his hands behind the bar. His shoulders in my hands, he who desired me above all others, to whom I was nothing. I'd had only a couple phone calls from my mother, my brother. Before Yahlie, he was the last person I knew.

Lawrence returns, has a bottle of something the color of a guava and four shot glasses. We pinch our noses and it tastes of mint and stickiness.

"I want to go outside," I say to Yahlie. We wander back to the front, the parked cars covered in dust so full of mica that it sparkles.

Yahlie points. A ways into the brush is a barn. "He said something about horses, remember?"

Something in the power of the lie leaves me as I follow. The barn is splattered with dust and is decrepit compared to the house. Yahlie pushes open its door; a pulley emits a squeak and the planks rattle. No light—the sound of the party drops away.

It smells of hay and manure, of candles burning, of oily rags. My feet sink into the ground; the dirt feels wet. The barn's ceiling seems to go on and on, as though we are at the bottom of a cavern.

Something breathes. To our left are stalls. Horses. As my eyes adjust, I see a wet, black eye. The horse hangs its nose over the stall door, its coat gleaming in the dark.

"Hey, pretty," Yahlie coos. The horse breathes. The stall door is covered with hanging leather pieces, bits, bridles. A crop, a whip.

Another horse rattles in a nearby stall and puts its face over the door. It is immense. A racehorse.

"Hi, handsome boy," Yahlie says. Gently she reaches to pet its nose. The horse twitches its head. How soft this is. How soft a place. How quiet. How far away I am, how the noise has drifted off. Just us and these creatures.

I reach to touch the white blaze on the horse's forehead, glowing at me. Its breathing quickens. I touch its soft coat, and what feels like a sharp bone under its skin.

Like a clap of thunder, the horse lurches, kicks, and I feel it before I hear—its hooves crash against the stall door, and it bites my hand, and I feel its teeth grip bone.

Yahlie gasps. We both jump back. The walls clatter. I grasp my hand and feel a trickle of blood.

"Are you all right?" she says.

I look at my hand. It stings, there's blood. Something shutters in my chest, a balloon of air rising. A sob comes out, my eyes have filled like a child's.

"Oh no," Yahlie says. "Oh no. Don't cry."

She puts her arms around me and hugs me. She kisses my cheek, her nose like a little cat's.

"I'm drunk," I mumble.

But all she says is, *shhh*, and pats my back. "I was free for a second," I say.

"You were," she says.

A lash of anger passes through me. I can't stand her pitying me.

"No," I say. And I shove out of her hug. Hard, the tensing of her shoulder underneath my hands.

A staircase emerges in the dark. Just before the barn's exit.

"What's up here," I say, and I climb its narrow stairs, covered in hay and dirt, to a second floor. A hayloft. A wide expanse, ceiling disappearing into blackness. I see another staircase. A beam of moonlight from above, through a hatch.

"I'm going up here," I say, but Yahlie is not behind me.

I walk toward it, and something brushes my shoulder. It is cold, soft, but dense.

Something hangs there in the shadow. An animal. Another scent, putrid and yet earthy, like wet leaves in fall, mixes in with the scents of the barn. Even in the dark, I can see its split insides, a great cavern where its breathing being was. Beneath it is a slick pool of drying black liquid.

Something like starbursts cross my eyes, but I keep walking toward the beam of moonlight, and the sky comes into view, a brush of dry night air touching my face. The peak of the roof is flat, narrow, like a balance beam, like I walked as a child. A weathervane perches on its apex. As I stand, the roof spins, the sky dips down towards me, then it passes.

Slowly, I walk to the far end of the roof where I can see the party down below. The people, their colorful clothes, the shiny cars, the gentle yellow glow. But I can no longer discern our purpose for being here. I am in a fog. A cloud of rotating planets, of silence, of noise, the beer, the cigarettes, the directionless circling. Perhaps between now and tomorrow, I could die. I won't have to choose between me and another me.

Then he descends on me.

Are you dead? I want to ask him.

"Are you dead?" I say to the air, to no one.

Somehow, I know that he is. I know that wherever he went, or the story that he told to leave me, whatever came next, it killed him. And I wished that I had gone with him, had done what he was doing, whatever thing or whatever place. A desire for him, fleeting, returns so strong that a shock runs down the middle of me, and shame rushes to my face—sweetness, that taste of nickel. I stick my fist into my stomach, and the spot where the horse bit me aches.

Four black crows were pricking my insides with their beaks.

My mouth seeps with a viscous fluid. Blood. I spit it out, over the cornice of the roof, cold like quicksilver.

I stand on top of the roof and try to say: No. Me. Me next. Help me. Help me escape. But nothing comes.

Down below is a pile of weeds or grass or hay. A soft mass. I imagine a rusted metal object buried under it. A plow.

A reaper. Underneath all that softness. If I jumped, it would pierce the center of me, and that would be it. Then it is as if the ground beneath the pile is not dry dirt, but painted sky, white with a hint of blue. But it vanishes, and it is as it was, cold, dry, gravelly.

I hear Lawrence's voice. He stands in the driveway. "Hey!" he yells from the ground. "Jump!"

"Katie?"

Yahlie stands on the roof.

I look at her, and there is no look of pity. All I have to do is cross the distance between me and her. She wants me to. His chipped tooth. In my mind, he was crouched on the floor of a kitchen. His boots, on linoleum. Our kitchen, in the house we shared, borrowed. A cold breeze came through the window. He was a rabbit, erect, its paws clenched, still, until it heard a predator. And something else comes over my vision. A mask. A surgical mask. Someone asking me, is your address wrong on this form? I thought, how's this form supposed to hold it all? They put that mask on my face, the light went off. A woman said to me, angrily, Would you just breathe in? The light went on, the light went off again, and as it did, I heard Pete say, I need to get my life together, and I heard Yahlie say, Come down, don't be scared. And my distant reply, But I am.

NOVIO, NOVIA

One shift—I'd gotten a job at a juice bar, wedged inside the big organic supermarket, one of the last of a string of jobs I had before I left that town—I tried to take one of the fifteen-minute breaks I was entitled to and went outside to the iron picnic table. I was thinking about how tired I was of all my smoking cigarettes, all my keeping it in perspective, my not being in love. But, I thought, if I could just stay right here, I could do it—I could have one good thought. I was trying to drift off into a dewy field somewhere. I had, for the moment, a job. It didn't seem that I had entirely wrecked my life. It was 6:40 in the evening. There were waves of golden sand nearby, and even though I was in a puddle of asphalt, and apprehension filled me everywhere I drove, I was, right then, enjoying myself.

So of course, after only four minutes, Izaul, the deli guy, came out and said "Katie. *Venga*." He had been asking me out on dates for a couple of weeks.

"What?" I said.

"*Venga*. They really mad this time."

I had taken off the white chef's coat I had to wear so I could lay it on the ground and ash my cigarette on it. I had taken off the hat, a Girl Scout beanie fused with a midshipman's cap. I followed Izaul back inside, through the spaceship automatic door. He pointed to a lady in a sun hat and a gray-haired hippie who was tapping his fingers on the counter, car keys thrust out of his fist. They were irate. Goddamn it, not this again, I thought. Every day I'd try to take a break and something would interrupt it.

"My supervisor said I could go on a break," I said.

Which wasn't true, there weren't any supervisors, just a triptych of evil bosses.

"But we were standing here!" he said. His mustache, Mark Twain–ish, ruffled. "We watched you leave while we were waiting to have our order taken. We tried to get your attention."

"Very rude, very rude," the sun hat said.

"I have a trick knee," I said.

"Are you deaf?" the man said.

I said, "No. Definitely not."

I stood there for a second watching their fuses shorten. This was the moment when the customer yells at me and I take it. I could see Izaul and the dishwasher watching me through the round window in the dish room door, behind the endless glass case of the deli counter. I could faintly hear the twitching merengue from the dish room's radio. I had flopped the coat and the hat on the prep counter behind me. Now I stood wearing my stale softball shirt, and surely that was pissing them off more. I took a step and knocked a wedge of coffee filters onto the floor.

"Whoops," I said.

I wasn't very good at working at the juice bar.

"Well," the sun hat said, huffing, her arms folded with her wrists jammed into her elbows. "I'd like a large Beta Bunny," she said.

"And I'd like an iced soy latte," he said. "Today. Preferably."

Beta Bunny. The juice of nine carrots, give or take. $4.99.

I gave the coffee filters a kick and snapped on a pair of plastic gloves and made their drinks, right there in the softball shirt. They seemed angry. Really angry, angrier than people usually got. I could feel it, a tingling in my stomach like when my father would yell at me for not loading the dishwasher the way he liked it. I tried to think about other things. The man had said *prefer*ably, but more like, *pruh for*, which got me thinking about how people usually say that word. I decided that the word fluctuates. The juicer made a noise like a Weedwacker with something stuck inside it, the espresso machine squealed.

"I want you to know this is the last time I shop here," he said.

"Seems fair," I said.

I put their plastic cups on the counter. He took a sip of his drink and the straw seemed to disappear into his mustache. "Come on, Laura," he said to her, his hand on her back. I wanted to say, He doesn't love you. They scowled at me as they walked away.

I stood at the prep counter, the bouquet of vegetables lying before me, soon to be decimated. This was a fancy grocery store, a cavernous place air-conditioned to meat locker. Bulk carob, sugar substitutes, a vat of shampoo made from hemp that you could siphon into your own container. A place where the price point had been sharpened.

Izaul emerged from the kitchen, pushing open the doors like Clint Eastwood. He leaned next to me, one elbow on the counter.

"They don't like you," he said. "*Que malo.*"

"What?" I said. "I get a break. You get a break."

"No break," he said. I could see several faces peering through the window in the dish room door.

"You don't take a break? You should, you get a paid break. That's part of the deal."

Izaul shrugged, grinning. One of his eyeteeth was capped in silver, and his skin was the color of cinnamon sticks. He said, "You lazy."

"Fine, fine. Skip your mandated, paid break," I said. "See if I care."

I bent to get the fallen coffee filters. He kept standing there, smiling at me, which he tended to do, and I kind of liked, even though I never smiled back, and every time he would ask me to do something or go someplace, I acted like I had no idea what was going on. He was laughing through his teeth, going, *stee, stee, stee!*

"What are you looking at?"

"*Nada, nada.*"

I reached into the refrigerator under the counter for a bundle of spinach, tied into a little bale. The juice bar was a lot of going up and down the stairs to the frightening industrial refrigerator for bags of vegetables, frozen bananas, flats of wheatgrass. I would watch the customers deplete the stacks of napkins and straws like ants, then I would replenish them.

Frankie, one of the bosses, came up and put her fists on the counter. She was a bulbous woman with a row of earrings trailing up the side of her ear and a pompadour. She always talked to me like I was stupid, and I always talked to her like she was stupid.

"Did you piss those people off just now?" she asked. Her voice had a hint of bullfrog in it. Behind her I could see the sun hat and the man sipping their drinks. The man shook his head.

"What people?" I said.

She snapped at Izaul. "You need something?" and he skittered back to the deli.

"I had to apologize," she said, jerking her thumb over her shoulder. "I had to comp their drinks."

"We got to do something about this break situation," I said.

"What situation is that?"

"I get a fifteen-minute break every four hours. I'm entitled to it by law."

"So, take it."

"I can't take it," I said. "There's never a fifteen-minute break in the customers. And there's no one to cover for me."

Frankie looked distressed. But then her face flattened and she said, calmly, "You know you're the only one who has this problem?"

She started nodding at me. I thought about the other employees. There was the kid working his way through acupuncture school. The morning girl who worked in a horse barn and tended bar at the Hotel St. Francis. The guy who ran a garden and sometimes carried the bags of vegetable shavings home in his truck.

"I can't keep apologizing for your behavior," she said.

"But, I get a break," I said.

"If there's no one to cover your break you could just teach one of these guys to do it."

"Why do *I* have to do that?" I said.

"It's about solving problems. Questioning things."

"I see," I said. "But maybe you could provide me with a diagram."

"Would you just watch it? You know, you could really do with a little more positivity. We don't have any room here for problem people and what you're turning into is a problem person."

"Sure, okay, fine, right," I said. "But I'm not going to work through the break I'm entitled to take. I'm not going to do that, no matter how much you keep on goading the other guys to do that and they keep doing it, because they're afraid of getting fired."

"You seem to know a lot about it, don't you?" she said. "That's a great attitude, a real great attitude."

"I guess it's the attitude of a problem person," I said.

"You definitely need a major attitude shift, my dear. Put your uniform back on," she said, pointing at the hat with a wrinkly pink finger. "I got my eye on you," she said, and walked away, her ring of keys jangling.

I could see Izaul and the other guys looking at me. He called to me. "They don't like you!"

"Oh, shut it," I said.

I stood there feeling satisfied with myself. I was right. But also, I wasn't. I turned back to the spinach. I chopped the ends off. The guys were talking in Spanish. I had college sophomore Spanish, so I could understand them sometimes, and somehow the French I knew made it easier. They were cleaning out one of the deli cases, prepping for closing time. Izaul and another guy opened up the back of the case and took wads of paper towels and scrubbed. I thought about Frankie squeezing her hands together and comping their drinks. She's very difficult, she must have said, very troubled.

I plugged the drain in the sink and filled it with water. I dumped in the spinach leaves and they all floated on the surface. I watched them sink, one leaf at a time. That's it, I thought. I'm having a cigarette.

"Hey," I called across the deli counter. I could see Izaul lurking at the pizza station, dealing with what we like to call The Camper. The late evening shopper. She was bent at the waist, pointing inside the case at the last few lingering things on display, probably saying, No, that one, that one. I waved at him, he nodded back. When the shopper had her pizza, Izaul walked over, a specter floating behind the counter, carrying a stack of pizza pans. He went into the dish room and came out, busting through the swinging door, leaving it wavering on its hinge, his squirrel eyes blinking.

"*¿Qué necesitas?*" He was wringing his hand in a bar towel and I could see him being somebody's father. I couldn't keep myself from smiling.

"Whas you problem, eh?" he said. "You get fire?" He made a slicing motion across his neck.

"Can you cover for me for a second? So I can go have a smoke?"

He looked at me blankly.

I blundered for the word. "*Fumar,*" I said. "*Espera aquí, y voy a fumar.*" I pointed at the floor, then I held two fingers to my lips.

"Good espanish. *¿Por qué?* You *perezosa?* Boss don't like you."

"No, no. Just so I can go have a smoke. *Diez minutos.*"

He flopped the bar towel from hand to hand. "You just smoke," he said.

"Come on," I said. "I'll give you some of the tips."

He stroked the fuzz that grew in the place of a mustache. "Okay," he said. "For some tips, deal."

I headed for the automatic doors. Frankie could bite it if she saw me leaving. The music faded as I stepped outside. Night was approaching and the air was papery. There was a wistful wind blowing and some cars lingering in the lot. I lit a cigarette and fished around in the back seat of my car for the paperback I'd been reading. Its pages were stiffened by a rainstorm that had blown in through the window one day. I never closed the windows because it didn't matter if anyone stole this car. In fact, that would have helped me out, sort of. And besides it barely ever rained. I sat in the front seat with the door open. I read eight pages. Then I went back inside.

Izaul stood at the counter and seemed to be looking at something far away. "Thanks," I said.

But he just stood there with his arms dangling.

"What?" I said, and started walking away, around the salad bar to the counter where the napkins and straws and lids were. There weren't any more straws. I opened the cabinet underneath the counter. I could at least put some more out for whoever was opening tomorrow.

I heard Izaul say, "Katie."

He always said it like, *kah ti*.

"What?" I said. Then I saw Frankie jangling toward me.

"Did you just go outside again?" she said. Now she was looking at me like I was lying. I considered what it would be like to lie. She would know. Inevitably, she would know.

"Yeah?" I said.

"News flash," she said, her jowls shaking a little. "That's it, we're letting you go."

I craned my head over the deli counter, but Izaul was gone. I turned back and my arm hit the box of straws.

"Damn," I said. "Seriously?"

"Seriously."

"You're firing me? I just worked a double," I said. "I've been here since 6 a.m."

"Right, that's when the shift starts," she said. "Now you can sleep in."

"For Christ's sake."

"Are you surprised? This is a gift."

"What's that supposed to mean?"

Her jangling keys were now still. She said, "Go off and do whatever you want. Since you don't want to work here, don't."

"How could anybody want to work here?" I said.

"Fine then, consider it a gift to me and everyone else who works here. Clean up and go home."

"Now?"

"Maybe I'm not making myself clear," she said, folding her arms across her chest, staring at me with an almost fascinated gaze, like I was a diorama in the natural history museum, and walked away, something unencumbered in her step.

I had to fight the urge to run out of the place. But that's not what I did. Instead I left the box of straws on the floor and went back behind the bar. I broke down the espresso machine, went to the kitchen and found the blade to the wheatgrass juicer and left it where the day girl could find it, resting on the blender, right on its rubbery start button.

As I walked to the back past the natural peanut butter, the shampoos, the frozen meats, the flower section, I thought, okay, no job. No job. No job. Jobless. I could maybe go work with Yahlie at the Blue Corn Cafe. I could get a shift at the town bar. But right then I was going to get in the car and later she and I were going to sit in a bar and get slowly drunk. Yet again I had proved myself to be incapable. Once, before I left home, I went to a temp agency. *Graduation date? Grade point average?* they'd asked. I'd made up numbers, watched a person scribble into a form. I had rolled up my life into a tight wad, and ended up here.

I went to punch out in the back where all the walk-in refrigerators were. Izaul came in.

"Where did you go?" I said. He looked at me blankly.

"When?" he said.

"Didn't you see? I just got fired."

"Oh no," he said. But then he started laughing. "I told you."

"Shut it," I said.

"Why you always say that?" he said. I had the punch card in my hand.

"I don't know. You're always teasing me. It's what you say when someone teases you, and if you're me, and you can't think of anything to say back. What am I gonna say? That they don't like you either? They love you. You're fantastic."

"You leaving now?" he said, leaning against the time clock, grinning at me. I held the card, about to punch it.

"Yeah! I'm leaving now! I got fired. I'm done!"

"Katie," he said.

"What!" I noticed the shirt peeking out of the top of his

chef coat. It was a soccer jersey. "Are you going to play soccer?" I said. "Football?"

He shook his head. The clock buzzed and ticked. I got paid for one more minute.

"*¿Quieres comer?*" he said.

The couple of other times he'd asked me to go somewhere I'd been able to wear the face of a stupid girl, pretend I thought he meant a friendly co-worker chat, which I didn't have time for, or feign that I didn't understand. Izaul said it like it was not a question. He smelled like we all smelled when we left, like cheese roasting on the bottom of an oven and lawn clippings.

"*Quieres comer. Conmigo.*"

"Now?"

"*Sí.*" He said something else I couldn't understand.

"*¿Comer?*" he said again, and made a gesture like lifting a fork, then mimed holding a drink, taking a sip. He was a good mime.

There was a fluttering in my limbs. I blurted, "I can't right now."

But he just stood there. Right then he reminded me of the boys I went to high school with, spastic but steady as the mooring of a dock, with some superhuman awareness of their bodies. Throw something at them and they would catch. But those boys had never wanted anything to do with me.

He started to whistle. Then he said: "Lady, I would like. To eat. With you."

I threw up my hands. I should have said no.

"Fine," I said. "Fine. You can take me out somewhere."

He looked sort of stunned for a second and then said, "Okay? Okay, we go. Come outside when you finish, okay? I drive."

"I'm already finished! I just said. I'm done! I got fired!"

"Okay, okay," he said. "Just wait. Five minute." He backed out of the door.

The time clock buzzed quietly. I could have stuck the time card in the slot and it would have returned, skewered. But I didn't. I slid it back into the rack of other cards, and the clock continued on with its ticks, its buzzes.

I walked out and saw him jogging back toward the dish room, far ahead of me at the end of an aisle. I was going to go out with this guy. The night ahead changed. Some old feeling returned, that feeling of screwing up a calculus test. You are useless, those tests seemed to say. In my head was a small war. I passed an endcap on one of the aisles, filled with six-packs of organic soda. Their shape called up to me stacks of wood my father had cut, waiting to be built into something. Toward the front, near the bins of little things people tossed in their carts as they headed to the checkout lines—lip balm, travel-sized lotions, candy—I knelt, as if to straighten something, and slipped a cigarette lighter from a small cardboard display box into my palm. How strange it was for them to be for sale there.

And all those things they make you sit through at employee orientation, those loss-reduction training videos. What knowledge. To know where they aim the cameras.

Then I was out of there, box of straws still littering the floor.

I waited for him in the parking lot, sitting on the trunk of the car in the tail end of the day's rapturous sunset. He came out after a while wearing the soccer shirt, three bright colors—red, blue, gold—soft Adidas on his feet. I had never seen him without the stupid hat. His head was round as a volleyball, shorn to number two at the barber shop.

I said, "I can't spend one more minute in this place."

"You wait," he said, and ran off behind the store to where the dumpsters were.

A gust of dry wind blew through carrying the smell of road tar and he drove up a minute later, music rattling the rims of the car. It was low to the ground, two-toned gray, a gleaming dent on one fender. A giant *H* was painted on the hood. A hundred little flags hung from the rearview mirror. He leaned over and popped open the door for me. Inside it smelled impeccably clean. I thought of a nice hotel. I must have smelled like compost. We drove down Cerrillos Road.

Something about that moment made the slide of freedom I always felt when leaving that place even better, like jumping into a perfectly warm pool.

"Nice car," I said.

"Thank you," he said.

"So, where we going?"

On the road in front of us, two guys in a sporty pickup jumped on their brakes. We fell forward against the seat belts.

Izaul said something I couldn't understand. I wished I could understand someone swearing at traffic in another language. That would be a thing to know. He shouted over the music, "Club Alegría."

"Never been there. What's this music?"

"*Merengue. Me gusta el merengue muy rápido.* Very fast."

Horns slid over three notes, a sound like a stick clattered across a fence. The car had a loud engine, I liked it. We passed St. Francis, where I would have turned to go back to my casita.

"Where you from?" Izaul said.

"I'm from Delaware."

"Delaware?" he said.

"It's wet there. Not like this. Not dry. Where are you from?"

"Guatemala," he said.

"How long have you been here?"

"*Ocho meses.* Eight months."

"You been working at the market this whole time?"

"*Sí*," he said.

We stopped at a light and I heard car radios, someone's sugary country music. It hadn't cooled down yet, and in the car I felt like I was being broiled.

"You miss it? You wanna go back?"

He glanced at me as he drove. We were turning onto Agua Fría, a road that eventually turned to dirt. Up ahead I saw a building I'd passed before, a shabby-looking warehouse.

"No," he said, shaking his head. "*No voy a volver.*"

He turned into the parking lot, a dusty clearing filled with a herd of cars parked in crooked lines. A concrete block of a building sat ahead, floodlights shining off its roof. We could have been going to the county fair. As we got out, he took a step toward me, but didn't come any closer. We shuffled through the dirt to the entrance, a dented metal door. A man leaned against a stool, taking five-dollar bills from the couple ahead of us, a guy in a pressed basketball jersey and a woman with a bushy ponytail. I heard the music from inside with the hollow beat of drums.

I reached for my wallet as we stepped up to the man, but Izaul put his hand out to stop me, took out a roll of cash the size of a double-A battery, peeled a bill off. The man taking our cash didn't look at us, just opened the door.

Inside, the place was full and a band played on a stage. A balcony overlooked the dance floor, the railings lined with people, dangling their drinks, nodding their heads. A bar against the far wall, a cloudy mirror hanging above, tipped forward, covered in red Christmas lights, reflected a million bottles, the crowns of people's heads, hands holding out cash. This music was what I'd heard blasting from car windows, from the dish room. On the stage the singer had a head of wavy black hair and sang, his vibrato a wave in a pool, holding something silver, like a cocktail shaker. He was desperate for something. It was the loudest sound. The musicians—all of them—moved left, right, and a ripple in between, each movement distinct. On the dance floor they were doing the same, only with twists, spins. One couple in the center ruled the show, their arms forming a diamond. Her hips moved sharply, but there was something soft—like the back of a horse's neck. The horns played a melody under the singer's voice, moving upward, upward. They swayed again and the trumpet player dabbed at the hollow near his throat.

It was the best thing I had ever seen.

"You wanna eat?" Izaul said.

"No," I said. "I want to drink."

He leaned his ear to my face and held my elbow. I shouted over the music. "*Una cerveza.*"

He motioned with his head and we made our way up a staircase. There was a miniature bar, a bartender in a halter top with silver rings on all her fingers. She stuck her ear in our direction, Izaul ordered, and she cracked two cans of Tecate. She looked at me and didn't smile. I let him pay, held the drink, and it cooled my hand.

The music changed and the crowd stopped and clapped. Everyone was sweating, wiping their brows. Izaul nodded his head and swayed.

"This is *merengue*," he said. "*Muy fácil*. Easy."

Izaul looked good in this place, in his shirt with the sleeves that dangled past his elbows, the way he slouched on the railing. I felt sloppy in my softball shirt that read *Spadaro's Plumbing*, covered in scum, yet when a group of men passed me, six eyes looked not at my face. Izaul was glued to my elbow. Next to the stage a window overlooked the pine trees outside, now black, turning the window into a mirror. In the reflection the room was doubled as though through a kaleidoscope, pine trees glowing, and I could see hands placing glasses on the bar, one after another, seedlings planted in rows. We were nodding our heads.

"*¿Quieres bailar?*" he said. "You want dance?"

"No, no, I don't think so."

"Come on," he said. "*Venga. Es fácil.*"

"No, no."

He reached for my hand. I pulled it away. Then he took a step and set his Tecate down on a table. He took my hand and squeezed, and my fingers felt like a paw, the can of beer still in my other hand. He took another step and put one arm around my waist, the warmth of his arm on my back. Then his face was right next to mine, covered in fine black stubble, and I thought, He could be younger than I am. I could feel him sweating. I put my hand on his shoulder and it was hot. A shiver ran up my arm and I shoved him away. He let go.

Certainly, the entire room was staring at me. I must have had a fluorescent bulb shining over my head. I must have had horns.

Izaul turned to face me, his back to the railing. I looked at the carpet, a galaxy of red and black shag, crumbs, the tab of a beer can, and felt him looking. He didn't move away. After a long second I glanced up and he was still standing, watching me. He had this look on his face, like a frustrated soccer coach. I could barely meet his eyes.

I should have wanted to dance. I should have been that girl who jumped right in, who shook my flat ass with all those curvy women. But I wasn't. I wasn't ever young and free. That seemed to have passed me right by. Instead, I had a broken heart, lurking right under the surface. All the people dancing—I dreamed of being that joyous.

I stared at the dance floor for a long time. I saw Izaul's arm move, like a gentle swimming stroke, picking up his beer, and he let me stand there. Like we were just two people taking a break from the dance floor. Like that's all it was. I could hear myself breathing. The band played a few more songs.

Then Izaul said, "Wha? You can't dance?"

"No!" I said. I was crushing the beer can a millimeter at a time. "I can't!"

He had an about-to-crack-up smirk on his face, laughing through his teeth, like he was laughing at me hunting in the dish room for a box lid. The radiator came back on inside my chest. I started to laugh, but maybe I didn't want him to see me laugh. I scratched my nose, I tipped the rest of my beer into my mouth.

"Look, I show you. *Es fácil.*"

Then he took my hand again and pulled and we were walking down the stairs to where the music was even louder and then we were on the edge of the dance floor in the crush of people. I couldn't move. What if somebody from around town was here and saw me, the day I got fired, failing miserably at having fun. Izaul started dancing and held my hand as though I were descending from a horse-drawn carriage and he was moving it, moving me, back and forth. He put his hand on his stomach and did a thing with his hips, an unrepeatable thing, a ripple, the hidden wave between beats of a drum. He wasn't tall. But the people around him would remember him, his short, lithe arms bent like the crook of an anchor. He let go of my hand and placed it against my stomach.

"You know," he shouted, "like this."

I tried to do what he was showing me. A couple people stepped onto the floor and bumped me and I thought I would have to stop.

"No, no," he said.

He took my hand and pressed it against his stomach, and he was dancing, and for one second, I felt it, I felt what everyone in the room felt, and I was out there, dancing. I could feel it. *Here. You step here.* Underneath it all was a throbbing. It lasted for just a moment, then the music changed. And I was still again, a pole in a cornfield.

"Okay," I said. "That's enough."

"You wanna go outside?"

I nodded.

Upstairs, a door led to a deck above the parking lot. The music was piped through speakers. We pushed our way to the edge. Izaul reached into the stretched-out pocket of his jeans and pulled out a pack of cigarettes.

"You smoke?" I said.

"*A veces,*" he said. The sun was gone, all that remained

was a strip of cloudy gray along the horizon. He stood against the railing, the floodlight illuminating a group of people all hunched over a table. They were all perfectly still. He tapped the pack and shook out two cigarettes. He fished around in his pockets.

"Hang on," I said. I reached into my pocket for the stolen lighter. That familiar sound, a knife blade hitting a stone. Its flame gleamed on his skin. We stood there, inhaling, exhaling.

"Good night," he said.

"That's true," I said. "Lot of good nights here."

I thought about saying something more about how I got fired. But I couldn't bring it up again.

"I queet the store," he said.

"You what?"

"I queet."

"What do you mean you quit? You went to work today."

"They tell me stay for one week."

"You mean you leave after one week? This week or next week?"

"*¿Qué?*"

"Is this week your last or is next week your last?"

He shook his head. We stood there squinting at each other.

"Well, damn," I said. "Good for you. Fuck them. Now neither of us work there."

"I fix cars. With my cousin."

I saw him hunched over the engine of a Honda, wrench in hand.

"Too bad for the store."

He snorted. "They say *nada*. *Nos odian*," he said.

It was a word I somehow knew. They hate us. He laughed into the sky, as though it was nothing, cigarette between his fingers, inches from his mouth. I got the sense that he was thinking about someplace else altogether, not here, not me.

"My cousin fix cars," he said. "Good hands. *Manos buenos. Mucho trabajo.*"

I nodded. I could feel my neck sinking into my shoulders. I heard his cigarette crackle. I was looking at my dirty tennis shoes. Then he said, slowly, "You have very pretty skin."

I stopped and looked at the end of my cigarette. Then at him. He seemed to be nodding at me, through the corner of one eye.

"Thank you," I said.

"Is like the color of a seashell," he said.

I felt a flutter behind my nose. An unfamiliar feeling had crept into my bones. For a moment I had an awareness of where I was, as though seeing my own self-portrait. Izaul seemed to disappear. Back then I had appropriate clothes. I behaved appropriately. I had organized study habits. I was a person who had asked to be admitted to the National Honor Society. But had not been. I had tried hard to get jobs, to keep jobs. I was standing on a deck with an unfamiliar person in an unfamiliar place. I wished I could have said that my mother, my father would have been disappointed in me if they had seen me right then. But they wouldn't have been, because I had always been invisible to them. It was this that I felt regret for. I could sit all day in the cupola of the library watching people drop off their books in a rhombus of sunlight and dust. I could pack up all my useless possessions and follow a truck to Alaska. I could see my own peculiar species of dishonesty. I was no longer me. I wanted to tell Izaul this. But I couldn't. I couldn't leave him with that, that broken wing. I could only lift my hand, take a drag.

Izaul said, "You wanna go in?"

I smelled beer and spice. The air had grown harsh as it tended to do at night, and I rubbed the skin around my elbow, grains of salt flaking away. The throb of bass from inside changed to something slower. There was one cloud in the sky, like a haystack in a dark field.

"No," I said. "I like it out here."

"Okay," he said. He looked like he was moving around the players on a soccer field, hatching a plan. I thought of him checking the expiration date on a jar of pickles, or politely packing a pint of curry chicken salad for some woman at the deli.

He dropped his cigarette on the deck, and I saw glints of orange pass through the space between the planks, watched it fall like a seed.

I thought about how I was going to quit smoking. I was going to quit tomorrow. I looked down at the filter between my fingers, to see what little was left.

WEEKEND TRIP

On our way to the yearly party Yahlie's friends throw, we encounter a woman and her baby. This trip turns out to be the last one we take for a good long while. The drive is one day to Amarillo, one to Austin. Maybe Yahlie and I do it in less, with our feet up on the dash and Styrofoam cups of soda in the cup holders. Texas feels like a step down from where we've come from, devilish and mean. She and I feel the need to get out of town. In our borrowed house, the stereo is broken and we can't find the cable to hook up the VCR we found. Her friend, Kirsten, said we could stay with them for a while, and we might. We still have $220 between us. I hear Kirsten is belligerent and doesn't listen.

We're out in the open. It's hot in Yahlie's shrunken white car. It's got a whole assortment of stuff in the back. A basketball, an enormous foam hand that fits over one's own hand, guitar strings, pennies. She's driving. We have the windows down and the air is coming in, filching our oxygen. Out here it's more yellow than gold, nothing at all is green, and everywhere unidentifiable objects are supplanting the landscape. A roly-poly silver mechanism mounted on a flatbed trailer, the size of a jet engine. A silo with a roof too big for its shaft. Where we have come from, one state over, is softer, redder. Out here it seems unkind. But I love the road. I love it like a lost pet.

The plan is to find better work when we get back, better than two banquet jobs. We'd been doing this thing where we'd try to get scheduled for the same shifts, then one of us would sneak out after a while and work waitressing at the Cowgirl, shifts we bilked from our friend who had a boyfriend she got free rent from. I'd say, Yahlie's in the back slicing lemons. Yahlie'd say, Kate's out back having a cigarette. It was getting three paychecks for two jobs. In honor of this, we'd sometimes order three plates of huevos for the two of us. I finally had a little money, which I was going to save to buy a car that was legal. In the meantime, I was always making her drive. I'd grown used to it, I liked it.

"I hear Ambrose Bierce is buried somewhere out here," she says.

"That must be true," I say. I stare through the windshield and its pockmarks, about to nod out.

"Where Kirsten lives is nothing like this," she says. "They have trees and lots of friends."

She gets this wistful look on her face. When we met, she had seemed very scared and I had felt somewhat assured. Since then, that had ebbed and flowed so many times that I was sometimes confused by who we were.

A ways outside Austin we stop and get sandwiches in a town with a carved wooden Indian at nearly every doorway and four shops selling the same things. The restaurant has a checkered tablecloth and the only light in the place comes in through the window. As we eat, mayonnaise expands in my mouth, the lettuce bruises as I touch it. We drink two glasses of soda so cold it leaves a ringing in my ears. We hear the air-conditioning, like a combine running. Yahlie eats in enormous bites, steals fries off my plate with her slim hands. The waitresses sit at the table near the window, staring out.

"You eat so slowly. When I eat with you it takes all day," she says.

"It does not. And what else have you got to do, anyway, besides eat with me?"

When we get inside air-conditioning, our conversations return to our usual, a little like Franz Liszt playing the piano, a little like captives. She waits for me to finish the BLT.

We pay the woman and thank her. Outside the heat is a force field. One cloud has appeared from somewhere to cover the sun. The sky's a hollowed-out bone.

Yahlie says, "Why does one have to go so far from the city, even a small city, to find a place where the values of mass production have not infiltrated the food? Why do we still eat everything out of a can? Instead of those delicious sandwiches?"

"Because we're broke," I say. "And you don't know how to cook."

She laughs her snorting laugh. "My belly hurts," she says. "I need to walk around."

I can tell she's writing a white paper on economics in her head as we walk off the food, belching. She twists one piece of hair between two fingers.

"We either have too much food or not enough," she says.

Except I could have eaten three more of those sandwiches. It wasn't too much. In our house we eat instant soup and apples that I cut open on my desk because the kitchen has no room for a table, shuffling my papers out of the way. Or we eat pintos and cheese from Felipe's, loaded up with the free parsley and green chile, dented cans of beer from the squalid bar in town, or the assortment of leftovers from the caterer. Twenty cold shrimp rolls. Half a tray of cut fruit, all the strawberries gone. A sleeve of melba toast.

We walk across the wooden walkways they've built around the town square—the kind that we'd thump across ominously if we were wearing cowboy boots, spurs jangling—a dry fountain with a couple trees in the center. A guy in a gleaming red pickup screams past. I can hear the metal thrumming out of his stereo through the closed windows. Then we pass one little store, a vintage store. I can see someone behind the counter.

"Let's go in here," Yahlie says.

Inside it's cold, dusty, with painted floorboards and a welcome mat. For sale is a Formica table, a carpeted couch, a velvet

Elvis, a twelve-string guitar mounted in a frame, a restored Radio Flyer, stuff rich New Yorkers might dispatch staff to Texas to acquire. Country-swing records, high-waisted Jordache jeans with gold stitching, Walter Mondale campaign buttons in a teacup on the counter. Gem of a store. The kind of place Yahlie and I could kill two hours in.

A woman stands behind the glass counter, a sack of price tags emptied out in front of her. She has a look on her face like she'd been dreaming something sweet, or randy. Perched on a stool next to her is a bassinet holding a gurgly baby. I smell stinking diaper.

"I wonder if all this stuff has been here since the forties," Yahlie says, "and they just put up a sign that says 'Vintage.'" She finds an entire rack of plaid shirts in absurd color schemes, each with three buttons on the cuffs, arrows stitched on the breast pockets.

"Oh yeah," she says, and picks one in khaki and Astroturf green. She tries it on behind a curtain in the back and when she comes out it's not quite too small. "You look like Patsy Cline," I say.

"All I need," she says, "are some white patent leather cowboy boots and a blonde wig and I'd be Dolly Parton. I'm buying it."

While she's changing, I wander back and pull open a brocade curtain hiding another room lit by a plastic chandelier, the walls wooden panels painted white, the ceiling shining tin. Every surface holding an object. Teacups, old suitcases, a yellowing needlepoint in a frame. I can barely move, like I might knock something over and ruin it. Like being inside a Christmas tree.

I find a wooden chair. It's the green of a penny at the bottom of a fountain, all chipped and crackling. Several others sit nearby, part of a set. But this one, it's rougher than the others. I look at it and hear some far-off jukebox reverb, see the sun go down over a bluff, dancers shuffling, a woman singing into a microphone in a hall lit by strings of lights. This was the one its owner sat in. Every night, till it had to be given up. The tag says sixty dollars.

"You ready?" Yahlie says. She looks at the chair. "Woah, sixty bucks."

We go to the counter to pay and the woman has the baby against her shoulder, a white towel on its skull like a nun. She holds it as she rings Yahlie up one-handed. She also has on one of the plaid shirts: two yellows. She kneels slowly under the counter and retrieves a plastic bag, struggles to open the crinkly cellophane with the tips of her fingers. She shakes it with her one free hand. She could be ten years older than we are. But still she seems young to have a baby. Yahlie asks, "How old is your baby?"

"Oh, she's seven months."

"She's adorable," Yahlie says. "What's her name?"

"Her name's Pearl," the woman says, and smiles like she has a secret, or that same randy sweet dream still on her mind.

It's a name I've only imagined people having, women who waved to ships with handkerchiefs.

"That's a great name," Yahlie says.

The woman finally has the shirt in the bag and slides it across the counter.

"Thanks," she says, "And look."

With her free hand she untucks the yellow plaid shirt, and on her stomach is a tattoo, the word *Pearl*, in a script I've never seen, a sweet, buttery flower of a thing.

Yahlie makes a little gasping noise. "That's amazing!" she says.

"She's the person I always wished I was," the woman says as she smooths down her shirt. "She's the chance I never had, so I gave her the name I always wished I had. We couldn't get any store space in Austin so we're out here, just us and our antiques. All the shops in Austin are picked over, nothing good left. I think I got all the Bakelite jewelry in Texas right here. You can buy these shirts in Austin shops but they're all from the eighties, John Travolta era. These are the real deal. You can tell from the tight weave, the heavy fabric, and the extra button on the cuff. Y'all should go out dancing."

She strokes the baby's back and takes the towel down, finally done talking. Her hair lies in sandy curls around her face, spilling down around the baby's head, which is smattered with fuzz in the same color. She rocks from heel to heel and Pearl blurbles.

"What did she say?" Yahlie says. "Cue ball? Did she say cue ball?"

"She says all kinds of things," the woman says. "Sometimes in her little talking I hear the weirdest words. I can't wait till she starts talking real. She'll say the most amazing things."

Right then she lifts up one hand and waves out the front window. We turn and see a man in a baseball cap waving back, ambling past.

I stand there waiting and Yahlie coos over the baby some more. I've never heard her do this, in all the time we've been kicking around like two birds in the same cage. Who are you, talking in this lilting, whiny swirl? You can light four cigarettes with one match, and drink six cups of coffee a day, and you fall asleep with the door to our house unlocked.

"We have dancing here in the veterans' hall, and every Sunday there's barbecue. Stop by, I'll take you if you're back by. My name's Beverly. Bev."

"That's a nice name too," Yahlie says.

The woman shrugs. "I don't know, it doesn't mean anything. It sounds made-up."

Something about the way Yahlie is standing with her shoulder to me makes me go to the back room and pick up that chair and bring it to the counter.

"Think I'll buy this too."

Yahlie is looking at me with that squinched judgmental stare.

"What," I say.

I take out my wallet. I have seventy-four dollars.

"Actually I think I'll pass," I say.

Bev says, looking at the chair, "This is such a nice piece."

I put away my cash. I'm ready to leave and edge toward the door. "It was so nice to meet you, Pearl!" Yahlie says, giving a little wave.

Then Bev says, "You all got a car running out there?"

I can't tell if she means, a car with the key in the ignition, or a car that is not a complete piece of shit.

"Yeah," Yahlie says. "We're driving my car."

"Hate to impose if you got somewhere to be, but I thought I'd ask if you might give me a ride someplace. Somebody owes me money and I think I can get it today if I could just get over there."

Yahlie and I look at each other.

"That is, I mean the two of us," Bev says. "I could give it to you for forty dollars, if that helps."

Somewhere in the store is a ticking clock. The baby makes a noise. Yahlie's eyes are open wider than usual. Bev seems impossibly big and curvy standing behind the counter. I feel small and scrawny. The sun looks unreasonably bright through the shaded windows. Bev has squinted eyes, deep, bloodless laugh lines. Yahlie and I are staring each other down. Sometimes, I'll think I know what thing she wants to do and instead she does another. I'll think she wants to leave, and she'll keep us sitting at the bar talking to two yahoos from Colorado Springs.

Before I have a chance to say anything she decides for us.

"Sure!" she says, like we've been invited to the moon.

"Well, thanks. Sure appreciate it," Bev says, wandering off to some back room. "Just lemme get Pearl's stuff," she calls.

Now Yahlie's smiling. "What about the party?" I say, mumbling so Bev can't hear.

"We'll get there," she says. "This is exactly what we need."

"Why?" I say. "Why is this what we need?"

"Why are you gonna buy that?" she says. "Why do you need that chair?"

"You don't like it?"

"I do like it; I do like it."

Bev comes back with a lumpy bag over one shoulder, a wad of keys in her hand, Pearl in the other arm. She puts her in the bassinet and fastens a buckle Then she holds out one hand, smiling. I take out my wallet again, and hand her exact change.

"Still your turn to drive," I say to Yahlie.

"All right!" she says.

Bev locks the store and we walk outside on the wooden planks, back around to where the car is parked.

"Can't thank y'all enough for this," Bev says, standing at my elbow.

"Sure," I mumble, thinking, at least I got a discount.

Yahlie opens the car doors and it's an oven inside. "Wait," I say. "This chair won't fit in here with all of us."

"Oh, that's okay," Bev says. "We can come back for it." Then she puts the bassinet on the roof of the car, takes the chair, Pearl baking, and scurries to the store, unlocks it, and sort of bumps the chair through the door.

"Okay," I say. We get in the car, Bev in the back with the bassinet beside her. The diaper smell swirls, like something wafting up from a sewer, with fried funnel cake, and for a second, I think I might barf. Yahlie's face is twisted, her nose crumpled into a sneer. She pushes the buttons in her arm rest and the automatic windows roll slowly down.

"She need a seat or something?" I say.

"No," Bev says. "Y'all remember how to get on Route 1?"

"Where we headed?" Yahlie asks.

"Past Roundtop. We're not going far. I'll tell you when to turn off."

I forget what "far" means out here, and we drive twenty miles on Route 1, to another town altogether, where street signs appear on the sides of the road with names like sons and daughters, Gretchen and Randolph and MacKenzie, and the asphalt is fossilized. In the back, Bev talks.

"I got a couple of cousins out this way, and they tell me there's a great place to get some pie around here. Can't thank y'all enough. I just got my car back from the shop last week and didn't drive it but two days before whatever they said they fixed wasn't fixed and left me stuck at my store all night. Fuckin' assholes, I'm going to give them hell 'til they give me all my money back. Plus I got this ex, he owes me money. Y'all know anything about computers? Somebody gave us one and I'm still trying to figure out how to turn it on."

Yahlie puts on the tape we were listening to, two guys singing over some reggae. The street signs roll past and the names change to German, Hauptstrasse and Augsburg. Bev bites one fingernail.

Bev and I speak at the same time.

"So who owes you money again?" I say.

"Where you two got to go after this?" she says.

I turn around and we wait for each other to talk. Yahlie answers before either of us. "We're going to Austin," she says. "See some friends."

Pearl starts to moan, but not really a moan, more like a hum, a hum with a skip.

"What's wrong, sweet pea?" Bev says.

After another couple of short hills Bev says, "That's it," and Yahlie has to hit the brakes. The tires burr. We turn past a mailbox propped on a crooked piece of rebar jutting out of the ground. At the end of a driveway lined with a few cratered trees and pieces of things—a stained mattress, a tricycle, a pile of skinny PVC pipes, cinder blocks—is a dented trailer. We're in a haze of dust. Yahlie stops the car.

"Actually it's right back there," Bev says, pointing, her finger between the front seats.

Yahlie inches the car forward on the road past the trailer until I see there is another house, adobe like our casita, cracked and sinking into the ground. "That's it," Bev says. On the walls of the house, on the outside, is a faded poster with cars and someone's face. A screen door with a hole in it. Yahlie stops; Bev climbs out.

"Could you hold her?" Bev says to me. She's holding Pearl out at me like she might shove her through the window, and I smell the smell again.

"Could I what?"

"Just hold her for one second while I run up there?"

She has a rolled-up piece of paper in one hand, like it materialized from nothing, tucked under her thumb as she holds Pearl, and it seems like if I don't take the baby, she'll just drop her there in the dirt and split, so I open the door and next thing, Pearl is in my hands. Bev gives me a punch on the shoulder with two fingers, like she's my crazy aunt, and says, "Thanks, doll," and walks fast through the dirt toward the house. I have my hands under Pearl's armpits, and she's making the same noise, *hum, hum*. She's heavy, like a full gallon jug.

Or a dictionary. If the dictionary were her and had a beating heart.

"What the hell is this lady doing?" I say.

"Dunno," Yahlie says. She giggles a little and shuts off the car.

Bev pounds on the door. She lifts a fist and beats, her arm like a mace, and yells. Between strokes she stands there, arms loose at her sides. She yells when she pounds so we can't hear what she's saying. She grabs the doorknob with both hands and pushes with her foot.

"What kind of a scam do you suppose *this* is?" Yahlie says, laughing, thumping the gas pedal with her foot.

"I think this is what's known as the breaking and entering scam," I say. "I tried to ask her, but you didn't let me. Goddamn, the baby needs a diaper change."

"Okay, okay," she says. "We'll go right after this. You're not comfortable with other people's discourses."

I never know what to say when she says stuff like that. Why use such a word? I feel like a flock of birds has flown into the cage.

After a minute Pearl mumbles again. Yahlie says, "One of her eyes is smaller than the other."

So it is. One an almond, one a skipping stone. Pearl twists her head back and forth, from my face to the house. I sit there with the door open, one foot in the dirt.

"And she's fatter than you are," Yahlie says.

She *is* fatter than me. She's like I imagine an elf would be. I am a skeleton compared to her.

Bev is still whacking at the door.

"Why isn't she crying?" I ask. "You'd think she would be crying, since her diaper's all shitty."

"Dunno," Yahlie says. "Poor baby with a shitty diaper."

"I think she must be used to this."

"Used to what? Being all poopy?" Yahlie laughs her sniveling laugh, the one she has when she knows I'm not going to laugh at her joke.

"No, being left with strangers. This lady's leaving her with *us*? She's not thinking straight. And I don't think that door's going to open."

Pearl squirms. I have her held away from me. I should hold her to my chest, but I can't. She seems to weigh more now. Pearl looks right at me, and I can see the way she'll be when she's older and looks at someone and says what she wants most in the world, and I think, I've got a person's whole body in my hands. A wedge of fear rises up into my rib cage. I can see myself in the rearview mirror, the back of Pearl's head below my chin. The two of us reflected together. Under my eyes are gray half-moons like bruises.

Yahlie says, "You want me to hold her?"

"No," I say. And it has that edge that happens, without my meaning to; I am shutting the door on her, that blister that rises up between us. "I can do it," I say.

"Okay," she says. "*Fine.*"

Bev is looking through the window, her hands around her eyes. I get a twinge in my chest and my arms are tired. Yahlie is sulking, leaning on the windowsill. I get the feeling like something is coming and I want to get the hell out of here. And if there's one thing I can't stand, it's Yahlie sulking.

"Okay," I say. "You hold her."

I give Pearl to Yahlie. She says, "That's right, sweet pea." I get out. Bev turns away from the house and takes a couple steps, like she's about to give up, then she sees me and stops. The scabbed yard between me and her seems like a long way. I should just let her give up. The place is a trap about to close. I walk across the dust and as I get closer I see her eyes, creases circling them, a wrinkle in her skin that isn't going anywhere.

"I can't get the door open," she says.

"I can see that," I say.

"You got an idea about how to do it?"

"You sure you don't want to come back later? Maybe whoever it is will be back then. Somebody could see us."

"Nobody's going to see us."

"How do you know?"

"Because I did it once before," she says.

She leans on the post holding up the awning built out over the roof. I put a foot up on the crusty patch of adobe that is serving as a porch. Bev isn't a bit scared, like it's all the same to her, breaking and entering, bobbling the baby on her knee. I want her to see that I am scared, but I realize, then, that I am not. The collar of her shirt is rumpled.

"How'd you do it that time?"

"It was open," she says. "I thought the door would be open."

I go to the door, rattle the doorknob. It gives a little, and I'm thinking there must not be any dead bolt. A weak lock.

I'll admit to one thing about this happening: Up until right then, I had only watched this sort of thing on television, and I didn't believe that I was strong enough to do it. But I know about doors—about roofs, and windows, chimneys. Soffit, fascia, rake, slope. From my father, who could build everything. And although he'd taught me nothing, somehow, I realize just then, I'd absorbed it. Yahlie doesn't know this about me, that I know anything besides where to buy tacos and how to pump my own gas.

I knew where to kick.

"You have to be fast, though," I say.

The sound is hollow as the heel of my boot hits the door. It doesn't open, I kick again, then it cracks open and hits something inside. I have to stop myself from saying, *Yes!* The door doesn't swing; I was expecting it to swing. The doorjamb is barely broken.

The foyer is dark, and smells of a thousand burned breakfasts and vinegary coffee and fertilizer, and daylight comes in from somewhere in the back. Bev stomps past me and tramples a pair of work boots on the floor. To the right is a dining room with a table full of papers, jars, a tarnished chandelier hanging. I can hear Bev thumping around, opening drawers. I squint outside past the drapes and can barely see the car, can't see Yahlie. The papers are all faded newspapers; the jars are all half-filled with liquid, something stewed and putrid. The smell knocks me away.

To one side is a dim bedroom, and to the other, through a cramped arch, is the kitchen. Dishes are scattered everywhere, the counters lined with soda cans. All Mountain Dew, all coated in powdery dirt. Another arch has an enormous chunk knocked out of it so it seems to droop. It leads to a room carpeted in brown shag, dark except for a flickering TV, set to the news with the sound down. Bev is against a wall lined with dressers, ruffling her hands through some drawers.

I say, "So what the hell are you looking for? Wanna find it quicker?"

"My ex owes me money," she says. She slams a drawer and walks toward where the daylight is coming from, what I suppose is another bedroom. She stops and stares in, her arms hanging.

The light streams through a sliding glass door, and in the bedroom is a man in a wheelchair.

"You didn't hear me knocking?" she says, in some twangy accent that wasn't there before.

His chair takes up almost the entire room. Another TV sits against one wall, a neatly made bed on the other. He is staring at us, frozen, frowning. Between his eyes—a green that seems to be almost yellow—between two dark eyebrows, is a line that looks as though it was drawn with charcoal. A plastic tube snakes downward from somewhere behind his neck. One hand is on the wheelchair's joystick, about to push it. He has a mustache and two-day stubble. There are Mountain Dew cans in here too. His other hand rests on a tiny tray attached to the chair's arm. He looks strong. A shakiness begins around my knees and I want to get out of there. Any second, a guy in a truck will roll up and see the busted door. Yahlie is out in the car.

"Arman been here today?" Bev asks. I can't understand what name she says. Armand? Herman? The man doesn't answer. His lips seem to be moving, closed, churning underneath the mustache.

"Arman taking real good care of you as usual, right?" she says, in a voice all sarcasm.

"Look," I say, "We've got to go."

She ignores me. She seems to be awaiting an explanation of some kind. On the wood-paneled wall, I see a shelf with a stereo and a lamp, some magazines, another Mountain Dew can. Outside are two squares of concrete. He has an okay view—the land slopes away from the house, must catch the sunset.

"Bev, let's go," I say, hoping he won't hear me.

"Just a sec," she says, a horse's bite to her voice. To him she says, "You can tell him I was here, that I came looking for what he owes me. He can figure it out for himself whether I found it or not."

The line between the man's eyes seems to stiffen, and he is not looking at Bev, but at me, and I can see that he will tell anybody whatever the hell he wants.

Then she stalks off, like she's made her point and that's that. I try not to look at the man as I follow her, but I do anyway, and his eyes are shifted as far in their sockets as possible, watching me. I don't say one thing to him. The shallowest thought pops into my head—can he move his neck?

Bev goes to the kitchen, starts opening cabinets, yanking on drawers.

"Okay," I say to her. "Now we really have to go. You didn't say anyone was here."

"I didn't know he was here."

"The dude's in a wheelchair," I say. "How could he not be here?"

"You don't know anything," she says. "Quit getting in the way so I can find it, okay?" She looks up at me, her iceberg of a jaw jutting away from her face.

She yanks on one more drawer. Inside is mismatched silverware—she pushes it around, finds an envelope. She flips it open and inside is a wad of what looks like tens and ones. She lets out a long sigh.

"See?" she says. "All done." She walks out the open door, crossing the long distance to the car. I could fix it, fix the door just like it was. There are no cars out front but Yahlie's. She's in the front seat with the baby. I leave the door, follow Bev out. She jumps in the backseat.

"Oh," she says. "Sorry." She laughs nervously. She stands up, twitters around to the front and lifts Pearl out of Yahlie's hands.

"Were you a good girl?" she says.

"Yes, she's a good girl," Yahlie says.

"Can we go?" I say, and Yahlie gives me a mean look.

Yahlie turns the car around in its wind-up toy way. As we go back on the main road, Yahlie driving cautiously, a rickety pickup blows past in the other direction, breaking the sound barrier, someone with his bare arm hanging out the window. In the rear view I see Bev whip her head around.

"What color was that?" she says. "What color? Blue? Blue?"

"Keep driving," I say.

"I *am*," Yahlie says.

"I know you are, I didn't mean it like that, Jesus."

The road winds back the way it came. A string of unimportant questions forms in my head: Can he talk? Does he watch TV? How does he take a shit? I try to push the feeling away. Yahlie doesn't turn the tape on. The two of them in the back seem to creep over my shoulder and I have to look out the window at the road's white line.

Bev sits in the back and starts singing to Pearl. She sounds like June Carter and holds Pearl's hands, teaching her to clap, singing, "The wheels on the bus go round and round, round and round." But then in the middle she seems to forget that Pearl is on her lap, and she looks out the window, starting another song.

"I do believe, in all the things you see."

The return drive seems to take seconds, a drive Bev might do every day. Maybe this is what she does every time she runs out of cash, and this is like going to the supermarket. We leave her at the shop. As she gets out, setting the bassinet on the ground to put Pearl inside, Yahlie asks, "Got a ride home?"

"Oh, sure. My friend picks me up when she gets done at the restaurant. But y'all did me a special favor, taking me out that way."

"What about the chair?" I say.

"Oh, right," she says, and we all get out of the car. She walks bumping the bassinet against her hip, sets it down again. She unlocks the store. She doesn't let me in. She skitters the chair out on the concrete, its legs screeching.

"Y'all enjoy."

The chair sits like a throne, ruined. The store is dark and she's gone and it's all over. Yahlie sucks air in and blows it out.

"Good thing you bought *that*," she says.

She is a cruel person sometimes. I think of just leaving it there. But it's mine, I bought it. I look at it, and I can't leave it. Separated from all the others. I pick it and wrench it into the back seat.

"Dipshit," I say, "It was your idea to drive out there to begin with, and you're going to give me a bunch of shit for buying a chair. What are we doing? It's like what, 3:30? And we're how far from the interstate? You're the one who wants to go to Kirsten's party."

"You are so impossible to be around," she says.

Both of us standing on the wooden sidewalk waiting for the other.

"You drive," Yahlie says.

The car whirs, and we can't go without keeping the windows down. The sky now a preposterous blue.

We drive for a while and I contemplate how to suggest that we skip the party, but it seems impossible, now that we've driven all this way. We stop at a casino gas station once it gets dark. Yahlie goes inside, frowning, counting how much money she has left. I stay behind.

Another time, we were at a rodeo with some guys. She hated it, the ropes, the shrieking; she thought the horses were frightened. I thought of it right then, sitting on the back of the car in the waning heat. She had sat hunched on the wooden bench and kept saying, "It's just so awful." I said, "You want to leave?" And she was so upset that she couldn't even shake her head no. I wasn't thinking about the horses, or her. I was enjoying the feeling of tapping someone's back in comfort. I wasn't being true. She sat there, her tan face turning the color of cantaloupe. My tapping her back seemed to do nothing. So I stopped and watched the calf roping. I had to leave her sitting there. Why did I do that? Why did I leave her there like that, staring at her feet while I watched calves being lassoed and tied?

I sit on the back of the car, clammy, with the casino flashing and the sense that a wasp is hovering nearby and must be shooed away.

When she returns, she says, "I'll drive," even though it was still my turn.

When we get to Kirsten's house, a ranch with paper lanterns rising across the yard, there are fifteen or so people under the carport with lawn chairs. Through the windows I see a lamp turned on.

As we get out of the car somebody shouts, "What took you so long?" like they've known us forever and have thrown this party just for us.

A girl with black hair and skin like a china saucer comes up and says, "Hey!" As we walk up the dying lawn something returns to Yahlie, that airiness of hers.

"We thought you were Todd coming back with the beer," the woman says. She hugs Yahlie.

"This is Kirsten," Yahlie says to me.

"You guys," Kirsten says, "later you should check out the installation in the carport. So glad you guys could participate."

I don't know what the hell she's talking about. Kirsten shows us inside. Two brocade couches and a plastic shelf full of books, two desks, one with two computers on it.

"Kirsten is writing her dissertation," Yahlie says.

"Yep," Kirsten says, "Write my dissertation, then get fucked up. That is my plan."

"Good plan," Yahlie says.

I knock my foot on an amp and pass a guy, a weedy stallion of a guy with a petulant lip, a Grand Canyon dimple, and an entire sleeve of tattoos, all tinted green.

"Cheers," he says.

I nod at the guy.

"Hi," says Yahlie.

"How are you, dollface?" says Kirsten, and kisses him on the cheek. Whatever languid game exists between women, with men as the spoils, she will be the winner. I look at Yahlie, since this is usually the type of thing we agree on exactly without having to say a word, but I can't catch her eye.

Kirsten informs us that at the last second there's no room for us to crash for the night—all the air mattresses and floor spaces are spoken for. But we can crash with Todd, she tells us. Yahlie goes off with Kirsten and I try to handle the chatter. I stand in the kitchen for a while, find a beer and drink by the stove. The guy with the tattoos comes up and stands near me, his arm on their funk-brown refrigerator.

He says to me, "So what's your story?"

I run through some possible answers.

"We're from New Mexico. Except I'm not originally, I'm from the suburbs."

"Cool," he says. He nods, a marionette head.

"What's your story?" I ask.

"I'm getting my doctorate in Latin American studies."

He nods his head, scratches a green tattoo. I open my

mouth to say one other thing but only air comes out. He looks at me from the corner of his eye.

"You have a nice laugh," he says. "Just the right amount of nervous. I like it."

Someone gets his attention. "Brad," they say, and he wanders off.

I stand there for a moment in the swirl of people in the kitchen, empties lining the countertops. The smell of that man's house returns to my nose and I want to run away.

I go to the bathroom and pull down my jeans. I look at my stomach, flat as a crushed tumbleweed. In the crotch of my underwear is a smear of blood. In the front of my stomach I feel a roiling. I piss and it feels cold. I try to think about what my laugh sounds like. I think of that man looking out the sliding glass door at the same wicked sun rising every day.

Back in the living room, I can't see Yahlie. I search for another beer and go outside to the carport. The art consists of antique science movies on 16 mm projected onto the wall. No one else is around. I sit on a lawn chair. The film is of black string, twitching. It reaches a picture of a mountain, then returns to the string. The same thing over and over. It must be broken. String, mountain. The audio still runs, stuff about moving glaciers, the extraction of oil from the earth.

After a while Yahlie comes out. "These people aren't anything like I remember," she says. She sips her beer. The light from the projector hits underneath her chin. She says, "I loved that lady's tattoo. She's alone in the desert with that baby and she was so happy."

"She didn't seem so happy," I say.

"You didn't ask me about the baby."

I try to think how to explain what was in that house.

"I'm sorry I called you a dipshit," I say. "I'm sorry I didn't ask. How was the baby?"

"It's okay," she says. "You were talking about yourself when you said that."

She pauses and looks out into the driveway.

"The baby didn't make a sound," she says. "Just stared at the door the whole time."

"Jesus," I say.

"I wanted to take the baby with us," she says. "Either of us would be better than that lady."

I look at her. "Not sure about me," I say. "But you would. You would be."

I catch her eye and it says, Thank you.

"Listen," I say. "I might be hungover tomorrow."

"That's right," she says. "Shit-faced again!"

"Great," I say. "Then you can drive us to Todd's. Or maybe we could get a lift."

I've forgotten which person Todd is. Another stranger to follow. She shakes her head no, and the light disappears from her chin. "I want you to drive," she says.

"Why?" I say.

"Because I drove all day. So," she says, lifting her hand in a lilting way, as though presenting me with some small object, "you should quit drinking now so you'll be sober when I'm drunk."

"Okay," I say. "Done. Herewith, my last evening beer."

She says, "Look, I can fix this." She gets up and fiddles with the projector. "Was the house creepy?"

"Yeah. It was. There were soda cans everywhere. It was creepy. It was."

She twists a knob and the projector starts winding. "Look at that," she says. "I got it."

She looks at the projector like it's a statue she just carved. The tape winds neatly, and once that mountain appears, the picture continues, a pan across valleys, a distant forest. I stand up and stick my hand in a crevice in the projector, illuminating my fingers.

"You want to go back inside?" she says.

"I'm thinking about it," I say.

The audio tape beeps and says stuff about molecules. The paper lanterns above us swing. A breeze has appeared from nowhere. I feel like for a second it might be winter. I walk behind the carport, look up at the roof of the house and the clean, golden line it makes in the sky. I feel the urge to go for a long walk in the dark and look for lights in the windows of other people's houses.

I sit back down and she is still there.

"You know what?" I say.

"What?" she says.

"You know what?"

"What?!" she says, and begins to laugh. That laugh.

I am tempted to tell her all of it from the beginning. Or the end. The man in his wheelchair. How he looked at me with that look that said, Everything is wrong.

"It's just that—"

"It's just *what*?" she says. "Stop fucking around."

"It's just that I wonder if I'll ever be pregnant again."

She has been twisting her hair and stops.

"That's all," I say.

She sits very still and I can see that it has ebbed again so that now I am the one who's afraid.

"Why do you say that?" she says.

I couldn't talk for a second. I had to wipe my face because I was crying. I was thinking about my laugh, and how it sounds compared to hers. But that wasn't what I was thinking about. Also, his look said, Things will be right. Then one of the lanterns sways in the breeze again and begins gently hitting the carport wall, ticking. A cicada clicks in the trees behind the house.

"It just might not be in the cards for me," I say.

What I don't say is, Because if I ever sat still I might die. Because I don't believe I'll ever be lucky, because I think I'm a slum. Because right here, it's enough.

"Yes, it is," she says, softly, her eyes ringed in gold.

The certainty of it! It felt like a gift. I wondered if this was the moment when a door might open, when this feeling would become something I could just pass through the window, or sell to someone for a high price, or just abandon on a wooden sidewalk.

THE POOL

I got a job at the weekly newspaper in that small desert town. Hot! All the time, hot! The editor I worked for, a woman with a face like a stately horse, terrified me to the point of nausea. Some mornings I would lie in bed in the casita I shared with my one friend, staring at the stucco ceiling, its points like whipped egg whites, and nausea would bloom in my innards. So perturbed was I by this woman. I'd been doing this for half a year. There were a couple dozen people working there, and none of them seemed irked by her. One Wednesday, I awoke and dashed to the bathroom. I knelt before the commode, but nothing arose, and I sat on the bathmat with a mouth damp with saliva.

In the kitchen my friend had left a note. She'd gone to Colorado for a few days. BUY CHARCOAL.

Not me! I thought. I could do no such thing. I had lost my capacity to do normal, average things like stop at the store.

All I could do was work. I brushed my teeth, extra hard, even though my mouth hadn't been sullied. I went to the office.

I could hear the art director and the ad sales guy arguing about the coffee maker. Doreen, the editor, paraded into the little area of the office where I hoveled and rested an elbow on top of the filing cabinets, who were my friends. In addition to looking a bit like a horse, she was also as tall as a horse. She smelled of a trace of her morning cigarette and the pricey hand cream she used. A smell like potpourri and tea bags and smoke.

"You better write a story about that gas explosion last spring. This week," she said. She waved a dusty clipping at me. I was in my chair nursing some coffee. The coffee made the nausea worse, but I couldn't stop. She whisked the clipping onto my desk and put her finger on it like she was pinning a butterfly. It was the story the rival paper had published when the explosion had happened, back in May. Now it was December, and it was dry outside like a bundle of sticks.

That May morning of the explosion, a woman named Jordan Jeppeson, thirty-two, had arrived at her job at Seven Hills Title & Bond. The office was on Cerrillos Road, a cramped wood building with paneled walls, filing cabinets, a dusty ficus, a watercooler. She was the receptionist, so was in early, before anyone else. It was an uncharacteristically gray day. The sun was trying to squirm through the clouds. At shortly before 8:20 a.m., she smelled gas and called the gas company. The phone call was recorded, Jordan nonchalantly reporting the smell. At shortly before 8:45 a.m. the building exploded, a fiery Nerf ball launching into the sky, burning out into a skyscraper of black smoke. Jordan Jeppeson was pronounced dead on the scene at 10:49 a.m. Cause, the rival paper had written: smoke inhalation.

Even through the clouds, residents reported seeing smoke as far away as Rio Rancho, as late as 9 p.m., blocking the purple scrim of the sunset. It took the full complement of the town's fire company and two engines from the company of a nearby town to control the blaze. Later, after countless more reports of the smell of gas from around the city, residents were evacuated. The cause, it was determined, was citywide system failure.

"See? Remember?" Doreen said. "Please tell me you remember. Please tell me you *read it*. That's a crap story."

"I read it," I said. "I remember," I said.

Doreen waved a press release at me that had arrived by fax. I would have overlooked it. I was a terrible journalist. It read: Report on explosion released by department of public utilities. She pointed to the date on the fax. "This report's been out for three weeks and nobody's written a damn thing on it. You better go get it right," she said.

This was an unusual day. Usually, she was berating me for not coming up with enough of my own ideas. Today she was giving me one of hers. But it felt like a trick. How anyone could write anything interesting about a three-week-old press release was beyond me.

"And you better do a better job than Gus would have done. Okay?" she said.

"I'll try," I said.

"Don't try," she said. "Please don't try. I hate trying."

She stalked away in tiny, prancing steps, back to her glass-walled office, where I could see the back of her head. I imagined a cartoon black raincloud hovering over her.

A couple weeks prior, Gus had walked out. He was the one person I'd met before I got this job. I'd run into him around town, broke and jobless, and he'd said, "You could try working at the paper. Someone's always quitting." He was the only other person there who also seemed afraid of Doreen. He liked to read science fiction and was good at covering the city council meetings, despite the fact that they were about as interesting as a lady talking to you about her azalea bushes. One day he'd gone into Doreen's office. He came out looking like he'd been told he had one hour till they were going to strap him to the electric chair. *I got an interview to go to,* he mumbled. He left, the door not quite closing behind him, and didn't come back. Not the next day. Not the day after. A week went by, and he'd called me at home to say he was going to stay inside and never come out again.

"What the hell, man," I'd said. "Did she fire you?"

"No way!" Gus said. "I wish. She said my story on zoning read like a mentally disabled person wrote it. I quote. Then she said, 'Are you mentally disabled?' I can't take it anymore."

"Jesus. Did she call you?"

"She called but I got the caller ID. So, I didn't pick up."

Then he'd laughed. I missed him for a moment. Now it was just me and Doreen writing the whole front of the paper. I had four more stories to do just this week. I had nothing! Another wave of nausea arose and I suppressed a heave.

I called the number listed on the press release to request a copy of the report. I got the machine, the office of someone named Alfredo Zuniga, and left a message. "What a name," I said, to no one.

I decided to go see Steve Brown, a contact of mine and the spokesperson for the gas company, WestCo. He liked to talk to me. He was extremely friendly. I got in my faded red hatchback with the dent in the door and drove to his office outside of town. At last, I'd jettisoned the black Volvo. I'd sold it for cash to a husband and wife who I'd met through a friend who worked at an auto repair shop, and also dealt in cars of dubious provenance. I'd told the husband and wife, listen, there's no title. I'd told them not to get pulled over. The husband nodded gravely with a touch of seriousness on his face, his eyebrows knitted together, but the wife, she looked at me flatly and resigned, as if to say, we know what to do, as she slowly extended a pile of hundreds toward me.

As I drove, sun shone through the thinning branches. It was a little nippy outside, which meant I was wearing a jacket the weight of a grocery bag, just an old army shirt. I liked it, its deep pockets that I wished I could put a mouse into. I drove down Cerrillos. I passed the spot where the building had exploded. A pad of scorch the size of a basketball court was surrounded by chain-link fence. Next door was a pool installation company with a pool sunken into the asphalt, gleaming with blue water. The day of the explosion I'd been at the weapons range in the mountains, interviewing nutjobs about gun control. By the time I'd returned it'd been dark. That was me. I'd missed the whole thing.

Steve's office was at the gas company HQ, surrounded by pine. Inside was a chamber of woolly cubicles, all the walls tagged with the company logo. WestCo. I always wanted to put an exclamation mark after it. WestCo! We manufacture West!

Steve was sitting in his office, blond and fit in a herringbone jacket four sizes too big for him. Sporty sunglasses dangled from a neoprene strap around his neck along with a company badge on a lanyard. I liked to see if I could get Steve to behave like a normal person and not like a spokesperson. It was like a little war we were having. I sat in his cushy visitor's chair.

"I'm here about the final report that was released," I said.

"Sure thing, which report would that be?" he said, the cleft in his chin moving up and down as he talked. I too had a cleft in my chin, but mine was more a dimple. His was horizontal, like his chin had mostly folded in on itself.

"The one on the explosion last May at Seven Hills Title & Bond," I said.

"I'm afraid that's confidential," he said.

"Confidential? It's city property."

He cocked his head at me. "There's a city report," he said.

"A public report? I never got a copy."

"Came out like three weeks ago," I said. "So. The company's perspective?"

"Weeeeellllll," Steve said, "Can't say I've seen it. Whenever you get ahold of it, maybe you can spike me a copy over the net. Then we'll get one of the scientists to sit down and explain everything, set you right up."

He popped his lips. Up-*pah*. Him and those scientists. The gas company always wanted you to talk to scientists. Charts, graphs. A glass wall had gone up around him. The cleft in his chin was deep and black, like a ravine.

"So what's it like to be the spokesperson for the gas company?" I said.

He squeezed his lips together, pitching his head to one side like he was listening to the wind. "Not sure I follow," he said.

"Was this always what you wanted to be when you were a kid?"

"Was being a reporter what you wanted to be when you were a kid?"

"Yes," I said. "It was."

"Well, that's great!" he said.

He flicked his pen against the knuckle of his thumb.

I thought for a moment about if that was true, if I had wanted to be a reporter. But I'd said it: *Yes, it was.* But maybe that was just a story I was telling myself. I couldn't tell if I was lying or not. I smiled my smiliest smile. In all likelihood, it probably still looked false.

On the car ride back to the office, I thought, *Dag nab it, I tipped him off.* I thought of his face. The slightest hint of concern had crossed that chin of his, like something had dawned on him. He didn't even know there was a city report. He was talking about some other, secret WestCo report. There must have been something they wanted to hide. I slapped my head at a stoplight. I went back to my desk and sulked for a while. It was time to eat, but I wasn't hungry.

Doreen stormed over to my desk. "Here's what you have to do!" she said.

She had this calm, unflapped expression on her face. A railroad spike of fear prodded the small of my back.

"You have to go out and talk to people who were evacuated the day of the explosion. You have to ask them if their businesses were affected. Have them tell the story."

"Uh," I said, "Okay."

"Were you going to do that?"

"Yes. Yes I was. I was going to do that."

"Really?" She exhaled at me, breathing out loudly, like a stallion. "That sounds like it isn't true, like you didn't think of it. That isn't acceptable to me. Next time, think of it."

"Okay," I said.

She gazed at me. "You should really answer like you're at least making an effort to have people not think you're stupid," she said.

"Mmm," I said, and she turned to go, the daily quota of injustice having been met.

"Also, can you go out and get me a baked potato?"

"A potato," I said.

"*Yeah*," she said. "A *potato*. From the potato bar at the big supermarket." She looked at me like I was something on the end of a fishhook. "You're saying it like you've never heard the word before."

"But," I said, thinking I had to try to get the city's report. But I could not get myself to disagree with her. "What do you want me to do first?" I said. "Talk to those people or get the potato?"

"Talk first, then potato," she said. "Oh, also. Have you heard from Gus?"

Her eyes had a droop to them. She made the gesture she always was making, straightening her long black hair, so black as to be almost blue, laying it on her shoulders like a pair of drapes. She was like the bored ticket taker at a carnival sideshow. I thought of her tearing my stories to pieces, clicking away on the puny mouse on her computer. If I said he'd called me, maybe a wave of relief would wash over me, and I would be transported to someplace where I could sit, my feet in some cool water. But then I looked at Gus's desk, the detritus of work scattered around. Paper clips, a letter opener. He'd called me a few times since I spoke to him that one time. But I hadn't called him back. I was afraid Doreen would find out we talked. A pounding began in my stomach.

When I spoke, my word was a whisper. I uttered the tiniest word, hoping, pleading into the air that it would go unnoticed.

"No," I said.

She raised her top lip into a sneer. She pointed her finger at me, pink, crooked.

"Well," she said. She spoke quickly, her words running together. "If he calls you, tell him to call me."

Then she was gone again. I gagged.

Gus had liked to water the office plant. He would take the coffee pot and fill it with water and dump most of it on the geranium that sat by the printer under the skylight. One day he did this and came up to me while I was drinking my coffee, grinning, and said, "Would you like a warm-up, ma'am?" I looked at him with the half-full pot of cold water, and we both laughed soundless laughs.

I opened the phone book. I read listings and for a while I just flipped the pages. Then I tried to search for Jordan Jeppeson's obituary, but I couldn't find one. I was filled with a pungent, oily fear that always dredged itself up from the bottom of me, the fear that I couldn't do whatever she was asking. I can't! Forget it! I tried to ask myself a question: Would you just fucking calm down? In the phone book, I found the address of a fancy shop for children's clothes that was on the street where things had gone all wrong the day of the gas leak. I got in my car and drove there. El Alamo Street, a block-long side street.

The store looked like a cupcake. At the doorway I stared inside. I was starting to sweat. I didn't really go to places where people did leisurely things like shop. I only talked to spokespeople, sources. But I went in, a bell tinkling. A blonde woman was putting price tags on jumpers. Clearing my throat awkwardly, I asked her, did she remember that day?

"We had to close for the entire day," she said, shaking her head. She wore a black sweater and a turquoise necklace. No one else was in the store.

"Tell me the story," I said.

"Well," she said, and put down the jumpers. "It was just my partner and me. It was busy that day, it was Friday, and it was the weekend of the choir concert in town. There were people already up for the weekend. Anyway. There was this smell, like pool chlorine, but also like rotten eggs, and rubbing alcohol. We thought something was really wrong, like we were being invaded."

"Wow," I said.

"Yeah," she paused. "We were really afraid. I feel so terrible about what happened to that poor woman."

I was scribbling down what she said. "Could I put you on record?" I asked.

"Listen," she said, speaking gently. "I don't want you to write about us like people who had something stupid happen to them and then acted like it was the worst thing in the world. I feel really bad about that woman."

"It's horrible," I said. "I know. It's okay. Everything's going to be okay."

She squeezed a turquoise bead on her necklace. She didn't look comforted. Which was apt, because nothing she could say would change how I wrote about it, and nothing I wrote would change how Doreen would edit it later, twisting it like a mobile, so I would recognize nothing. Even the quotations would seem fabled.

I thanked her and as I left the bell chimed against the tidy glass door. In the shop window was a pram, covered in lace. The street seemed dark. I thought about what she said. I can't do anything for you, I thought.

I shoved my notes in my jacket pocket, as deep as they would go. Then I took them out again and read what I'd written.

We were really afraid, I read.

I drove to the big grocery store. I had to get the potato. I went to the potato bar, which had a sign over it that said, Potato Bar. All those toppings, laid out on a steaming barge under foggy sneeze guards. I had no idea which she wanted. Maybe she wanted none. I got her a little separate container of all of them, neatly arranged in rows. I got a duplicate for me.

I went back to the office and approached Doreen's office like a wraith. She was on the phone. She turned and saw me. I raised the bag, tried to smile, pointed at it.

Put it there, she mouthed, and jabbed her index finger at the art director's desk. The art director, sitting there, glared at me, her hair a maze of yellow spikes, and I scurried back to my desk.

A few minutes later Doreen came out carrying the potato, eating with a plastic fork.

"What's all this?" She held up the extra baggage of toppings.

"Accoutrements," I said.

The phone rang.

"What the fuck am I supposed to do with all this?" she said.

I pointed at the phone. "That might be Utilities calling me," I said. Doreen left, and I was free.

"Hello, the *Weekly*," I said.

No reply. "Hello, the *Weekly*!" I said again.

A withered voice answered.

"I am Alfredo Zuniga," a man said. "You will come today at 4 to pick up your copy of the report. You are the first request. We are happy to serve."

"Oh yes," I said. "Thank you for returning my call. Where do I come to get a copy of the report?"

"To my office, of course. 4 p.m."

I tried to ask what number, what floor. I'd been through this before. But he hung up.

It was 3:25. I got the phone book again, flipped through some pages while I ate the potato. I batted the pages of that white section, the directory of public agencies, the reporter's best friend. I found the address, wrote it down in my skinny white notebook. No doubt, Steve Brown had filed a request for the report by now. I felt sick again. I had thirty-five minutes.

The Department of Utilities was stuffed among the historic square downtown, a building I'd overlooked, with dark wooden beams protruding from its facade. Inside a floor of yellowing tile led to a wide staircase, and at the top, an elevator with a mesh sliding door stood open. Wind blew in from outside, a piece of newspaper flapped in the corner. A metal wheelchair lift was installed off to one side of the stairs, the blue wheelchair logo plastered on it, a red button marked up.

I stepped into the elevator. The floors were marked like a European building. I was on floor zero. What floor? Might as well start from the bottom. I hit the button and the thing jerked into action, clanking, groaning, the yellowing tile drifting away.

As the elevator rose, I recalled Gus talking about this building. He'd written about utilities, not me. Water mainly, this being the desert. He'd been here. He'd called it "The Tower."

I stepped out and the floor was a chamber of offices with gray steel doors. One of them was ajar. Inside a man in a cardigan sweater looked at a dusty computer, holding a mug with something steaming in it.

I felt like I was inside a third-world bus station.

"Pardon me," I said. "I'm looking for Alfredo Zuniga's office."

"*¿Qué?*" he said.

I pulled out the press release from my jacket pocket, looked for his name.

"Alfredo Zuniga. Director of Gas Importation and Distribution."

"For the City or the County?" the man said.

"City," I said, pointing at the city logo, dusted in a fax haze.

"Ohhhhhhhh," he said, "You want the fourth floor. In that elevator you wanna press five. That elevator doesn't work sometime."

"Thank you, sir," I said.

He shrugged, slurped at whatever was in the mug.

In the elevator I pushed five and it clanged and whinnied to the top. There was a windowless hallway, a massive iron gray desk covered in a mountain of multicolored notepads, fluttering from air coming in from somewhere. All the doors in the hallway were signless, and I walked, trying each of the doorknobs, until I reached the far end. There was a clock on the wall there behind a steel, clock-shaped cage. It was 4:05.

On an etched black plastic placard was the name: Alfredo Zuniga.

I tried the knob but it was locked. I knocked and a slot in the door, just below eye level, as if for a gnome, slowly opened. A pair of eyes gazed down. Suddenly they darted up and stared at me, angrily, and the sound of tympani went off in my head.

"I'm here to pick up the report about the gas explosion," I said. "I'm Katherine Hight from the *Weekly*."

The slot slowly closed, and a man opened the door with a sharp tug. He was nattily dressed, in a pressed white shirt open at the collar.

"I am Alfredo," he said.

"Katherine. Kate," I said. I stuck out my hand and he shook it and the weight of his hand was a heavy, cold octopus. The room held only a table with four steel chairs, a rickety photocopier, and some cabinets with glass fronts. All filled with black books with no titles on the spines. Reports, I thought.

"Here is the report," Alfredo said, and lifted a thick document from the table, shrouded in a black plastic cover. "That will be nine dollars," he said, "for the photocopy."

I rifled through my pockets until I found a wrinkled ten. He took an Army green lockbox from a shelf, opened it, and handed me a crisp one-dollar bill, moving slowly as though half asleep.

"Can I get a receipt?" I said.

"Of course," he said. He removed a receipt pad, only one receipt remaining. He walked to the photocopier, laid the pad down, carefully aligning it, and hit the start button. The room gleamed momentarily as a blade of light shone against the glass cabinets. What seemed like minutes passed, and the machine ejected a sheet of paper. Alfredo, removing a pen from his shirt pocket, entered the information, his signature a sharp-lined oval.

He pressed the receipt neatly on top of the black-covered report.

"You are welcome," he said, his voice, having lost its rasp, boomed like he was a wizard. The clock read 4:25.

On the way out, on floor zero, I encountered Steve Brown. He was removing the sporty sunglasses. His cheeks were pink, his blond hair was combed and seemed Brylcreemed. Behind him was a man in a pressed black suit, sweating, who had the demeanor of a spider.

Something was all bungled. Steve was chasing the report—something in it had to be chased. On his sweating face, I saw a frightened look. He was panicking. For a second, I thought, maybe I was in the lead.

"Hello, Steve," I said.

"Hello, *Katherine*," he said. "What's that you have in your hand there?"

"What you're here looking for!" I said.

"Well, that's *great*! So when's your deadline?" he asked.

"Wouldn't you like to know," I said.

I saw that the sweating man had a folded baby-blue sheaf of papers in his hand. Court documents.

"You look like you could use a cold beverage, sir!" I shouted at him, but the man only grunted, making a sound like a rusted gate, moving. Steve began to chuckle, making a noise like *Yuck, Yuck, Yuck*.

"Soooo," he said. "How's about we talk before you hit that old deadline of yours?"

"I'll consider it," I said. "I'll read this. I'm sure it's fascinating."

"What office you get that from?"

"I'm sure you'll figure it out. You're smart boys," I said. "Oh. Elevator's broken. You'll have to walk it."

Steve started up the steps, the sweating man gazing at me angrily. "No problem!" he said.

With any luck, they'd pass Zuniga on his way down as they were on the way up. Closing time was 4:30, and municipalities are timely in their office hours.

At the office, I sat at my desk, potato detritus everywhere. I opened the report. Pages of administrativity. The board of inquiry. The jurisdiction. Available for public review upon request. Stuff, stuff, stuff.

Doreen walked over. I could hear the echo of her clomps as she came to my spider hole. Her underbite seemed to have gone even farther under and her jaw preceded her like a royal parade. This, I knew, meant she was angry. She had a proof in her hand.

"What the fuck is this?" she said.

"What?" I said.

She pointed at a printout of a story I'd submitted the day prior. A string of words came out of her mouth. NO CLARITY. MISREPRESENTATION. STORY? ANGLE? It seemed to go on for minutes, maybe hours. The grinding nausea in my stomach switched again. The arts editor had turned around in her chair to look at me.

At last, Doreen was finished.

"Okay," I said, and I stood.

"Don't walk away from me when I'm talking to you," she said.

"I'm sorry, I thought you were finished," I said.

"I have no idea what this person is saying in this quote, or what that has to do with anything. This needs a total overhaul. I'll be here all weekend."

I couldn't say anything. I sat again. I thought I would have diarrhea, right there, in the chair.

"So, what are you doing," she said.

"Gas explosion. I'm reading the report," I said. "I talked to some people. And I got you the potato. Oh, you already knew that. You already ate it."

She stared at me. Somehow, she looked calm, shaking her head, adjusting her hair.

"Well, do a better job on that one than you did on this trash."

When she was gone, I went to the bathroom. I thought I would throw up, but again still nothing, even though my stomach felt full of nails. At the sink I splashed some water on my face, heaved once more, and returned to my desk. The sun had gone down. I thought of Zuniga, at home, or in his car, undoing his cufflinks. Perhaps he was cutting loose. I opened the report again.

I got to the serious part. The tone grew direct, scientific. There were footnotes, photographs, references to scientific journal articles. A section entitled "Findings, Section 6," began: "Fittings found to be ill-maintained. Pressure allowed to drop. WestCo employee stated that monitoring as of 6 a.m. the morning of May 29 was incomplete." Then there was a word that had been bolded, in a niggling sans serif typeface: "Negligent."

"Report submitted to State Attorney General office. Committee recommends criminal action be taken against WestCo. Internal Audit Board commenced." Then, an oblique yet clear sentence of instructions. "See further detail in Appendix B, attached."

I turned to Appendix B.

It was an autopsy report. Jordan Jeppeson, age thirty-two.

There were photographs. A hand, black char blossoming up the fingers, its fingernails pristine, like the insides of conch shells. A body, partially burned, a scrawl of wet, blackened feathers.

Something in my stomach toppled, like a bowling pin, falling.

Cause of death, it said in the same bolded typeface: "Drowning."

I closed the document. That demo pool in the parking lot next door. She hadn't died from smoke inhalation. I began to feel faint. I stood and ran to the bathroom. Then, at last, in the stall, everything that was in my stomach finally unrolled itself. Hideous, pumpkin-colored liquid dotted with acorns of food. I heard the noise I was making, a splattering into the surface of the water. It was a little like crying. And when I finally stood, I was no longer nauseous.

"Oh," I heard myself saying. "Thank god."

I returned to the desk, picked up the phone book, and found the letter *J*. I scanned for the name. There wasn't anyone there by that name. There was no other Jeppeson. Jordan was the only one. I could have met her somewhere, in a bar. In the filmy clipping of the article the rival paper had run there was a blurry picture of Jordan sitting at a picnic table. I read it again. There weren't any quotations about her, no friends, no family. I thought of her family. Maybe her parents were divorced. Maybe they lived in Colorado, or Utah. Maybe they lived back East. Or, maybe, she was just alone. Whoever they were, what had they done when she died? *Nothing*, I thought. Because they'd believed it was an accident.

I stood and looked into Doreen's office. I could see her there on the phone.

I was sick of her talking to me like I was a turd.

I watched her for a moment. Turn around, I wanted to say. There was no longer any sun coming in through the skylight. Only the screen glare of computers. For once, I knew exactly what I would do.

I wrote the story. I sat there without moving and wrote. The only thing was, we had to ask the company for a comment. I left a space for it. *Insert quotation from Steve Brown here.* I sent it to Doreen. In the subject of the email, I wrote, "WestCo found to be negligent, City gas lines at risk for future damage." There would be nothing to rewrite.

Then I picked up the phone.

"Hello, *Steve*," I said. "It's me. Katherine. I'm calling you. Did you get a copy of the report? Perhaps you did. Or maybe you didn't. Any case, I'm calling you. You know, for a comment."

As soon as I placed the phone down, it rang again. I jumped.

"The *Weekly*!" I said.

"Kate," a voice said, and I knew it was him.

"Gus. What are you doing calling me here? You know she sometimes answers whatever phone is ringing. I could have been her."

"I know, I don't know what I was thinking," he said. He was talking from a quiet place. I imagined him buried in his house, blocking the sun with the drapes. "You never called me back."

"I'm sorry. I didn't want to get you in trouble."

"I saw you earlier. You were coming out of The Tower. I tried to wave to you but you were gone. I was getting a pie at Rollo's."

"I have to write this thing about the gas explosion."

"Oh," he said. Something shuffled in the background. Paper creasing.

"Are you there?" I said.

"Last spring? You mean, Jordan Jeppeson?"

"You remember?"

"Of course I remember. I, uh, sort of guessed."

"How did you guess?"

"I don't know. I just did. Something stood up on the back of my neck."

We were both silent. We were both afraid. Then he said, "I wanted to see if you were still there."

"What do you mean?"

"I was hoping you'd be gone."

"What are you talking about?"

"Why are you still there?"

I couldn't answer, I couldn't figure out what he wanted. What did he want me to do?

But then I asked, why *was* I still there?

I heard a thump; Doreen had backed up her chair into her glass wall. She was standing. Her door opened, she was marching over.

"Kate?" Gus said.

"She's coming," I said. "I have to go."

When I hung up, there Doreen was.

"So, what are you doing," she said.

"I'm trying!" I said.

She opened her mouth, about to speak.

"It's done," I said. "You won't have to change a thing. This is just the first one."

"First one what?" she said. "What the hell are you talking about?"

"Just go read it," I said. A whole string of stories unspooled in front of me. Hearings. Wrongful death lawsuit. The stories would go on for years. But it wouldn't be me who wrote them all. Even then, I could see: This job, this boss, would be the last before I left this town for good. Doreen opened her mouth again, and her eyes widened, her nostrils flared. But I held up my finger, as if to say, just wait.

The phone rang. In all likelihood, it was Steve. Here it came.

Before I picked up, in front of me, there was a woman. The woman had made some tea, on that oddly cloudy day. Jordan had picked up the phone. She'd said, "There's an odd odor in the air. You'd better send someone out to check on it." Maybe thirty-two was young enough to still expect everything from life, and maybe she believed that Seven Hills Title & Bond was a way to someplace else. Or maybe, thirty-two was old enough to have stopped expecting, having grown afraid of watching things deflate like a sail. She'd said, Thank you, and hung up the phone, and those would be her final words. I could see her say them. *Thank you.* Then she'd smelled smoke, she'd heard a snapping noise and the walls became covered in blue heat, and it'd happened so fast and so painful she'd almost laughed, saying ha! and she knew what to do, tried to escape, even as the building shattered, littering the air with cheap wallboard and carpeting. Then I was watching her run, I was watching her jump, her limbs coated in brilliant crimson, and she flew, until her body pricked the surface of the rippling water, still chilled from the night, running for the sky, that hot, risky air, one last time.

ROAD'S EDGE

At our mother's new townhouse, a brick-fronted split-level, Danny and I found her out front in her bathrobe at three in the afternoon, carrying a box. The contractor renovating her bathroom had left tiling unfinished and the water disconnected, and she was unable to shower—she was displeased.

As she set the box down on the asphalt, we froze. Seeing her in daylight, in a plush mauve bathrobe, her legs bare, startled us. This was a woman who had dusted her face with powder and put on lipstick twice a day, no matter what, even in the long year after my father died when she barely went out. Danny tried to get her to come to his cluttered house in Baltimore, which he was slowly rehabbing, and where I was living.

"You can shower at my place," he said, but she waved him off.

"Here, take these," she said, shoving carboard boxes at us. "Maybe one day you'll be glad I saved them." They were filled with things of ours that she hadn't thrown out before vacating the house where we'd grown up, and was now insisting we come and take away. The boxes' flaps wobbled like unsteady wings—Danny's vinyl, my books and old school papers. On top was a music book of mine: *Method for Clarinet*. As we loaded Danny's car—a sporty silver hatchback that he was fond of saying looked more expensive than it was—she handed me another box.

"And this one too," she said, resting a box in my arms. "Katie, take this."

Her eyes narrowed, turned slightly blank, and she went inside. The box was small, densely packed, and its flaps were crisscrossed into a kind of flower.

Danny followed her to the doorway. "Come to my house," he insisted.

"I just said I'll shower at the gym," she said. "Now get going before it gets dark."

It was early September, a scalding Indian summer. As we pulled onto the highway Danny said, "She goes to a gym?"

I shrugged. "I never would have thought." But more than that, I was thinking about the look on her face when she handed me that last box.

"I need a drink," he said. "Pool?"

I said absolutely to playing pool, and we proceeded to do what we did from time to time, which was go to Bad Decisions—truly, that was the name of our local bar. We parked in front of Danny's narrow rowhouse of mismatched stone, didn't bother to unload the boxes, and walked up the patched asphalt, past tall trees and short houses and overgrown alleys. The sun of the early evening streamed through the bar's open door and onto the mottled floor. The black vinyl stools occupied by other neighborhood day drinkers. It wasn't until Danny had racked a round of nine-ball on the green felt and we had two cold beers in front of us that I thought to check my flip phone.

There was a message that I'd have to pay by the minute to listen to.

The week prior, I'd had a phone interview with a publishing house in New York. To think how I lunged for the phone when they'd called amuses me now. The message was from the chirpy woman in HR, asking if I could come to New York for an in-person interview. I nearly replied, Yes, goddamnit, even though it was just a voicemail.

I was chasing a job, any job. I thought having a job would make me peaceful, untroubled. Although the situation should have been peaceful enough. Danny wasn't at the house most of the time. He had a girlfriend—substantially older than he was, which I presumed he found exotic—who had several children and lived way out in Virginia, and he seemed happy spending his abundant information technology money on them and on one rehab project after another. Between my intermittent waitressing and temping, days would pass during which I did not put on shoes.

I particularly wanted this job because Yahlie had just moved to New York to start grad school.

Yahlie was simultaneously adept and inept. She never had anything she needed—tissues, a hair elastic. She would blow her nose on a piece of notebook paper. But she was always on time, always wore a watch. She would become absorbed in a project and forget everything else. She would want to talk the whole time she worked on it, exclaiming when she, for example, found a lost screw.

We'd been out of touch. She'd moved around—Israel, Europe—while I'd drifted through jobs and towns that didn't suit me. We exchanged stray emails, swapping facts of our lives, but we'd only managed to talk occasionally in the past few years and we only planned visits that never happened. But even when we didn't talk, she was always there, in the background of my life.

Danny was chalking a cue. "Hey, I got a job interview," I told him.

He looked at me sidelong, his large brown eyes seeming even more bulbous, his knobby hand freezing on the cube of chalk.

"So you may yet become a solvent adult," he said. "If you jump through the appropriate flaming hoops."

He cracked the cue ball, and after a while it got dark and the bartender gave us a buyback.

"You take too long lining up those shots," he said on our third game. "Just shoot it."

Between turns Danny prattled on about the girlfriend's kids, who he spent his money on and yet was constantly annoyed by, and I had a pang. A pang that if I moved to New York, there wouldn't be this thing we did together. That was the first time it occurred to me that *this* was a *this*. Or that I could ever miss it. That is, if I moved to New York.

I thought about it as if I were a different person: one day she would grow nostalgic for Bad Decisions, nostalgic for Danny's grumbling about taking a cranky four-year-old to the zoo.

We went back to the car and carried the boxes up the shallow concrete steps that served as a porch and into the house, which was short on windows and headroom. The week prior, I'd helped him tear out the last of the wall-to-wall shag. The two bathrooms were like twin stars of disrepair—one had a sink but a broken toilet, the other a brand-new toilet but a pipe where the sink should have been. My mother would not have wanted to shower here.

Danny went out to the crumbling deck off the kitchen that he called his white trash patio. I heard a scraping sound; he'd been slowly chipping paint off the outside wall, one brick at a time, it seemed. Our father's ability to build anything had rubbed off on Danny, sort of. Danny had knocked out the wall between the kitchen and the living room, but hadn't yet put anything in its place. Instead, the boxes my mother had given us were strewn across the scuffed hardwood. I should unpack them, I thought. But it seemed pointless in the clutter. The rusty orange of the dusty shag carpet piled in the corner reminded me of a rug Yahlie and I had taken from a street corner. The phone was heavy in my hand: I should call her.

But I didn't dial—calling was probably pointless anyway. She hadn't answered the half dozen times I'd tried her before.

Maybe she was too busy for anything other than the approximate floating around each other's lives we'd been doing. And yet, the notion of a new situation, of being in a new city together pulled at me. I had moved back east because there never seemed to be jobs in any of the towns I'd lived in that I had any business doing. Danny's house had just the right amount of impermanence to make me want to move out. The time had come to exit the wretchedness that the languor of my youth had become. And so, I dialed.

When I said hello and she heard my voice, she let out a sharp gasp.

"Been a while," I said, and told her about the interview, that I'd be in town.

"Yes!" Yahlie said. "I'm so impressed you got a job interview."

"I doubt it will last more than five minutes," I said.

She laughed her cackling laugh. "Oh please," she said. "When do I see you? Can we meet after the interview?"

And just like that we made a plan.

As we talked, I stalked around the kitchen, and the achy, petulant feeling I often had when it came to Yahlie flooded back, one she didn't really deserve. I wanted to ask where she was staying and how long she'd been there and why she'd never called me back. Maybe the plan we'd made the moment before would never materialize, just like all the other times. Well, you could have called, I yelled at her silently. But I was craving that groove we could fall into, like a needle on a record. I missed it. So I held my tongue.

"Can't wait," I said, and we said goodbye.

"Who was that?" Danny said, and I jumped, startled by his low voice.

He was peering at me through an open window that looked onto the patio, his face obscured by the screen, his forehead a glowing cue ball. At last, now that he was almost entirely bald, he'd finally cut off his straggly brown ponytail. I was twenty-five, he was about to turn twenty-seven, and yet to me he seemed far older, certainly more like a fully formed adult. He lumbered inside, pushing open the screen door with one pale arm, and let it slam behind him.

"Dude," I said. "You scared me."

He shrugged and asked, "Must you leave this window open?"

"It's hot outside," I said. "That was Yahlie. Gonna see her when I go to New York."

His eyebrows seemed to slide most of the way up his forehead. "Ah," he said. "Presumably for this job interview? One of the most expensive cities on the planet. Well, not my problem if you want to give up on a cheap city. And presumably they will be paying you. So you may not be completely broke."

"It's publishing. And entry level," I said.

"Good point," he said, and wandered to the living room, stepping around the boxes. Probably I should have been thanking him for letting me stay in exchange for groceries and cleaning—the least I could do to prevent the entire place from becoming engulfed in mold.

Danny edged the boxes around with his feet, sat, and began rifling through one of them. After a moment we began to unpack them.

I pulled out a French textbook and held it out to him. Our father had made us learn it. When he wasn't listening, Danny and I had repeated words to each other that we thought sounded the most ridiculous in our cartoonish French accents. *Stupide. Le fromage. La mort.*

Danny held up a yellowed workbook, *Wheelock's Latin Third Edition*, his name written on it in black magic marker—D. Hight—then a tattered copy of the *Aeneid*, flipped to a page. "*Caput inter nubila*," he said, reading.

"*L'idiot lit la poésie*," I said.

He sniggered, began flicking through a stack of records. "Look at this one," he said. *Figure 8*, the title read, amid a swirl of black and red. Danny's house had only one working toilet and an unplugged fridge on his patio, but his turntable was plugged in and ready.

The little box, the one with its flaps folded, was pushed off to the side. As the chords rang, I gently undid it.

I expected there to be more of our things inside. Maybe our father's. But there weren't. They were our sister's.

Our sister Amy was a thing we never spoke about. Any of us. A scent of aged paper and the faintest hint of cherry wafted from inside. On top was a model of a horse, no taller than my little finger, its coat a mottled gray with even white circles, like stars. Its head was bent, one hoof raised, as though about to charge. As I held it aloft, the song ended—*everything means nothing to me*—and Danny crouched over me, his eyebrows raised in astonishment.

As we unpacked the box, everything from the day slinked away—Yahlie, my future plans—and the fact of *her*, our sister, returned. How my mother had pressed that box into my hands. She'd held it as though, perhaps, she'd almost kept it behind.

A faded page torn from *National Geographic* showing a desert valley, labeled: Morocco. A child's toy watch, imprinted with hearts. A report card, all As.

Danny laughed gently. "Damn," he said. This was a feat neither of us had achieved, ever.

A stack of flashcards, written in a hand with a flat *O*, a curvy *A*. *Cantle, corona*. Was this her handwriting? I turned one over: *Hackamore—a bitless bridle, for training*.

And then: A photo of her, perhaps at nine or ten, at the edge of a riding arena, beside a towering horse, holding the reins. The horse was the same as the miniature, its legs thick and coated in deep fur, its white mane braided with red ribbon that spilled over its rounded muscles. Her smile—there was nothing in my scant, weak memories of her with that smile. Her hair, though, it was mine, a dark brown. Pulled into two tails that spread down her back, in the dangling half-curl that mine, too, formed whenever it rained.

"I didn't know she liked horses," I said.

"Maybe she gave it up," Danny said. "Maybe it was a kid thing."

Then, there was the clipping from the Baltimore Sun. *Delaware teen killed in hit-and-run.* Danny and I crouched on the floor reading. The filmy, yellow paper sent a memory rising that had long been buried, and it spoke to me as if a newspaper reporter were asking me questions. *How old were you when she was killed?* I was eight, Danny was about to turn ten. My parents had gone out. I don't know where. They left my sister to babysit us. Some time went by, and then my sister went out. She'd just turned sixteen, she'd gotten her driver's license perhaps a week prior. *So she snuck out?* Yes. So we were alone in the house.

"I never saw this article," Danny said. "Did you?"

I shook my head no, and as the facts from the article tumbled in front of us, my memories of that time unfolded, slowly, as something being told by another person. I, she.

It was hot, wet spring. The sort that left a feeling of drip on one's skin. Amy was at home with her two much younger siblings, in the house that still smelled of newness: drywall yet to fully harden, the plasticine odor of carpet adhesive. A tract home, the trees shaved down to nothing, and new ones planted. The children's parents went out, thought it would be fine to leave them together in the house for one night. With her shiny new license, Katie's sister left the house in the parents' other car.

Katie—me, I—went to sleep first that night. She remembers her sister closing the door, shadowed by a child's nighttime lamp. Maybe her sister told her brother she was leaving. Sometimes Katie's sister yelled. Maybe she had yelled at Danny that evening, or maybe she was gentle and told him she had to run out, told a lie, saying, *We're out of milk*. Perhaps she wanted to leave, to be alone without the ankle weight of her little sister and brother, of her mother, of her father. Although maybe Katie's sister remembered their father as moving, or even joyful, as tall and walking and running. Not as the inert person Katie remembers him as.

When their mother and father came home, Katie's sister had not yet returned, and she didn't return the day after, or the day after that. All of the people in charge—police, a social worker—took some time to believe she was missing, and to find her body.

She. I.

Amy had gone to another town almost fifty miles away, to a house party. She'd parked on the side of the road, the police guessed, and a car hit her. Most likely, as she opened the door. She'd parked near a culvert at the road's edge, and most likely, the car bounced as it was hit, tipping oddly on its side. She would have seen it coming, in the thin frame of headlights on the asphalt. The other car sped off. A tire track. Heated asphalt. A dense spring fog had descended over the country roads from the lush fields nearby. The car was not visible right away from the road. The police interviewed the residents of the house, the neighbors, and tried to find other partygoers. None had any memory of her at the party. She'd never gone inside the house.

As I held the delicate clipping, in my imagination a heavy hand is grasping a fist of my sister's hair. So brown as to be almost black, straight, but never really straight. An open car door, a line of blood. That car that became not a car but an imaginary place. I had the feeling of touching bone, of holding a sharp jaw.

A noise came from the back of the house. The sound of a flat metal object hitting something soft and dense. It made both of us jump. But maybe it was just the neighbor, slamming his back gate.

I put away the scrap of newspaper; neither of us could look anymore. Danny sat against the couch, his hands against his forehead, and I could tell he was thinking of how our father had become angry, saying, *What did she tell you*, and Danny had revealed that she had been gentle. She hadn't yelled.

"She said, I'm just going to get some milk. I just want to drive the car one more time," Danny said, repeating to me words that I hadn't heard since that day. "She said, 'I want to try it in the dark.'"

Our father, at the table, shoving his thumbs into his own eyes.

Danny reached into the box. He pulled out a wallet—red plastic. He opened it. Inside, her driver's license.

A glittering smile. Sixteen forever. Her name, in solid black type: Amy Hight.

Underneath was a stack of documents in a worn manila folder, and he began paging through it.

"I don't remember what kind of car it was," I said.

"A Civic. This is an accident report," Danny said and flipped a page. "Look at this. A complaint letter. Five years later. From mom and dad to the police. They wanted them to keep searching for the driver. All this time I thought they had stopped trying."

Behind the folder lay one final photograph. It was Amy and a boy. A boy who was approaching being a man. Also with dark hair, and ivory, nearly translucent skin. Who needed a haircut. But who had the undeniable rakishness of eighteen or nineteen. Leafy trees behind them, the photo paper gone yellow with time. I lifted it to Danny, and he shook his head as if to say he didn't know.

Her smile, though, was different. It contained a hint of danger. But also, an urge. An urge to look right at whoever was taking the picture and say, *It's me*. It said to me that this was the someone who'd been waiting for her at the party.

Maybe it was this photograph that made me angry. And maybe it was the image that had already started to form of what my future self might look like. How there was—against all odds—the potential for that self to be something other than what I was right then, a person who sometimes didn't put on shoes for days at a time. Maybe it was seeing her name—Amy Hight—and the spilling of my memory. The sensation was as though water was seeping around my bare feet. Maybe it was my mother's face that afternoon—the way she had met my eyes, turned away, as though she were trying to send her mind back to a blank space. I recognized this had always been her way: Put it in a box.

Maybe it was all of this that made me blurt at Danny: "Why is it that we can never, ever talk about this? Why is Mom giving us this stuff, like the ark of the covenant? Don't you want to ask?"

His gaze rested on the turntable as it spun idly. "Sometimes," he said. "But I think I remember her more than you do."

"Like what?"

"I remember she took us to the pool that day," he said.

The crisp, blue square of the town pool came back to me. The memory arose without distance. As though I could feel her body in my presence. She and I had been there together. I jumped off the pool's edge into her arms. I felt the splash, felt her arms around me until I could see her chin. She and I, and my father, we had the same chin, with a dimple in the center, hers and mine small, his deep and hollow. She had acne. She pulled orange inflatable floats up my arms. We stood in line out front on the hot pebbled sidewalk, puddled with the drip of kids in wet swimsuits, where she bought us two orange Creamsicles. *You're getting that everywhere*, she said, not smiling. Her legs protruding from the bottom of denim shorts.

"I remember the pool," I said. "But it might have been a different day." A memory of that night did return to me. Danny and I had watched a movie, a clever detective movie. I loved it, but Danny said, "This is stupid." He wanted to watch in the dark. I never liked that, the flickering blue like a demon. But he turned the lights out anyway. In the kitchen, my sister unwrapped a frozen chicken pot pie and put it in the microwave. When it was finished, a bell sounded. She ate some, but then sat crushing it with her fork. I wanted her to share, but she slid the rest into the trash. I wanted to say, don't throw it away. My memory of her was loose, fogged. I only felt her sadness. But, just then, in Danny's house, what I felt more was envy. Because after she left, our father was unknown to me"Sometimes," I said, "I want to grab Mom and make her explain why we can never say one damn thing about her."

I pictured my mother in the kitchen, when I had asked her about Amy, when once, I'd summoned the nerve. She changed the subject, to, I don't know, dinner, and clattered clean silverware into a drawer and slammed it shut.

Danny went to the kitchen and opened a beer, the cap tinkling on the countertop.

"You will remember the line, no doubt," he said. "Talking won't help."

This he said precisely in my father's husky voice, and I pictured my father saying it at the dinner table, and him biting into a piece of bread that had been toasted to nearly black, the way he liked it, the sound of his teeth crushing it to crumbs.

"He said it about everything," Danny said. "Talking won't finish your Latin."

He sat back down and paged through the documents for a while longer, but I couldn't look away from the photo of her and the boy.

"It seems that I have consumed nearly too many of these," Danny said, and set his bottle on the floor. As he stood, the slouch he had acquired from being a tall person who tried to hide his height seemed to sink even deeper. "Go to sleep before you drive yourself mad," he said, pausing on the narrow staircase.

I took this to mean, Maybe our father was right.

Upstairs, I lay down on my mattress. I wished I could remember her smiling as she had in the photos. She constantly told me to grow up. She said I smelled. Was it possible she wasn't nice? But that was standard big sister; and, maybe, one day, she could have been nice. I shut off the light and the city's gloam filtered in through the alley. I thought of the party—the one my sister almost made it to. Dozens of teenagers drinking cans of National Bohemian from a cooler. I drifted off feverishly, one thought remaining.

She never got to go inside.

The next day, I awoke to loud bangs. It was noon. Downstairs, Danny's beer sat on the floor where he'd left it.

On the white trash patio, Danny, still in his pajama pants, was hanging fence boards. Hammer flying, nails clenched in his teeth. I drained what was left from his beer into the sink and tossed it into the recycling.

In a few short days I was on a belching bus, whizzing up I-95.

THE DAY OF THE INTERVIEW, in the apartment of an old college friend who was out of town, I woke with a jolt and lunged for the clock, convinced that I had missed my interview. I lay with the clock on my chest until my heart slowed.

I showered and stood in front of the air conditioner, rehearsing questions again and again. I put on my interview clothes, which, being black on black suddenly seemed like a terrible mistake. It was scorching and I feared it made me look like Johnny Cash. Or a witch. As I passed through the neighborhood—some blocks from the Flatiron Building jutting into the sky, on a street where flower vendors crowded the sidewalk with boxes bursting with color—a feeling came over me that this could be the life I would soon inhabit. The mingled scents of eucalyptus and jasmine and refuse and exhaust set a story moving of a future self, a self I was not yet, but might become: *She left her apartment on 26th Street, swerving around a coffee cart, and went downtown.*

I was early for the interview. The building had a towering daylight-filled atrium with red-painted columns. As I waited, I fidgeted with the flip phone and I saw there was a message.

It was from Danny. He'd left it late the night before. I hadn't heard it ring. "Is today your job interview?" he asked, his tone almost jovial. Probably, he'd been out with his idiot friends and had had too many glasses of brown liquid—this was how he referred to a whiskey or two. He cleared his throat loudly into the phone. "In any event, I wish you good luck. Do not screw it up."

I flipped it closed and realized I was smiling. For him, this was as much of a high five as I was ever to receive.

In our adolescence, Danny and I had never exchanged anything about our personal lives. Sometimes I was surprised that we talked at all. But somehow, the silent strife had slowly abated. My annoyance at listening to his tedium was there alongside a pleasure, of sorts, that we were there listening to each other. I wanted to be more certain that it would last, that we wouldn't drift apart. I thought for a moment that maybe I shouldn't leave.

A voice called: "Katherine?" Then a woman with straight red hair—the editor—was showing me into her office. The room was a cool cave. She'd turned off the overhead fluorescent light.

At each question, I felt my answers rising so easily that I could just hand them to her like paper napkins. As though I was not answering about myself but speaking about another, different, eminently qualified person. Katherine is an exceedingly quick reader. Her eye for fit within market is superb.

The editor grinned and ran a smoothing gesture down her perfectly blow-dried hair.

"And you went to St. Mary's, I see."

Only during this one moment did I falter. *This question left Katherine feeling like she had a pulsating letter A on her chest. She'd told this lie passively many times. But this was the only time she truly cared if anyone found out. It'd become barely a lie, but a detail, edited out. She thought of Amy. I'm just going out to get some milk.*

Then I answered. "Yes, yes I did."

When it was over, the editor walked me to the front desk and shook my hand. There was a glint in her eye when she said, "We'll be in touch!"

The corner where Yahlie and I had picked to meet turned out to be a swarming mass of tourists and shoppers and people who moved so fast they seemed to be fleeing. A nervous anticipation nagged at me; maybe she wouldn't show. This had happened before.

Another half an hour passed before my phone rang from a number I didn't recognize, and Yahlie's upturned voice was suddenly in my ear. She was calling from a stranger's phone because hers had died. She'd confused West Broadway and Broadway, and was blocks away. Could I walk to her? As I did, I let out a huffy sigh. By the time I arrived I was mopping sweat from my brow.

I spotted her on an opposite corner. Even from a distance I could see her hair was even shorter than the last time I'd seen her. Before I could let go of my irritation with her, she ran across the crosswalk and threw her arms around me, squealing.

"You!" she said when she let go, her eyes so filled with excitement and love that I thought I would have to turn away. I had spent too many days in my brother's dispiriting house.

"It's me!" I said. "We made it!"

As she let go, I saw how thin she was. Her face, with its diamond shape, seemed longer, taller, fiercer.

She said, "You look exactly the same."

"No way," I said.

We strolled around the neighborhood—the far West Village—past basketball courts and shops and bodegas. We found a vacant bench near a school, underneath an overhang of brush that had been trimmed into a topiary like a green awning. I told her to tell me everything. She'd been in Israel trying to write a thesis.

"But it's still unfinished," she said. "Now I'm about to start Columbia. Maybe leaving wasn't a good idea."

Her worry, the same as mine. Using one thumbnail, she cleaned under the fingernails of her other hand, a gesture I'd always enjoyed; it was so at odds with how messy she was otherwise.

"I don't know how I can miss it so much and be happy to be here at the same time," she said. "I wish someone could explain that to me."

"Sorry I can't," I said. "I was just having the same thought. I'm worried I shouldn't leave either. It hasn't been so bad living with Danny."

I took off my jacket and shoved it into my bag. A woman in heels walked by tiredly, holding a blazer in her right hand. She unlocked the door of an apartment near us and went in. Could this be me, fishing keys from my purse after a long day at work?

"He seems miserable and happy at the same time," I said. Yahlie sighed a long sigh. The fenced blacktop of the school was filled with the sound of kids playing, the muffled drumming of balls being dribbled. That sigh, I'd always appreciated it. It meant that she thought I was right, and wasn't going to try to convince me of anything other than the nihilistic thing I'd just said.

"You know what I kind of want to do?" she said. "Smoke a cigarette." She grinned. Like it was a party to end all parties. And so we jumped from the bench and went to the bodega.

A cat languidly waved its tail as it sat in the doorway. We had to step over her as we left. We returned to the bench, lit two, and sat, like two old men.

"This is making me feel high," Yahlie said.

"Me too," I said.

She took out her camera, a little silver battery-operated thing. She held its tiny viewfinder to her eye, shot a picture of the vines overhead.

I asked her about her graduate program, which was in social justice. She was going to focus on the environment, she said. Ecoterrorism, networks of power. Somehow, I couldn't picture it. As she spoke, I realized I'd always hoped she'd do something with objects—sculpture? Design? It wasn't her path, as it turned out. For a brief moment I thought I could teach myself to fix things like her, like Danny had, and maybe even be good at it, like my father. But I was clumsy, I had no spatial sense. As she spoke, I realized it was me who wished I'd done it.

"So, wait," I said. "Did you come back to the States at all?"

She dropped her cigarette on the ground, snubbed it out under her sandal, and shook her head. Not even to see her parents, with whom she'd always been tightly wound. She sheepishly shrugged.

"I got involved with someone they hated," she said. "And then, of course, it blew up in my face."

She looked unsurprised; she and I had both had many a thing fall apart. I could guess what had happened. She crossed her arms and legs, as though warding someone off.

"I wasn't going to not go," she said. I sensed an uncertainty in her, but also, determination. Neither of which were quite what I remembered.

"Well, who cares?" I said. "You could do worse than Columbia. Maybe I'll get this damn job and come here too."

She gripped my arm, reached for another cigarette. "Oh, Katie," she said. "You have to. I don't know anyone here."

As we smoked another, the future self that I had conjured that morning emerged again: *Kate met her best friend after work in the West Village for dinner and a drink. She fished out her keys, she went inside.*

As the sun went down, we walked and encountered a bistro. I doubt I could find it again. Le Quelque Chose. I saw white tablecloths and bottles of wine and I wanted nothing more than to sit.

"Let's sit down," I said. "Let's have dinner."

"That sounds so fun," she said, sadly. "I have almost no money."

Sometimes it was she who dragged me someplace, sometimes it was the reverse. I was hungry, and already, that feeling of New York had overwhelmed me, the sense of a vast world outside, steaming and clapping, and that being inside ignoring it was a kind of foolishness. That feeling has been with me, probably to my detriment, ever since. So she humored me, and we got a table.

As soon as we sat down, we were astonished to discover that there was a happy hour until 6, and *moules-frites* and bottles of house white were half price. "It's 5:49!" Yahlie said. "What luck!" We decided to order it all, a bowl for each of us and the wine and even a salad to share.

But when the waitress arrived, she began to change her mind. When we'd gone to the taqueria in the town where we'd lived, she'd always been decisive and order the same thing— pintos and cheese, as if it were suddenly new. Now she deliberated about the salad, asking the waitress half a dozen questions. Even once we'd ordered, she pinched her chin, as though we might have done it wrong.

"It's always surprising how the brain is able to hold two feelings at once," she said, turning the conversation back to where we'd left it hours before, like kicking a ball in another direction. "Like missing Israel but being happy to be here. Or what you said about your brother."

I nodded. "It's like an egg," I said, and she cocked her head at me. But before I could explain, the waitress brought the wine. We both stuck our noses in and inhaled, sipped. I said I couldn't think of one time I'd eaten in a restaurant like this. I'd only eaten in restaurants that were suburban copies of this very place.

She held up her finger. "But this is a copy of something French, isn't it?" she said.

"I was only saying—" I was about to answer, and the salad arrived, with a jewel of a poached egg on top.

"Oh!" Yahlie said, so loudly that I glanced around, worried we were causing a scene.

"The brain has one feeling—happy to be here—and another feeling—worried you shouldn't leave," she said. "Like an egg—one feeling is the yolk, the other is the white. I get it now."

She smiled at me and took out her camera as I raised a forkful of greens to my mouth, and snapped a picture.

"Hey," I said. "I look ridiculous."

"You look great," she said. Changing the subject, she asked, "How is your mom?"

"She doesn't like being around people, like she used to," I said. "And maybe she never will again. But surprisingly, to Danny and me, she seems almost happy."

I thought of her handing me that box. Maybe it wasn't blankness I'd seen on her face, but something more like peace. As though she could finally rest. She asked me about Danny, and I told her about his recent awful visit to the zoo. Dropped ice-cream cone, sunburn. We laughed about it for a while.

"I'm nervous about whether I'll get that job," I said. "Because, you know. That thing with my diploma."

Almost before I finished my sentence, she held her glass in my direction and said, "That whole thing? You had all those internships and temp jobs. They won't even notice."

She wasn't wrong; I had in essence quit caring that it wasn't real. And someday, I guessed, when I had some money, whenever that was, I'd finish my credits.

"It's like a video game," she said. "You were, like, one jump from level nine, then you found a secret loophole to level ten."

The waitress arrived, and we were silenced by our bowls of *moules-frites*. Her brow furrowed in a sort of wonder as she ate. I thought, Why can't this be real life? If I got the job and moved here, perhaps it would be. But doubt crept in. Maybe she would disappear, even if we lived in the same city again. The doubt was prompted by the contrast—my delight in our ease of being, against all those times she'd been silent. I pictured myself in Danny's house, with its unpainted Sheetrock and its carpet remnants, listening to the phone ring as I called her. At the time, I'd brushed aside the hurt I'd felt. Like flipping a switch, I was overtaken by a sort of bitterness, and the hurt returned.

"Did you think that about me?" I asked, abruptly.

"Think what?"

"Did you have two feelings about me?"

"What two feelings?"

"I called you all those times," I said. "But you never picked up. I thought you forgot about me."

She pricked at the bottom of her bowl with her fork. "What are the two feelings?" she asked.

"I mean that you want to see me, but you don't—you avoid me."

She ripped a crust of bread and ate it quickly. In her long pause, I could see I'd been right. She'd seen my calls. I wondered then if I'd become just someone who floated through her life. Perhaps our ease would be just one other thing that disappeared. And maybe she'd be better off without me. Or maybe I would be better off without her. Maybe she'd seen some flaw in me that I'd never see, something she could only stand some of the time. Something about me that no one else could see. I had an urge to say, *Tell me.*

I sat folding and refolding the corner of my white napkin, trying to make it into a perfect triangle. The waitress brought the check. We muddled over it, and paid.

My phone rang with Danny's number. Yahlie waved at me to answer.

Danny spoke in the combo of skepticism and optimism that I recognized. "Well," he said. "A message has been left on the machine here. It would seem those people have offered you the assistant editor position."

I must have exclaimed loudly; the waitress looked up sharply.

"I got the job," I said to Yahlie. She clapped.

On the phone, Danny said, "Not sure why they called my house and not you."

For a moment I nearly snapped back at him, Does it matter? in the spastic, irritated tone he can always pull out of me. I suppose it would have been out of habit more than anything. But just then not even he could interrupt the relief I felt.

"Dude, how should I know?" I said.

"Well, in any case," he said. "Now you must join the ranks of office drones like the rest of us."

The waitress's annoyance turned to a celebratory grin, and, although we'd already paid and finished that bottle of wine, she brought us two glasses of champagne on the house.

"I'm happy," Yahlie said. "Really."

"I am too," I said. "Really."

"And I'm sorry," she said.

"Me too."

We clinked our glasses. At last, something new.

What I remember, too, is what Danny said, right before I hung up.

"Good job, fool."

Outside, the weather had cooled at last, and we walked around the leafy neighborhood. We passed a church, its white facade almost glowing in the setting sun.

"Remember those dogs?" Yahlie said suddenly. "They ran off into the desert and we ran to look for them?"

"Oh god, in that house where we were housesitting," I said. "I think about them all the time."

"I do too!" she yelped. "Those dogs didn't have a happy life, I don't think."

"Nope," I said. "That house though—it was free."

Yahlie laughed, the sound thundering up into the trees.

"And that lady we gave a ride to. With her baby. Where were we going?"

Yahlie talked, trying to piece together which day was which. On the street, a small, burnished building sat between two hulking brownstones. I gazed into the hollow of its door.

At that moment, a man ran up to us. From inside the building across the street, into which I'd been staring.

"Excuse me," he yelled. He was rumpled and sweating, in thick glasses, and wore a harried look. "Can you please help me turn on this light?"

He pointed at the building nearby.

"I cannot turn on this light," he said. He moved toward Yahlie, reaching for her, gesturing Come.

I began to back away, feeling hassled. "Sorry, no," I said. "Let's go."

"It's Friday," the man said. He jabbed his finger upward. At the tip of the building was a turret, jutting into the sky.

Yahlie stopped.

"Oh!" she said. "It's Friday!"

The man was backing toward the building, gesturing. She ran off, following the stranger, and they entered the building.

I was about to run after them. But then, I paused. As they ran inside, the concrete, asphalt, and brick of the city fell away, and an image came to me, of Amy, rising from the driver's seat of a Honda. It was as though the contents of the box my mother had handed me had begun to move like figures on a carousel. A scene unrolled in my mind. The party. Crushed beer cans. Someone had been waiting for her. She would have switched off the ignition. The engine would have ticked a little as it cooled. She would have pressed into the car door, about to exit, to go to whomever was inside. That smile in the photo of her and the boy, the boy we'd never know.

I opened my mouth to call out to Yahlie. Walking closer, I saw what the building was: Temple Beth Israel.

It dawned on me: It was the Sabbath. The man was observing. He would do no work, he would turn on no lights. The doorway through which Yahlie had run stood open, showing a gaping dark stairwell. I grinned at Yahlie, running up those stairs into a stranger's study.

As I gazed up at the synagogue, I thought perhaps none of the people who would come in and out of our lives would know us as well as Yahlie and I knew each other right then. I allowed myself the thought that maybe this closeness wouldn't disappear. The thing that she and I had in common—the thing that made us jump on a bus, follow a stranger into the desert or up some stairs—I realized then that I shared it with my sister, too. What happened to her should have made me more careful of where I was led, and by whom. But it hadn't. It made me hopeful, made me let everyone in. Sometimes it made me cracked and hollow. But it made me know who I am. The pang returned—maybe I shouldn't move away. I'd already done so much leaving and staying and leaving and staying. My heart held two feelings, one encased in the other.

Then I chased Yahlie through that dark doorway, hoping to catch the moment when the lamp was lit.

.

SPINE

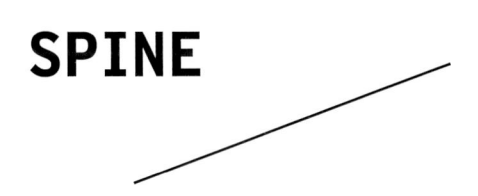

I was having problems with my shoulder, probably from using the computer too much. I was also having problems with men, cause unknown. The shoulder was unsurprising, working hunched over a computer, as I did back then, when I was in my mid-thirties, at an office in a crook of lower Midtown, on a block that seemed not so much like a street, but like an opening between buildings.

Around that time, I had to participate in the many ministrations of Yahlie's wedding. The day of her dress fitting, group emails about the plan for that evening swarmed like lions to an antelope. Yahlie asked, again and again, what time I was leaving the office, and what was the story with my plus-one?

The plan was to meet at a hulking, silver bridal shop far uptown. My reply all: See you there/then. I tried to whisk her questions and the rest of it away like crumbs, while my shoulder throbbed. There'd been two engagement parties and a wedding shower, at which I'd cleared glasses and clapped as presents were opened. Shopping for various dresses. Much discussion of what the rules were, and which she'd break. (Very few, in the end.) It was spring, just when the days began to lengthen; her wedding was in late September. She and the fiancé were constantly talking about children. Which in practicality meant I was constantly hearing about how soon she wanted to have kids, and how he was waffling. Lately she'd been relaying questions to me that she wanted him to answer. Once she'd asked, should they move to an apartment with a nursery? Inside, I barked at her, Ask him, for god's sake.

In all this it was hard not to remind her that I had once been pregnant; that I had not kept it. But that day, the pain in my shoulder that had been there for months was keeping me from thinking about anything else.

Through the sliver of window from my office cube, I could see the city's tableau of water towers and cranes and silver flashing on the roofs of other buildings, a view partially blocked by the scaffolding that had encased the building for years. My phone rang—Yahlie was calling.

"Do I need a physical therapist?" I asked her.

"Just go to your regular doctor," she said. "You getting these emails about the fitting? We have to get there at 5:30. That's the last appointment, they close at 6:30."

Her tone suggested she didn't think I'd leave work on time. She wasn't wrong. I was reliably late.

"I just replied," I said. "I'll be there. You on campus? If you're at home, we could go up together."

The apartment she shared with her fiancé was near my work. We'd meet in the park in the middle sometimes. I liked it when we did; it got me out of the office. By then I had my own list of books to acquire and an editor working under me, and would often leave very late. I'd exit when the day had entered a sort of between-time, and I'd find myself perusing some steam table at a deli, selecting the least unappetizing thing to eat, too late, as it was, to cook. Yahlie's apartment building had the feel of a newly built dorm, with its bland lobby and residents who were all about the same age. But their apartment had a terrace and a sunken living room, and I loved its warmth and clutter. We'd sit on the couch and her fiancé would clear out while we had long, rambling conversations. There was a bottle of whiskey that she'd written our names on in marker—Yahlie and Katie. We would often start talking before I took my coat off and spend half the evening standing in the kitchen with tumblers.

"I'm at school," she said. "Reading awful papers."

She was a professor at a university where the tuition was high and the students, except for the PhDs writing dissertations on stipends, were rich. The awful undergrad papers were the worst part, she said. She studied things at the intersection of the environment, politics, economics, et cetera, and wanted to do her research, wanted tenure. I often thought of her at her crowded but orderly table, writing in her miniscule handwriting. The contrast between this image and the shitty, borrowed places we'd lived in in the desert was delightful. Now I pictured her at the same table, only piled with ribbons, glassware, and metallic envelopes like Hershey bar wrappers.

"You still haven't answered about your guest," she said. "Who are you bringing? And don't say no one." In the background I heard clicking. She was probably frantically replying all. I wished for the other Yahlie.

"I'll have to let you know," I said. "Sorry."

As we hung up, I caught my reflection in the screen and smoothed a wisp of hair, which I couldn't seem to keep from looking frizzled. Waffling over the guest was absurd: I was seeing a married man. Kenneth.

Yahlie didn't know about him. I hadn't known he was married when we'd gone home together. He hadn't been wearing his ring; he'd slipped it off. He'd put it back on the next morning.

"Ah," I'd said, from the bed, the sheet pulled over my shoulders. "That wasn't very nice, taking that off like that."

"We're not doing well," he said. "We're taking a break, I guess."

"Naturally," I said, hearing the thickness of the pronoun: *we*.

I thought he might take my nonplussed response as a signal that I wasn't interested. He was another book person; he worked for a competitor, which was how I met him. I was introduced to him at some bookfair party at which we wore plastic nametags around our necks. He made even that look alluring, wore it flung like a set of dog tags. His blondish hair was often mussed, except when he combed it neat like a Dartmouth student. He had a dilettante air, and the circles under his eyes suggested he'd been out all night, somewhere better, probably because he had. He wore tweed pants and oxford loafers. He didn't take the hint that first night, and called me anyway. I can still remember the delicious, tawdry rush that arose when he phoned. His calls made me grin; I wanted those calls. I was letting myself go after what I wanted.

That drive was working. I kept getting promoted at the office. But the amount of work kept outpacing the promotions. So I was wanting other things. Our regular affair had been going on for several months, and I craved it still.

Once, he'd invited me to go to a museum and we spent an afternoon looking at de Koonings. I'd enjoyed it. I liked him.

Even still, I probably should have stopped kidding myself: I would bring no guest. Reaching for the keyboard, a twinge ran through my shoulder. I picked up the phone and called my doctor.

Naturally, Yahlie was right. I didn't leave early enough to make it there by half past five. Some task had to be completed. And of course, I had to smoke a cigarette in the park. I should have been able to go straight there, but I couldn't—even though I knew this would make me even later. Sometimes the only thing I could think of to make the transition from work to anything else was a solitary cigarette. I exited, passing under the scaffolding that blocked the building's gold awning and dripped cloudy water perpetually, even when it wasn't raining. I had a vague memory of two small brass pillars that had once stood by the entrance, their tops filled with sand for extinguishing cigarettes. The sinking afternoon sun cast a glare up Fifth Avenue against the side of the Flatiron Building. I put on my sunglasses and headed to the park. In the center of the park's oval meadow was a sculpture that I often gazed at. Three gleaming silver spires, like fingers. I needed a moment before entering the wedding vortex.

Much of it had little to do with me. And yet hearing about all the details, it did. I liked the man she was marrying. He was a classic trust funder, and I could never remember from what this fortune extended. Furs? Gherkins? Maybe I thought gherkins because of the engagement party, where, during the endless toasts, I drank glass after glass of champagne, looking down into a dish of cut cucumbers. He was declining the trappings of the wealth—he worked, for one. He owned a beloved antique shop, was hip and disorganized and their apartment was filled with beautiful objects they'd both collected. I think they fell in love over recycling. His mother, who Yahlie found irksome, lived on Central Park West.

The park was fairly empty and I sat on a bench in the shade. I found my cigarettes in my shoulder bag and rummaged for matches. They were not there; I pawed inside, shuffling every item. Not finding the matches, the things I had in there seemed stupid. Half a dozen partially stamped loyalty cards from coffee shops? Bug repellant? Nail polish? All my useless possessions swelled up around me and I grew heated.

It was 5:02—I should have skipped the cigarette altogether. But, no, I thought. Not today. I scanned for someone smoking.

Nearby, a man in a ball cap leaned over a book. He flicked some ash. I stood and went to him. As I did, he dropped the cigarette and lightly crushed it with his sneaker.

"Pardon me," I said. "I'm sorry to bother you, but may I borrow a light?"

He half-glanced toward me, reached into his back pocket, and pulled out a gray lighter. He rotated it in his palm, so that its red plastic switch was under his thumb.

"Can you *borrow* a light?" he said. It was not a laughing tone, but rather, a critique. A truck passed, a crashing sound, interrupting the gentle-sounding waves of traffic. I leaned down, he flicked the lighter, its flare arose.

It was right then—those two, in sequence, the sound of the truck, and the nearly silent flick of the lighter—that I was flooded with a fleeting embarrassment at being mocked by a stranger, and with a crashing sense that this was not a stranger who was lighting my cigarette. I knew this man.

This was the father of the baby I had not kept.

I had known this man's very fibers through to my own. He'd not been a man. We were children. In that instant, I was transported to that pungent moment of peace, when he was merely a stranger on a bus, when I didn't yet know him. Before my whole life had been colored by him, his greenish eyes, the slope of his shoulders, by the primal, animal quality of him. Before we became fused, like barnacles to a ship. Even though the time I spent with him was a few short months, that time had always rippled in the background of my mind's eye, whether I desire it or not. As I saw his thumb, pressing the lighter's notch, I knew that fusing had happened all in one moment, fifteen years before, at the moment when that bus collided with a buck, decimating it, and he turned to me as he gripped the armrest of my seat. I knew it because when he raised the lighter, I thought that fusing would happen again. I thought I would become swept outward once more. All he would have had to do was look at me.

Wes.

But he was looking at the end of my cigarette.

His eyes were obscured by the hat's brim. In the second that it took me to breathe in, for the tobacco to ignite, for the orange tip to begin to glow, a doubt crept in. Surely it wasn't him. This was a trick of memory, just a feeling brought on by the wedding, surely. I was overthinking the unhappy state of my own love life. I mumbled a polite thank you and the flame flicked off. He put the lighter back in his pocket, and I backed away, turned, walked to the more vacant side of the park. I began to circle the playground. I passed a kid bouncing a basketball and sipping a red drink, a woman in sneakers with a pair of pumps in her hand.

The last time I'd seen him was in a rental on the fringe of the Mission with doors painted in cracking brown paint.

The building's entrance opened onto the back of a gas station's parking lot where the ground underfoot always held the slight slickness of motor oil. The last time I saw him, he walked out. He was impermanent then, I was impermanent. I never saw him again. It had flung me into a period of nervous wandering, until I met Yahlie. For a time, she'd been my home.

In the brief time it took me to circle the playground, the image of his thumb appeared, flicking the lighter—the straight, deep line where the fingernail ended, the sharp, square cut— and I knew. It was him. It was no trick of memory. Had he not even recognized me? Then again, I did look different—I wasn't the twig I'd been when we'd met. And I was wearing the sunglasses, which I hastily took off, like removing a disguise, and shoved in my overfull bag. The past stretched out ahead of me like a canvas unrolling, and pinned to it was a future where I had not backed away, had taken the steps backward to see: Would he pull me in, as he once had? The people near me—the boy with his red drink, the woman carrying her shoes—they could not know they were in this map of two futures, one where I let him drift away into their nameless number, and another where I returned, where I faced him.

I felt an unseen force propel me forward, saying, You walked away once. I quickened my step, toward where he'd sat.

Just as he came into view, he turned over his book and closed it. He slowly stood and jammed one hand in the pocket of his jeans. I quavered—it was in the rise of him, the arc in his arm, that gesture. Then he removed his hat. Even at that distance, I could see. The dark brow, the deep eyes. He walked away, his head turned toward the three silver spires.

He began to walk quicker, exiting the park into the swarm of people who were crossing in and out of the shadow of the Flatiron Building, and began walking down Broadway. I could still feel the cadence of his distinctive step—a raise onto the tip of his foot—from holding his hand. My hesitation had been long enough for him to be nearly out of my view. As I tried to keep up with him, we passed through the neighborhood, which was so familiar to me—the overpriced Italian restaurant with sidewalk tables where I went with the few coworkers I could stand to have a drink with. The deli where the cashier from Lebanon in her headscarf often stood smoking out front. Wes reached for the bins of flowers out front, brushing his hand through petals. His urge to reach for the greenest thing in sight. With him so close, the streets became unfamiliar, as though I'd entered a new map.

He approached Union Square, its grid of hexagon tiles strewn with people. A man selling flying toys pulled a cord and one flung into the air. As Wes waited at the light, watching it float to the ground, I thought I would catch him. But the light changed, and he entered the crowd and turned down Fourth Avenue. Quickly, that became the East Village and its smoky, hawking mess.

His shape was the same as it had been fifteen years ago. A sloping triangle. Only now it was not hidden in loose, careless clothes. How I had loved knowing the shape of his body beneath those clothes. Everything he had seemed worn, muddy, as though he'd just stepped from a long walk along a brook in spring. The brownish apartment, the last place we were together, with blocks of glass that lined the bathroom and ceilings so high that they always seemed full of fog. The house in Noe Valley that we stayed in, borrowed from his cousin, with its white gate, and a view of the bay from the bed.

The way you said certain words: *bag*, the trace of the Midwest in your voice, the *a* turning the word to *beg*. I wonder if you still have it. Or if you ever went back.

Somehow I knew he hadn't. The farther we walked downtown, the more loudly the things I'd never said to him churned through my mind. You left me alone, you left me no choice. It was as though the old me, the one I'd been when I met him—frightened, frozen, yearning—overtook who I'd become. Whatever strength I had to raise my voice and call out to him was slipping from me—no, I told myself, and walked quicker.

But then, just past the bakery at the corner of Eleventh, he made a left, jogging across the street. I was trapped, waiting for the light to change as cars streamed past, and he slipped from view.

At last, I was able to cross and walked faster until I could see him. I wanted to catch him, to call out to him. And yet, I wanted to keep him, suspended, in my sight and memory. He passed botanicas, basketball courts, a graveyard, as if he knew his way. Through Tompkins Square Park, he gazed at the chess players—he would have admired their skill, but for him it was too dull. He needed movement. I was almost close enough for him to hear me—I took a breath, about to shout. So often I had thought of him saying my name in his soft, dusky voice. But now I thought of him turning toward me, mouth opening to answer me, and I pictured not the face I'd dreamed of so often, but one that was ghostly, wide-mouthed and fearsome, and his name caught in my throat.

He turned a corner, and another, and then we were on Avenue C.

We were the only two people on the block, which was mostly occupied by a school. *Now*, I thought. *Now*. At the school's end was a small string of apartments, and he climbed the stairs of the last one. He dug in his pocket, unlocked the door. He was about to disappear into the building. No. Wait. I was too far away to catch him before he was gone from view. I ran, hoping to catch the door before it locked me out forever. But the latch clicked behind him.

I was only able to catch a glimpse of him, through the window in the door of the crotchety building, climbing a set of tilted stairs painted a dull red.

I squinted through the window, crossed with security wires, at the mailbox. His name was not there. *Damn*, I screamed at myself inside.

I pushed all the door buzzers, one at a time. Half of them didn't ring—busted. One person answered, a woman, who shouted into the intercom, "Yes?"

"Is Wes there?" I answered.

"Who?" she said.

As I stood on the steps, staring at the fading paint and the steel cage of trash, thinking what to do, it came to me—the dress fitting.

I scrambled for my phone in my bag. As I did, my shoulder wrenched hard. I cried out in pain.

Yahlie didn't answer her phone. It was 6:24. The store was about to close. I'd missed the whole thing.

I see myself standing in the crisp shadow cast by the awning of the building across the street, looking in every window, for lights, for shadows moving. In the end, he never came out.

When I returned to my neighborhood, on the border of an industrial zone in Brooklyn, I couldn't face my apartment alone. I'd lived there for years, a stunted railroad with a bricked-over fireplace in its kitchen. On the building's first floor was a bar where I spent an inordinate amount of time. I went in.

The place had a wooden ceiling and a rotating cast of bartenders, all of whom I knew well. The corner chair I liked was occupied, so I settled for one pressed against the window and ordered a whiskey and let it and the empty recognition of the bartender's greeting nurse me.

My phone buzzed. It was Kenneth.

Hey I'm in your neighborhood, the tiny message said. *What are you up to?*

There was a time when the appearance of his name on my phone would make the space between my legs feel hard. I had always answered. But right then, it only made me feel exhausted. An image arose of Wes's olive skin, his chest, rippled yet hollow, on a bed in a dim room. His dark brown hair grown out. As he put his hands on my hips, his top lip curled into a snarl, and his chipped tooth, like a fang.

I jabbed at my phone, and sat shredding the wet napkin around my drink with my fingertips. I took a long, sharp gulp. The ice tinkled—almost empty. The music had grown loud. The bartender came to me smiling, shouting.

"What?" I said, and he didn't answer, only refilled my glass.

I knew where it would lead with Kenneth that evening. I would fall into it like tripping into an empty pool. I should just go over and apologize to Yahlie, I thought. Maybe she hadn't answered because the fitting was a ringing success, it was a white that would show off her tan skin perfectly, and even the mother-in-law loved it. I picked up the phone again and found Kenneth's text, pressed the tiny trash can. I scrolled to Yahlie's name and called. No answer.

As I hung up, I heard a voice softly speak my name. A man's voice. No, I thought, you're dreaming. But then there was a tapping on the window from the outside. I started—it was Kenneth. His face was covered in fuzz that he must have been growing the last few days, and the streetlamp made his dark eyes look racoonish.

"Oh, fine," I said, into the air.

He strode around the corner with his wide, slack steps, flung open the door.

"I thought I'd find you here," he said, taking the stool in the cramped unoccupied space next to me.

"Here I am," I said.

He rested his elbows on the bar, sleeves brushing his skinny wrists. I'd taken him here once before. I suppose he'd gleaned that this was my place. He signaled to the bartender with an upward nod of his chin, with that magic power he had to become the center of any attention to anyone who could bring him a drink.

He looked at me over his arms. "Sup," he said.

He was flirting. Teasing.

"What are you doing down here?" I said.

"Oh, this and that," he said. We never did this, talking about our day. The bartender brought his whiskey, and as he lifted it to sip, I saw his left hand. He'd removed his ring.

We sat drinking our drinks for a moment. And then he kissed me, that way he had, that we had—stolen.

At that point of our few months together, things had just begun to have a hint of the routine. We'd sit somewhere like strangers, saying nothing of consequence, as if we were seeing each other for the first time, until one of us would be unable to resist any longer and we'd kiss each other like we were throwing open doors. But as I felt the heat of his hands, I slowly pushed back.

He didn't say anything at first. He only took another drink.

"You okay?" he said.

"I screwed up," I said.

"That's you, a total screwup," he said, teasing. "How so?"

"I missed my friend's thing," I said. "I was supposed to be there. But then—"

With one hand he stroked his beard, with the other he made a gesture as if to say, then what?

"Something happened, I never made it. I got derailed."

I hesitated, squeezing my glass.

"It was for her wedding. Her dress fitting."

He stopped stroking his beard.

"It was my fault," I said. "Now she's not answering her phone."

He mumbled that he was sorry. He stared into the bottles on the bar, rubbing the fingers of his left hand.

We never talked about it—his marriage. We had our ritual. And I had never asked. His shoulders hunched, and he dropped his head. I realized then that I'd been too weak to ask, that I didn't want to know. And I realized too, as he stared into his lap, that if I pressed, he would want me—not his wife. I would only have to want him. But I didn't. I took his hand from his cocktail. It was damp from the chilly glass.

He jerked his head up and said, "Come on. You think because you're talking about a wedding I'm going to get all worked up?" He leaned in again, into my neck, and kissed. "Come on, let's not worry about all that."

His pencil-thin lips touched my skin in little, preening kisses. We'd had this shared space between us that was perilous, but also, an illusion. All at once, I was revulsed by it. As though a bad smell that had slowly been creeping in had wafted at me full force. That space, the one between us, just then, I could inhabit it no longer.

Even still, even though I was certain I was barely hiding my revulsion, he wanted to go upstairs. I sent him home.

On the sidewalk, he began hailing a cab, his arm swinging stiffly, as if doing semaphore. He looked small, rumpled. I glanced over my shoulder as I walked away, to see if one had stopped for him. He was looking at his phone and dabbed at his nose with one hand.

At home I called Yahlie. I sat with one lamp on, the rest dark, still with my coat on. I often did this—I would enter the apartment and stay with the day on me, my coat, my bag, my shoes, as though home was merely some way station between the end of one day and the beginning of the next.

She finally answered.

"Where were you?"

"I—"

I tried to find the words to tell her.

"You what?"

"It's kinda complicated."

"Complicated? What does that mean?"

"That's the wrong word. Maybe I mean it's complex. You'd understand—"

"I'd understand? I don't think so. I had to choose without you. I needed you," she said. "But I guess whatever you were doing was more important."

And she hung up.

"But—" I said, into the phone, which was already dead.

Wait, I wanted to say. I've been at every damn thing.

I went to the kitchen and poured myself another drink.

It's funny to think how the day would have unfolded if I hadn't insisted on smoking. If I wasn't a workaholic, fending off task after task like a dog. If I hadn't learned, slowly, to paste over the tedious, frantic work with one, single cigarette. If I had been a more selfless friend, a more organized person.

If, if, if.

Another drink was absurd. I did not need another drink. I raised it to my mouth, and as I tilted my head to swallow, the pain in my shoulder rang through my whole skull. The glass slipped from my hand. I didn't even try to grab it. I only watched it shatter on the linoleum.

The next day, I did what I'd been doing for years: I threw myself at my job, where I was competent to an exaggerated degree. I had to run some terrible meeting—I was in no shape to be in charge of anything—but I showed up with a stack of crisply printed agendas, which I furiously passed out. A hissing stream of heartburn shot through my chest. I could taste it. And yet I drank more coffee and ate next to nothing. The intern came to ask me something, and I was so sharp with her that a crease formed between her eyebrows and her chin trembled. She was the niece of an old friend of mine who worked in foreign rights.

Wait, I'm sorry! I wanted to call after her. But I didn't even do that. I think of it now and I picture myself flung against the desk, punching keys.

When I thought of Yahlie and the wedding, I grew angry. I'd been there to discuss every miniscule decision. How had my friend of twenty years become demanding, wanting me at her beck and call? The way she'd used that word: *important*. I heard it again and my stomach cramped, as though it was being squeezed through a tube.

I was thinking of anything that would keep me from thinking about how I'd been only a few feet from Wes. And I had not said one word. My mind sank like an oar, and toward the end of the afternoon, I lay my head on the desk.

In the quiet, the computer whirring in the background, I finally grasped that all this time, beneath the bare facts, lay a heap of sentences that I yearned to hurl at him: I had a life connected to you, with all the potential that contained, a life I hoped could let me jettison my past. When you disappeared, you destroyed that hope, like it meant nothing to you. And you never knew.

I jerked my head up off the desk, sending shooting pain up my shoulder. I stood and grabbed my things.

Someone was at the door, wanting something. "Kate, could you—?"

"Later," I said.

Outside I began to retrace the path through the city. I'd ring the broken buzzers and wait on the steps if I had to. I plunged forward, through Union Square, which today seemed polluted and damp and shifty, across the crowded sidewalks of St. Marks, the smoke of hookah and exhaust giving way to the perfumed incense of boutiques, and I made my way to Avenue C.

As I made a line to that battered rowhouse, I had every intention of saying the words that had finally come to me. I barreled on, steeling myself against seeing Wes's face in anger, or of an indifferent smile, or as a ghostly mask.

But then, before I came to the house, a figure entered the boundary of my sight. Of all the people on the street, who rushed or strolled to work or school or a bodega or into rooms and buildings I'd never know, of all of these people, my mind caught this one.

I stood, frozen, as he turned a corner, gone from view.

The trace of humid mist in the air obscured his figure somewhat. But it was Wes. He walked on the opposite side of the street, back in the direction from which I'd just come. He was carrying a duffel bag—I could tell it was him by from the way he held it. Gripping the two handles across his right shoulder, his back bearing the bag's weight. It was how he'd carried anything. The bounce in his step tamed only slightly by the weight of the bag. For a split second, he glanced to one side. I could picture his smile that could be as sinister as it was seductive, and in that instant, a shard of hesitation crept in. And his hands—the flex of the muscle between his index finger and his thumb, the tension of his grip. He had always insisted on carrying everything. Although he was thin, he was strong, and he seemed to gather everything he needed into a bundle around him, ready to stand and leave. It'd been his way in the world. He was, at his heart, a drifter.

It dawned on me—he was leaving. This was it. I'd seen it, many times.

I made a hairpin turn and followed him.

In my final moment of hesitation, he'd walked up the street. He raised his arm—he was hailing a cab, his back to me. Just then was a moment of stillness. As he looked into the direction of traffic, a cab drifted to him and stopped.

He turned. I took a breath, about to call to him. But then he opened taxi's door, and as he did, he froze. He lifted his head, and saw me. His face had grown rounder, a shape that made it almost plaintive. There was the small, wine-colored birthmark, like a spot of dried blood, on the bridge of his nose. I was looking into the deep hollow of his hazel eyes.

In that instant I was transported back to a dark San Francisco street, when he had opened the door to a black Volvo for me, and that door had stood between us momentarily, like a barrier at a checkpoint. *Get in*, he'd said, *I'm waiting*. And I did, even though I never should have. Then, I'd only been able to summon a half-hearted attempt to walk away from him. Now, the door to the taxi was not between us—it was open.

I had readied myself to see his face once more. But until that moment I did not know that I would be ready to hear him say my name. I thought that if I heard him call to me, in that dusky voice, which had once signaled to me both shelter and harm, I would turn and follow him anywhere.

"Katie," he said.

In the short silence that followed, I was seized by a current, urging me to slip into the stream he was in. But in that moment a speck of something I can only describe as power expanded in my mind. The furious words I had longed to say to him turned quiet. And the sound of my name began to clang, a warning. I decided, for once and for all, to listen—it was saying, *Halt*.

I turned on my heel and walked the length of the sidewalk away from him. Briefly, I halted.

"Katie."

I began walking away, and I did not turn.

I walked back through Tompkins Square Park. A noise arose, of chants, drums. The square was thronged with protestors and a sea of black and red banners on sticks. A springing rage filled the air, giving off heat.

Justice, justice, they called.

I went to Yahlie's apartment. She didn't answer the buzzer, but the doorman was in the lobby vacuuming. He recognized me and opened the door.

When I rang Yahlie's bell, she answered. She stared at me through the inch she'd opened the door, the corners of her mouth down. She let me in.

She sat down at the table where she worked. Amid her papers, a large white wicker basket sat, filled with objects and more papers, with a gold ribbon on its handle. She ignored me and began clicking at her laptop, the silvery screen glowing back at her. She was in the black suit jacket she often wore when she had to teach. Her hair was different. She'd decided to grow it out for the wedding, from the short cut she'd worn since she'd chopped it off to delete a bad dye job. Now it had grown to a new shape, an oval around her face.

"Hey, so," I said. "Thanks for letting me in."

She didn't answer. Her finger clicking the touch pad grew quicker.

"Listen," I said, taking a step closer. "I'm sorry I didn't show up for you. I wish that you'd picked up so I could tell you what happened. I'm really sorry."

She flicked her eyes toward me, hollowed by the glare of the screen, a hard, cold look. I felt a jolt of how cutting she could be when she was angry, how that warmth of hers could disappear like a sparkler being stomped out.

"I need to tell you what happened," I said.

She grasped a piece of her hair, now long enough for her to nervously shove behind her ear. She shrugged.

"Okay," she said. "Tell it."

"Remember how I was that summer? The summer we met. You took me to the clinic."

She began rifling papers, fidgeting with them noisily, and shoving them inside the already overflowing basket like files.

"There were all those people with signs. They said—"

She paused, seeming to slip into memory. "Murder. The signs read murder."

I swallowed hard. "Yesterday when I was on my way to the bridal shop, I was in the park, and—"

"And?" Yahlie said, a hint of tenderness returning to her voice, her face softening some.

"I saw him. The father."

Her hands froze amid the files. "I followed him," I said. "He disappeared into some building and I waited for him. But he never came out. By the time I realized what time it was, I was too late."

The pain in my shoulder pressed again, like a needle about to puncture my skin.

"I'm sorry I wasn't there. I didn't mean to miss it," I said. "He got in a cab, he was leaving."

Her arms were crossed over her chest in a tight squeeze, and she was holding an object plucked from the basket—a small, silver tube covered in shiny flowers. Gripping it she raised it to her lip, held like a pen, like I'd seen her do a thousand times. Until, at last, her face softened into pity.

"The way you said that, though," I said. "*Important*. How what I was doing was more important. Are we always going to be in a war about whose thing is more important?"

She sighed, in that way that meant she agreed with me and wasn't going to argue. "I know," she said. "I shouldn't have said that. We'll have to try not to be at war."

"Remember the week you took me to the clinic?" I said. "When we were staying in that weird house?"

"You made us that delicious dinner one night. That was a fun day. We went to the riverbed and shot arrows, and you were so good at it."

"But remember we fought about the dinner. I was horrible that day."

She slowly uncrossed her arms and brushed the piece of hair to her ear once more.

"It was a good reason to be horrible," she said. "It's over now."

The way she said it, she was not comforting me. She was saying, You missed it. We faced each other in silence for a moment, until at last I asked—what happened with the dress?

"All my friends—" she said, "and his mother—they all had so many opinions that in the end I couldn't care anymore."

She had clutched the silver tube again and was twisting it in her hand. All of a sudden, she flung it toward the full wicker basket and missed. Down it went, hitting the table's edge with a sharp rap. She picked it up and held it delicately, gazing down at it in her fingertips. Then she exhaled deeply, put her hands over her face, and began to cry.

"His mother," she said. "She thinks I'm doing everything all wrong. And I just realized, he agrees with her."

When she took her hands away, a great globe tear spilled over her black lashes.

"Maybe he isn't the person I thought he was," she said. "But I don't think I could walk away. If I lost him, I'd die."

I did lose him, I thought, I lost him, and more. And I did die. But even back then, I knew he could be no father. I had spared us a bad fate. And I resurrected. So would she.

I didn't say all this. I took her hand and held it, and told her it was all going to be okay.

I tried to get her to show me the dress. She wiped away the tears, and brought out the zipped bag, a luxuriant, shiny satin, but didn't open it. Instead, she went to the kitchen and opened a cabinet. "I know what will fix this!" she said, and took out the bottle of Old Overholt with our names on it.

As we drank at her counter, she still held the silver tube.

"What is that thing?" I said.

"A confetti cannon. You give them to the guests," she said, and looked down at it in disgust. "You know what I kind of want to do? Shoot this."

We threw open the door to the terrace and leaned out into the damp night air. Yahlie shoved up the sleeves of her jacket and picked at the label on the tube.

"So," she said. "Plus-one?"

I shook my head, and she looked relieved.

"Can you imagine me giving these out?" she said. "They shoot *plastic*. Why does one have to burn so much oil to have a wedding?"

"I can upcycle my dress," I said. "Turn it into sofa cushions."

She had finally gotten the tube open and aimed it out over the skyline. "If it shot flower petals it would be better," she said.

Just then, my memory pitched me backward, to my mother in the basement of our suburban house, long vacated, counting seeds for her flower beds. Once, she'd found me down there, looking at our family photo albums. How frightened I'd been to ask her about what I'd found there. *Put those away*, she'd said, wrapping her robe tighter.

Yahlie pulled its silvery string and it exploded open with a pop. The air filled with pink and gold plastic flakes, and Yahlie's laugh. Her loudest laugh. Bright caws, bursting into the air like fireworks.

As we watched the plastic float to the ground, she asked, "What's his name? I don't think I ever knew it."

I was suddenly too warm; spring was coming. I felt bound in my coat. I took it off, hung it on the railing. Yahlie picked a fleck of gold plastic from its sleeve.

"Wes," I said. And then I began telling her about that day on the bus.

As I left Yahlie's, I fumbled through my bag and lit a cigarette. In all of this, I somehow managed to get another lighter and not lose it. How organized of me. As I hoisted the bag, my shoulder jerked so hard that I gasped and doubled over.

That same week I saw Wes, I sat at the conference room table, impatient for the afternoon meeting to start, so it could end. I had to leave for the doctor's appointment for my shoulder. Words blinked on and off the video screen: *Wrong SPID on*

Line 6. My coworkers filed in, and the meeting began. Production schedules. Riders to contracts. I answered a dozen questions. Yes. Absolutely. Absolutely not! My voice sounded calm, even as things became mildly heated, disorderly. Their questions sounded like villagers shouting in the town square, until at last there was a lull.

"I think that's enough for today," I said. I took my things and left the room.

I went downstairs for a cigarette. On the street, a cabbie leaned on his horn. A woman's high heels clicked. I did not walk to the park; I couldn't go there again. I stood in front of the building instead. The doorman who worked the evening shift appeared. He and I were often friendly, owing to my frequently being there so late. He carried an enormous floral arrangement. He grinned at me, and said, "Not for me."

We laughed for a moment, and then he handed off the flowers to a delivery guy, and said to me, "Have a great afternoon, Kate."

In all that time, I'd never known he knew my name.

"You too, Louie."

When he was gone the traffic quieted momentarily. I gulped a breath of fresh air, and it was as though the scent of flowers lingered in my nose, mingling with woodsy smoke. I looked down, and saw a tiny dish of sand atop a gold receptacle. Like a pillar. I gazed into it, and, all at once, I saw an old me. I can't even think of her as if she is also me, which, of course, she is. She is floating alongside me, twenty-one and living nowhere.

There was no way she could have kept that little life. She would have stood at the sink of a rest station bathroom in the desert, washing the feet of the baby, changing a diaper, strapping the baby into a car seat she bought at St. Vincent's thrift store.

I was, in that moment, filled with wonder at having become someone other than who I was at twenty-one, and at the same time, remorse. The two feelings—joy at my good fortune, and the remorse—lay cradled together, two open books, resting one on top of the other.

All of a sudden the cigarette tasted terrible, like mud, leaves. I put it out in the sand.

I looked up and saw the gold awning of the building—something was different. Why were these gold pillars familiar? Had they always been there? No, I realized, they had returned. Abruptly I glanced around, at the dry sidewalk, the unblemished sand, the bright metal, and realized what was new. At last, the scaffolding was gone.

At the doctor's appointment, I had an X-ray. Then I sat in an exam room until the doctor arrived, a fit man with string bracelets on his wrist, as though he'd just come from summer camp.

"Let's see what we have here," he said. He moved my arm a hundred different ways, not reacting when I winced.

"I see," he said, his rubber shoes squeaking as he turned. "Ever had problems with this before?"

"Just since last winter," I said. "I'm sure it's from working at the computer."

"Uh-huh," he said, skepticism in his voice. "It's not your shoulder. It's your upper back."

He pointed to the X-ray. "You have a deformity there. The insertion angle in this joint—well—it's not great," he said. "It's putting pressure toward your spine where it's not supposed to."

He named other things—ligament length, cartilage deterioration, arthritis. I should really know this, but I don't. In the moment, I tuned out. I asked what I should do.

"Listen," he said, as though I'd misunderstood. "You can't cure this. The ligament is inflamed because every time you move, the extension is wrong. The only thing we can do is manage your pain. You put it off for a while. I'm surprised it's never hurt before. That's, really—I don't know."

They'd do an MRI to be sure, he said, but for now the only thing was a steroid injection, and he sent me to another, dimmer room, where a nurse instructed me to lie face down, staring at the dark gray floor. I must have nodded off. Maybe I was dreaming. But suddenly I was on my back, and a pain arose in my lower abdomen.

A voice said, *You won't feel anything in a moment.*

WARNING SIGN

That night, the dogs run off. We're afraid to look for them; fear we'll find buried wedding dresses, the skeletons of mammoths, Billy the Kid's grave marker. My tan-armed friend has a housesitting job in Galisteo, some friend of hers roped her into it. That night she calls. *Come stay with me out here, it's darker than Russian coffee and the dogs keep barking at something. The other night the neighbor from I swear three miles away came across the piñon to say hello, just to say hello.* After my shift I drive out there on Highway 14 with the windows down, dusk coming in, past the prison. Sign out there that says "do not pick up hitchhikers." I am trying to fly out the window. Sky can't consume us whole. Or can it. I may wake and find I'm Jonah in the whale.

It's earth that scares me. It's the sound of my tires on her driveway, the sun's devilish colors. She's in the doorway of a busted house when I get there, and the dogs, Chulo and Rocky or whatever their absent owner named them, are furious. Chulo's little with spots, Rocky, something like mastiff and Labrador, is red all over.

She comes out to greet me holding an oven mitt, she is raiding the pantry, boiling water. She takes my bag, leaves it on the carpet to attract dog hair. We find we're peaceful and manic. *Rule is you can't leave the bathroom door open or the dogs will get in,* she says. *I cleaned in there, but no place else. This woman's shit is amazing. We'll have to clear a landing strip. That bathroom, it'll be our safe haven.*

The dogs lick and lick. *Sorry about the dogs,* she says. *These dogs need love. The girl left me these complicated instructions. She said there's a cage out there for them, but I can't find it. They just lick my feet, they won't stop.*

Who would put these dogs in a cage? I say.

I reach down and try to pet Rocky, the lumbering red one, but he shakes his head and flings my torso full of spit. He steps on my foot and through my boot it feels like the tip of an old man's cane.

Hey watch it, fatso, I say.

Just let him be, she says.

We clean up this woman's kitchen and marvel at her spices. Three half-empty containers of something with no label. My friend laughs, sticks out her arms, aghast. *Who knew she was such a slob*, she says. But who are we to talk, two professional dirtbags. Living in our shitty casita in town, passing cans of Mexican beer and odd jobs back and forth. We fix a bowl of boiled noodles and eat standing in the doorway, trying to fend off the dogs, listening for the neighbor approaching. Then we hear that no one is coming but crickets. We go to the patio and sit on crusty wicker chairs, drinking soda, bantering, only the bugs zoom and there's no beer. We wander through the cluttered rooms, laugh at the one sullen cactus in a terra-cotta pot.

Like we need any more cactuses, I say.

Cacti, she says.

I'm uneasy among this woman's stuff, gym clothes, computer, pile of sheet music, and the waning light coming in from somewhere, except I can't find the windows. *Dogs, quit,* my friend says. Chulo pouts.

Then they hear something we can't hear—then they're gone, out the open door. They flee through the piñon, Rocky with his haunches rippling like a thoroughbred. We step out into the driveway, looking for the source of their fear, our banter halted, sodas dangling from our hands. I imagine a man dragging a murdered bride toward us, or a hawk materializing overhead, a strange car with a chainsaw engine pulling onto the gravel driveway. I want to grab her arm, say *Leave the bags, let's go, now.* Then Chulo, the little dog—he slams on his brakes for a moment, turns to look at us, *Why aren't you fleeing the monster too?* Then he disappears into the brush.

We stand in silence, till her soda bubbles. *Where'd you go? Damn dogs.* She's afraid, arm bent up as if warding off glare, even though the sun's gone. Her sweater falls from her waist, she calls and calls. They're really gone. She looks at me. *What if they don't come back? Where will we find them? We might have to go look for them.* I want to plead: *What is that thing we don't hear?* Her feet crunch on the gravel, I stare at my knees. *You hear anything?* she asks.

I shake my head no, and I want to flee too, hop in the car and head for the brightest gas station with no red-rock dust in sight. We're not on this planet. We're buried beneath it. I feel like a kid who just watched a horror movie at a slumber party and craves candy.

I think they'll come back. But if they don't we'll have to go find them. It wouldn't be that hard. We could grab long pants from our bags.

I'm not going out there, I say. *Maybe we could go get the neighbor. I heard once that in South America you shouldn't approach a quiet house in the country 'cause you'll startle whoever's inside. You have to clap first, from three miles away. Maybe he's on his way. Maybe they heard him clapping.*

She looks back at me, her arm drops anchor. *Where the hell did you get that?* she says. Then she's laughing, sucking air through her nose. But the dogs are lost. *We have to find them,* she says. *I'm going out there.*

She is the brave one now, even though I am the one who smacks a roach in our casita and tells the guy who comes up to us in the bar wanting to kiss our hands to fuck off. She is thinking only of the dogs, their licking, scattering their needy drool all over the ground like chicken feed. I am thinking of a lurching car, rolling silently into this driveway, and the fear tastes rich like sopaipillas and grilled ribs.

Fine, fine. I say. We forget about the long pants, tromp out into the field, the earth burying our booted feet. My eyes open up wide as Niagara Falls. She is the kid who'll open the basement door and search for the monster. She gets ahead of me, feet straight on, crushing the brush. We walk for a while, calling, *Chulo, Rocky, here boy.* She veers left, then starts to run, like she sees them. *Wait! Don't run off, I'll get lost out here!* I yell. I lose her over the bushes. The earth sucks up all the noise. I catch my leg on a piñon branch. *Shit.* It's almost dark, sky turning a leathery brown.

Hey! I yell. Nothing.

Hey, where the fuck are you? I say. I look behind me and can't see the house, can't see anything but the brush. I near the tree line. I am about to be lost. But no, all I have to do is turn back, I think. Then my foot chinks on something metal in the dirt. I look down and the tip of my boot is against a grommet in the sand, a metal line threaded through it. In front of me is a cage. But it's like a circus cage, a square of solid steel bars, bolted down by steel cables, big enough for a grizzly bear. Inside are leather leashes, dangling. I step closer and on the ground inside is a rusted chain. A stream of something sets itself moving in my chest, like creosote burning. I put the tips of my fingers on the steel and it's as cold as the lip of a dead man.

In the distance I hear a roar. The dogs? An 18-wheeler flying off the highway? I have to find my way back. Then I hear her voice, its squeak.

Hear them? she says.

I see her head over the piñon. She is not lost. *Let's go back, they'll come back*, she says.

So we tromp back to the house. When we return it's flooded by dark, except for the eerie porch light throwing out a dirty yellow haze. We wait for them.

You scared? Look at your leg.

On my calf is a red slash, blood dripping like tree sap. I look at it and it starts to throb with a familiar pain.

Did you find the cage? she says.

I can't tell her that I found the cage and that my knees are trembling, that I can almost feel the meaty, gnashing jaws of a dog clamped around my leg. I can't tell her about the cage, because then she'll want to go look for it. She'll be her fearless self. I'll be here alone.

Nope, I say. *I don't think there's any cage out there. Who would put those dogs in a cage. It would be impossible to put those dogs in a cage.*

We stand there, feet sinking into the ground, looking to the limit of the porch light, like the dogs are there, just out of sight, watching.

Guess it doesn't matter, she says. *Because I don't have the key.*

We call out to the dogs one last time but they don't heed. Nothing arrives, no car, no neighbor. Then we find there's no coffee for the morning either, and we realize we can talk ourselves out of anything, rise up from under the ground. It's clairvoyance, the power to escape. We are on the patio with a porch light and the coffee sky. We sit around, wade through the mess, try to string a guitar we find. I crack my foot against a guitar amp and we disintegrate in laughter, my eyes watering, but then I think about the grommet in the sand and as she laughs, I want to ask her to sit with me quiet and scared, until my chest warms, but I can't. We make up the bed. Next to it, we assemble a frame she finds, wrangle a futon onto it like a bale of alfalfa. She lies in the bed, and I lie on the futon among sheet music. She turns out the light. She says, *There is power in some fear*, and I say *yes*. In other fear there is only a sulking, needing dog.

About the Author

ANNE RAY was raised in Ellicott City, Maryland, and has worked as a waitress, a gardener, an English teacher, and a fishmonger. She's a graduate of the creative writing program at Carnegie Mellon University and the MFA program in fiction at Brooklyn College. A two-time fellow at the MacDowell Colony and the Virginia Center for the Creative Arts, her fiction has appeared in many literary magazines and has been awarded a Pushcart Prize. During the daytime she's the managing editor at Reveal Digital, a project of JSTOR, where she oversees several digital archives of radical and historical press materials.